The Christmas Leap

Also by Keira Andrews

Contemporary

Honeymoon for One
Beyond the Sea
Ends of the Earth
Arctic Fire
The Chimera Affair

Holiday

The Christmas Leap
Only One Bed
Merry Cherry Christmas
The Christmas Deal
Santa Daddy
In Case of Emergency
Eight Nights in December
If Only in My Dreams
Where the Lovelight Gleams
Gay Romance Holiday Collection

Sports

Kiss and Cry
Reading the Signs
Cold War
The Next Competitor
Love Match
Synchronicity (free read!)

Gay Amish Romance Series

A Forbidden Rumspringa
A Clean Break
A Way Home
A Very English Christmas

Valor Duology

Valor on the Move
Test of Valor
Complete Valor Duology

Lifeguards of Barking Beach
Flash Rip
Swept Away (free read!)

Historical

Kidnapped by the Pirate
Semper Fi
The Station
Voyageurs (free read!)

Paranormal

Kick at the Darkness Trilogy
Kick at the Darkness
Fight the Tide

Taste of Midnight (free read!)

Fantasy

Barbarian Duet
Wed to the Barbarian
The Barbarian's Vow

The Christmas Leap

BY KEIRA ANDREWS

The Christmas Leap
Written and published by Keira Andrews
Cover by Dar Albert
Formatting by BB eBooks

Copyright © 2022 by Keira Andrews
Print Edition

ISBN: 978-1-988260-88-4

This is a work of fiction. Names, characters, businesses, places, events and incidents are either the products of the author's imagination or used in a fictitious manner. No persons, living or dead, were harmed by the writing of this book. Any resemblance to any actual persons, living or dead, or actual events is purely coincidental.

Acknowledgments

Many thanks to Leta Blake, Angela O'Connell, Rai, and Samantha for helping make this novel the best it can be. Special thanks also to Scotty Porter for his help with the Scottish lingo and dialogue, and Elaine and Sharna for their Aussie expertise. I appreciate all of you so much!

Chapter One
Michael

THERE WAS AN old saying about best-laid plans. It was probably Shakespeare, and the point was that no matter how carefully you tried to get your ducks in a row, those little jerks had minds of their own.

"I can't break up with him at *Christmas*!" Jared's voice rose incredulously.

Earlier in the day, I'd decided to take the afternoon off work for an early start to two glorious weeks of vacation time over the holidays. After running a few errands, I'd eased open the door of our townhouse to call out to Jared that I'd brought home a surprise—our first Christmas tree together.

But now I strained to listen over the thudding of my heart.

It had to be the TV. Sure, it had sounded exactly like Jared's smooth, slightly nasal voice, but... It couldn't have been. After working my butt off at making this relationship a success, I couldn't have overheard my boyfriend talking about breaking up with me.

Not just my boyfriend—my *partner*. I wasn't a kid anymore. Jared and I were partners. Maybe this was a bad joke. Some kind of terrible, out-of-character prank?

Ho-ho-ho?

Jared muttered, "I know." It sounded like he was in the kitchen at the back of the townhouse. The hardwood floor creaked—

which drove Jared nuts even though I thought it added charm. Warm light spilled into the hallway, flickering with his shadow as he moved restlessly. I could picture him pacing by the granite-topped island.

Jared sighed. "There's no good time to tell him. That's true. Still. I have to wait until January. He's so excited about our first Christmas together here. I can't do it." A pause. "I know I'm not a Christmas person, but it's fine. It makes him happy."

I stood there clutching the twine-bound tree, my nose full of pine. The paper shopping bag on the bristly outdoor mat beneath my feet contained an artisanal mulled wine kit and chestnuts for roasting. And wait, Jared didn't *like* Christmas? I knew he wasn't a fan of tacky decorations and cheesy songs, but...

I'd stashed boxes of tasteful gold and silver ornaments that would fit Jared's minimalist style under the bed yesterday. I knew he wouldn't like the idea of dropped needles on the floor, so I'd bought the newest automatic watering system for the tree. The trunk of my Hyundai hatchback was crammed with gifts and rolls of the classiest wrapping paper I could find.

I had planned every detail of our Instagram-worthy Christmas.

Jared exhaled loudly. "I know, Steph. He must see it coming, right? Unless he's in denial. Fuck, I hate this."

Oh, god. I'd thought everything was perfect, and now it was disintegrating in front of my eyes. Well, my ears. Rigid, I waited for him to say more to his sister.

I'd always gotten along with Stephanie, or at least I thought I had? She was only looking out for Jared, and it wasn't about me. That didn't make it hurt less.

And okay, *perfect* was a strong word for my relationship with Jared. But everything was pretty good, wasn't it? I'd been so careful since I moved into the townhouse to keep everything running smoothly. All the experts said compromise was key, and I'd compromised like a champion, hadn't I?

"It's only another couple of weeks. I'll tell him in the new year." A pause. "I know." Another pause. "Steph, I couldn't do it before because we went to Tampa to visit his folks for Thanksgiving. We had plane tickets, and they took us to Universal. And yes, I hate theme parks, but I couldn't back out."

I tasted acid. I'd been so proud to show off Jared to my parents. Proof that I was indeed a responsible adult now, and they didn't have to worry about me or lend me money. They could live their best retired lives.

For too long in my twenties, I'd drifted. Working okay jobs with no future for advancement. Dating okay people while nursing my impossible crush. I had a steady office job now with benefits, and my impossible crush was a hundred percent over.

Gripping the teetering Christmas tree, I braced for thoughts of Will, which were the last thing I needed. Will was straight. He was never going to love me back. I'd had to put distance between us— at least while I got over him. I'd made a plan, grown up, and figured out my life. I was no longer in love with my best friend.

Whether Will *was* still my best friend was another story, but my hands were full with problems at the moment, including being stabbed by pine needles through my thin gloves as I fought to stay quiet while keeping the Christmas tree vertical.

Jared groaned. "I was hoping... I don't know. That it would all magically work out. Of course, I should have ended it months ago."

Months?!

I'd only moved into the townhouse in March. Which meant Jared had decided humiliatingly quickly that he didn't want me to stay. We'd dated for more than a year before living together. I'd been so freaking careful not to jump into anything. Should I have seen this coming? *Had* I? My head spun, and I clung to the tree.

"I just feel so sorry for him."

I jerked violently—then scrambled to keep hold of the tipping tree. Needles clawed my cheek as I tripped backward.

See above, re: *best-laid plans*.

Kicking over the fancy paper bag on my way down, I hit the shoveled stoop, my jeans offering no protection and my peacoat not much more. Glass smashed on the freezing concrete.

The tree pinning me, I sank back in defeat, my head perilously close to the edge of the top step. The jagged granules of rock salt I'd sprinkled over the walkway that morning dug into my skull.

Jared appeared in the open doorway wearing his favorite dress pants and black silk sweater, a furrow between his thin brows before they shot up. "Babe! Are you okay?"

I nodded, struggling to retain a shred of dignity. Jared hauled the tree off me, his handsome face transforming into a familiar smile as he laughed and cracked some joke I couldn't make out over the buzzing in my ears.

My throat swelled painfully, tears burning my eyes. If I hadn't just overheard him, I wouldn't have had a damn clue anything was wrong. I was so stupid. I'd had no idea he wanted to break up with me. That he didn't love me anymore. God, did he not love me?

Do I love him? Or did I only want to love him?

"Mike? Shit, babe. You *are* hurt."

Choking down a scream/shout/sob, I pushed myself up to sitting while Jared wrangled the tree into the narrow foyer. When he turned back, his eyes bugged out.

"Jesus! Are you bleeding?" He lunged out the door in his Italian leather slippers. Dropping to his knees, he groped my left thigh, and I blinked down at the dark stain on my jeans.

"Wine," I croaked. "Careful—you'll get it on your pants."

Jared pressed a hand to his chest, seeming to notice the red-soaked paper bag for the first time. The wine had sloshed all over the stoop, and my hip was wet with it.

He exhaled noisily. "You gave me a heart attack. I don't care about my pants."

"There's broken glass."

He ignored that. "You're sure you're okay? What happened to your face?"

I dodged his hand, squirming away and almost sliding backward down the handful of steps to the tiny front yard where I'd proudly planted a row of petunias that had lived half the summer. I swiped at my smooth cheek—now scratched to hell.

My blond facial hair grew patchy on my pale skin and took forever, so I'd learned to lean into my baby face. Maybe it would scar, and I'd finally look thirty and not like I was still in college. Swipes of blood stained my gray gloves.

Jared reached for me again. "You're hurt. Let me help you."

"What do you care?" I half shouted, cringing at my patheticness. Was that a word? If it wasn't, it should have been.

"Babe, what's—" He blinked, glancing back at the open door. His concern morphed with resignation to form a sad, defeated expression. "How much did you hear?"

I shrugged, ignoring the flare of pain in my shoulder blade. "Enough."

Jared rubbed his face, his stubble scratching audibly before he ran his hands through his gelled brown hair. Somehow, it still looked only artfully out of place. He was rarely messy. It was one of his wonderfully mature qualities I'd been attracted to.

He muttered, "Shit, babe. I didn't want it to be like this. Especially not at Christmas." He carefully stood and stepped back over the broken glass to the beige interior welcome mat, rubbing his slippers on it. "Let's talk inside. It's freezing." He reached out his hand.

I let him haul me up and inside the foyer, where the pine took up almost the whole space. I stopped on the mat, the door still open behind me. Jared shifted from foot to foot, crossing and uncrossing his arms.

"Why?" I asked, the single word scraping my throat.

Deep down, I knew the answer, didn't I?

Jared blinked back tears. "It's not you, I swear. You're great. But it was a mistake to move in together. I should have known better." He held up his palms. "Again, not because of you. Because of me. I love living alone. But like I said, you're great, so I wanted to try." He sighed. "It's not working for me. *We're* not working. We rushed it."

"We didn't! We were together for more than a year. We didn't jump into this without thinking. There was a plan."

"Was there, though? You got evicted by that shitty landlord that sold to a developer, and I thought it was time to stretch my boundaries and get out of my comfort zone." He shook his head. "I'm sorry. I really like you, but..."

"Like. Not love." My mouth flooded with saliva. I was going to hurl all over our scotch pine. Though not *ours* now. There was no more *us* and *we* and *ours*. Just like that.

He dropped his arms to his sides. "I wanted to love you. Honestly."

All I could do was nod. It would be too humiliating to sob.

Evidently having hoarded these words for months, they spilled out of Jared now. "I really do like you! But we don't quite fit. Come on—you have to know that. We don't like the same kind of music or TV shows. I hate that true crime shit you're addicted to."

"So we compromise!" I shouted with a burst of frustration. "Haven't we compromised?"

"Yes!" He stood straighter, fisting his hands. "We compromise on everything. Don't we deserve to get what we really need? What we really want?" He opened and closed his mouth a few times, sputtering before blurting, "I mean, we both like to get fucked! You can't stand there and tell me we've ever really clicked in bed even though we were really attracted to each other at first."

My face was so hot my cheeks had to be bright red. God, did

we have to talk about this? "I told you I don't mind topping. It's fine."

And it was! It wasn't like I didn't get off. I'd penetrated plenty of my exes. Giving other people what they needed *did* turn me on. Maybe not quite as much as some other stuff did, but that was okay. It was!

His mouth tugged down, and his voice turned pleading. "You shouldn't be settling for 'fine.' And if it was only about sex, sure, we could talk about options for an open relationship. But it's about everything being 'fine.' As much as I care about you, 'fine' isn't enough. I don't want to settle."

I really was going to puke.

"Haven't I done everything you want?" I cringed at how small I sounded. How young.

Jared exhaled, his face creasing like he was in pain. "Yes. You're so sweet and generous, and you've bent over backwards for me. At first, I thought you were my dream come true. You're the most caring and thoughtful guy I've ever dated."

"Then what did I do wrong?" I was practically begging.

"You didn't do anything wrong. But catering to my whims isn't healthy. I feel like you're walking on eggshells trying to keep me happy. Trying to be this perfect version of yourself. You're too…careful. It makes me feel like shit. Like I can't be real with you. Ba—" He cut himself off. "Mike—"

"I hate being called 'Mike,'" I blurted. He wanted real? There.

He blinked. "What?"

"My name is Michael."

"But everyone calls you Mike." He stared, eyes wide. "Why the hell didn't you *say* something?"

All I could do was shrug. "I'm used to it."

"See, this is the problem! You settle all over the place!" Groaning, Jared shook his head. "Fuck, I hate saying this to you. Which is why I've been putting it off. Also, because it's Christmas, and I know it's a big deal to you to do the cozy, snowy, traditional thing."

"It's not a big deal," I insisted reflexively.

Jared looked down pointedly at the fallen tree at our feet. "Tell me you weren't planning on decorating and taking pics of us in cable-knit sweaters sipping cocoa and pretending we don't have any problems."

"I just thought it would be nice!"

"Because you actually love Christmas or because you want everything to look perfect on Insta?"

I flinched. As much as I wanted to argue, I couldn't.

"We need to face facts," Jared said more firmly. "We can't settle. You're thirty, and I'm thirty-three. We can't coast along in a relationship that's not working. I think we really liked the *idea* of us. The reality? Not so much."

All I could do was nod.

He shivered. "Shut the door. Come on, let's talk this out."

What else was there to say? Broken glass crunched under my boots on the landing and chestnuts rolled down the steps as I escaped, leaving my now ex-boyfriend—ex-*partner*—a nine-foot organic scotch pine, and the life I'd wanted so desperately to be mine in my wake.

"MIKE?"

I would have hit the roof of the hatchback—not hard to do since there were only a few inches of clearance—if I hadn't been wearing my seatbelt.

Cursing myself for spacing out, I focused on Zoe squinting at me from the bungalow's porch. She wore fluffy Ugg boots but no coat, holding her cardigan closed at her throat, the icy wind blowing her dark curls into her eyes.

Zoe's muffled voice came again as she called, "Mike? Is that you?"

The key was still in the ignition, but Zoe was already picking her way down the slick driveway. It sloped just enough to be treacherous in the winter, which I'd learned the hard way more than once back in the day when I'd lived here with Zoe and Will and a few roommates.

Her parents had bought the house as an investment property so she had a safe place to live during college. With prices skyrocketing now, it'd been a smart move.

What was I even *doing* here? In my aimless driving around Albany, trying to process that my hard-earned relationship with Jared was over, my brain's muscle memory had apparently brought me back to my former home. I'd lived in a couple of apartments between this house and moving into Jared's, but it seemed neither had made a lasting impression on my subconscious.

Great. I hadn't seen Zoe in person in a few years, and now I was sitting outside my ex-girlfriend's place like some kind of creep in my extremely recognizable orange car, which glowed like a beacon even in the quickly fading daylight.

Her pretty face creased in understandable confusion, Zoe knocked on the driver-side window, her solitaire diamond engagement ring glinting in the rays of the setting sun. The glass was tinted enough that it was only once I rolled down the window that Zoe saw my scratched face.

She gasped and clapped her hand over her mouth, her cardigan flapping open in the wind. "What happened? Are you okay?"

"I'm fine! It's nothing." Shit, my face must have looked worse than I'd thought. I flipped down the mirror on the back of the visor and grimaced.

Yep, dried blood streaked over my cheek and the scratches had swelled. Was I suddenly allergic to Christmas trees? That would be just my luck after how today had gone.

"Did you get in an accident?" Zoe pressed.

I shook my head. "Christmas tree wrestling. 'Tis the season."

"Right. Okay. So…" She frowned. "Is everything all right with Jared? And work?"

Ignoring the first part, I said, "Work's great! I got a promotion last month."

"Yeah? You're still at that e-commerce company?"

"Yep. Still responding to customer complaints, but now I'm training and monitoring new staff. I've got vacation time until the new year. It's a great company."

"Cool." Her sculpted brows met. "What are you doing here? Did something happen with Jared? I thought everything was going well. Thanksgiving in Tampa looked awesome. You seemed really happy finally."

Could I just drive away? I toyed with the option before dismissing it and confessing, "We broke up."

"Shit. I'm sorry." Zoe tensed and reached through the open window to grab my shoulder. "Did he do that to your face?"

"No. It was the stupid tree. Jared's not like that."

She relaxed and let go of me. "Okay. I thought maybe Will was right."

Blood rushing in my ears, I squeaked, "Will?"

"Our former roommate? Your best friend?" She arched a brow. "Ring any bells? Or did you ghost him right out of your memory?"

"I didn't ghost him!" Hot shame washed over me. Vomiting was definitely back on the table.

"Then why are you being so defensive?"

"I'm not! I've just been busy."

Zoe's dubious expression was sadly familiar from when we dated. "If you say so."

"Why? What…" I swallowed thickly. "What did Will tell

you?"

She shrugged as an older woman's commanding voice called out, "Is that Mike?"

"Here we go," Zoe muttered, rolling her eyes. "You're still her favorite after all this time. My parents just arrived for the holidays. We're renovating the bathroom, god help me."

For a stout woman with chronic back pain, Mrs. Schmidt-Wong moved like lightning, appearing at Zoe's side in a parka three sizes too big—likely belonging to Zoe's dad—with her blonde curls flying wild in the wind.

It was her turn to gasp. "Did you get mugged? Or was it a cat? You can't trust cats. Even if you feed them every day their whole lives, they'll eat your corpse without a second thought."

"It was pine needles. Not a cat. No big deal. Christmas tree injury." I tried to smile at Zoe's mom. Torn between formal politeness and reverting to what I'd called her when Zoe and I were a couple, I stupidly said, "It's nice to see you, Mrs....Janice. I was just driving by and..."

Come on. Think of something. Anything. Literally anything.

I had nothing. At least I stopped talking.

The wrinkles around Mrs. Schmidt-Wong's eyes deepened as she gave me a playful smile. "You're here to win Zoe back? Not that I have anything against Peter, but he's not as cute as you."

Zoe smacked her mother's arm, the parka surely taking the brunt. "*Mom.* Peter is extremely cute. Well, he's *handsome.* Distinguished." She glanced at me. "No offense." As a car approached with a rumble, she stood straight, then leaned back down to the window. "Shit, he's home. For real, tell me what's going on?"

"Nothing. I was just...um, around, and I stopped to check a text. I didn't even realize it was your house." Considering I'd previously lived here for several years, it wasn't particularly plausible. I leaned into it anyway. "Texting and driving kills."

"That's true," Mrs. Schmidt-Wong said. "Mike was always very responsible."

Zoe hissed, "*Peter's* responsible! He's a nurse!"

Mrs. Schmidt-Wong conceded, "True, true." To me, she whispered, "He's just a little boring if you ask me. No sparks."

Ignoring her mother, arms wrapped around her middle, Zoe frowned at me. "Seriously, are you okay?"

"Yeah," I lied. "Had a sh—crappy day. Just driving around. It's good to see you." It was—we'd managed to stay kind-of friends after we'd broken up. Before I'd made the worst mistake of my life. Mistakes. Plural. "I've got to get—" I choked on the next word.

It wasn't home. It had always been *Jared's* townhouse, and as much as I'd tried, he didn't want me. I suddenly didn't have a home. Jesus, where was I going to *live*? My heart hammered. I'd been so preoccupied with my failed relationship that I hadn't even considered the immediate issue.

"Are your parents okay?" Zoe asked, still frowning suspiciously.

"Absolutely! Living their best retirement dream." Before she could ask, I added, "My brothers and their families are all great too."

I'd been a surprise baby, a full fourteen years younger than my next oldest brother. My brothers were all miles ahead of me, and I'd thought I'd finally caught up somehow.

"Everything's great!" I cleared my throat. "Merry Christmas!"

As I turned the key and the engine sputtered, Peter—who was definitely handsome if you asked me—joined the party at the window. Good thing this sleepy street didn't get much traffic. I nodded to him, willing the damn engine to catch. It took a minute sometimes.

Zoe introduced me as I stepped hard on the gas, the engine making a sad *whoa-whoa-whoa* whine.

Peter exclaimed, "Oh, the bi guy, right? Hey, man. Great to meet you." He stuck his hand through the open window.

We shook, and I let the engine rest a few seconds since I was about to flood it. "That's me. Good to meet you too."

Squeezing closer to Zoe, Peter apparently caught a better look at the Christmas tree wounds on my face. "You okay? Looks like you were bleeding."

"It's nothing!" The smile hurt my face. My laugh sounded manic.

"Are you coming in for dinner?" Zoe asked—a sort-of invitation that wasn't overly enthusiastic. Completely understandable.

Mrs. Schmidt-Wong said, "There's plenty! Yes, you must join us."

I shook my head. "I can't, but thank you."

Aside from imposing on them and how awkward it would be, my jeans were soaked with red wine. I didn't want to explain why I was such a mess. I turned the key again, willing my rust bucket to just do me this one more favor and get me out of this ridiculous situation I'd put myself in.

The cosmic engine gods were in a benevolent mood. The engine roared to life. More like sputtered, but I'd take it. I jammed down the button to raise the window. "Merry Christmas! Say hi to your dad and the rest of the family."

They stepped back, and I waved as I escaped, turning at the corner and racing out of the neighborhood as fast as I could. I headed out of town, eventually ending up on a lonely two-lane highway in the darkness.

Night came so early this time of year. I'd imagined Jared and I would be decorating the tree with jazzy carols playing, sipping mulled wine and roasting chestnuts in the oven since the sleek, modern fireplace was electric.

In my pocket, my phone buzzed. I'd received at least ten texts since I'd run away from Jared, but I hadn't looked at the screen.

Maybe they were just spammers trying to trick me into giving them my bank account information or social security number. Maybe Jared wasn't even worried about me.

I couldn't stand to know.

Where was I even going? Where was I going to stay? I mentally ran through the possibilities of local friends. My closest friends from college aside from Zoe had recently had their first baby, so they were out.

Some people from high school were mutuals on social media, but we hadn't spoken in years. I was only friendly with people at work—not *friends*.

And obviously, I couldn't ask Will.

Ghosted.

Shit, was that what I'd done? I'd needed to take a step back from hanging with Will all the time. I'd needed to finally move on from my hopeless crush. All of our friends were getting engaged, and he'd started dating a girl he was crazy about. I couldn't keep treading water.

But it wasn't like we'd had a fight. We were still friends. I hadn't *ghosted* him. I was waiting until I was sure I was over him to reconnect. Will was fine! He was too busy dating gorgeous women and traveling for work to think about me.

Of course he was. We were older now. This was the way life went. We didn't have time to hang out the way we used to.

"Fuck," I muttered. All my justifications aside, I'd had to stop torturing myself. There was only so long you could secretly love your best friend before self-preservation kicked in. I'd never have gotten over him if I still saw him all the time. And it'd worked! I was very much over him.

I slowed for a curve before accelerating. Everyone was busy with parties and holiday plans. The thought of showing up on anyone's doorstep—let alone Will's—was honestly mortifying after the encounter at Zoe's house.

I'd find a hotel. I'd buy what I needed for the night and deal with returning to the townhouse for my stuff tomorrow. I needed to hole up and lick my wounds.

In silence but for the rough rumble of the engine, I followed the road even deeper into the snowy forest. The pavement was clear with snowbanks rising on either side.

Where even was I? It was time to turn around and find a place to crash. There were chain hotels and motels back in town, and I wasn't picky.

Though there wasn't much traffic, I didn't want to pull a U-turn in the dark on a twisting road. Surely there'd be a driveway or another road soon. I kept going, my mind replaying everything Jared had said yet again.

He was right—I'd been in willful denial. I'd wanted so much for it to work. I'd thought it had all fallen into place with Jared. Granite countertops and a comfortable, functional relationship! Ticking all the grown-up boxes.

Even if it wasn't perfect, I'd decided Jared was the one. Clearly, I was mistaken. If "the one" even existed. What if life was only a series of disappointments and failures, and I never—

I gripped the wheel as the distinct smell of smoke reached my nose. Before I could launch into a full-blown existential crisis, the cosmic engine gods announced they weren't on my side after all.

Chapter Two
Will

A S THE NARRATOR described how the killer slipped into the house through an unlocked patio door, my phone buzzed.

Making a sound I was relieved no one else heard—something which could only be described as a "yelp"—I jabbed the button on the steering wheel and accepted the call, leaving the notorious serial killer poised outside the victims' bedroom with thick shag carpet muffling his deadly steps.

"Hi, Mum."

"Hello, love! Oh, it's so good to hear you. Just what the doctor ordered."

She'd said this, her voice resonant with sincerity, every single time we spoke since my parents moved back to Glasgow when I was in uni.

I smiled in the darkness, warm with affection, and checked my blind spot before changing lanes. The sea of red taillights had thinned and the exits on the freeway became farther apart. The recent storm had dumped a ton of pristine snow on the hilly landscape, but the pavement was clear.

I said, "Haven't missed you at all, actually."

"Bugger off. How was the drive to… Where exactly are you going?"

"I'm still on the road. Just gettin' oot o' the city now." I added, "No much traffic," slipping into Scots now that I was speaking to Mum. "Nae idea where I'm heading, but the address is in the GPS. It'll be a hotel or resort of some kind. Angela always goes all out for these holiday family retreats."

"All bosses should be so generous."

"Aye, but mandatory festivities aren't everyone's cup o' tea."

"Oh, bah humbug! You used tae love Christmas as a wee boy. Mandatory festivities will do you some good, laddie. If you'd come home for once, I'd make your favorite Christmas pudding, you know."

"I was just there in October for three weeks!"

She sighed. "I know, love. Cannae blame me for trying, can you?"

"Not to mention the fact that it was you and Dad who moved us over here when I was too young to have a say and then cruelly abandoned me."

"Wheesht, that's enough of your cheek."

I laughed. "Did I hit a nerve, Mum?"

"Fuck off, ya wee shite. You're no too big to get a skelped arse."

It had been her visiting professorship that had brought us to Buffalo when I was sixteen. I'd gone to uni in Albany and stayed rather than going back to Scotland. I loved visiting, but I had a home here.

Well, at least I'd had one at the time. There'd been a few golden years living with Michael and Zoe and the others, but we'd all moved on.

"William?"

"Aye, I'm here."

I sipped lukewarm coffee and ordered myself not to fall into the endless, cruel loop of wondering why Michael had ghosted me. The simple answer was that he'd fallen in love. I certainly wasn't the first person whose best friend had become distracted by their new partner. It wasn't as though we'd quarreled. It wasn't about me.

Somehow, that didn't make it easier.

"Hello?"

I realized Mum had said something else. "Sorry, the connection's bad. What was that?"

"I hate to think of you alone at the holidays."

"I'll be with Seth and his husband Logan on Christmas Day, remember? Not alone."

"Aye, of course. And I'm glad you've made such good friends at work, but... Are you sure Logan and Seth don't know someone special? Doesn't Logan have a sister?"

"Yes, Mum, he does. Jenna's my colleague. Also a happily married mother of two. Unless you want me to have an affair—"

"Don't be a bloody numpty." She *tsked*, clearly trying not to laugh and failing. "I forgot about that. Oh, love. I just don't want you to get too stuck in your ways as a bachelor. It's time to take a leap."

I rolled my eyes. Mum's philosophy of life was a delicate balance of risk averse and adventurous. "I've taken plenty of leaps. I took one staying here in America."

She grumbled. "Not what I had in mind, as you well know. But yes, I admit that was a leap. So, when's your next one coming? If you get too comfortable, you'll miss out on life."

"I've signed up for sky diving lessons. Plenty of leaps in my future."

"Fuck off. It's not nice to torture your poor old mum."

"You're fifty-seven. Not old yet."

She groaned. "Tell that to my lower back. And honey, you can't coast along being a ladies' man forever. Even George Clooney couldn't."

Gulping my coffee, I tried to ignore the unsettling rush of... I didn't know what. Wrongness, I supposed. Honestly, I wasn't sure how I'd gotten that reputation: *ladies' man.*

Sure, I'd dated my fair share of women since high school, and I'd had a few girlfriends. Those relationships hadn't worked out for various reasons, and a mythology had built up that I didn't want to settle down.

In reality, I'd been happier hanging with Michael. Going to quiz nights at the local bar, watching the Mets, bingeing true crime shows, and playing video games. Until he'd suddenly started doing those things with Jared instead. Presumably. I'd never actually met Jared.

Mum sighed. "I just want you to find the right woman. How's Michael doing? He's coupled up with that lad now, isn't he? Zoe's engaged, and didn't Brittany and Eric have a baby?"

"Mmm." It was best not to engage when she got on this topic. Fortunately, it wasn't often. And I hadn't mentioned that Michael didn't talk to me these days. I'd spoken to Zoe about it once and regretted it. Her sympathy had only made me feel worse somehow.

"I know, your old Mum's nagging. It's just hard not to worry. You've got to put some effort into it. You dinnae want to be left behind while all your pals move on. Have you looked at any flats this month?"

"I was too busy with planning for Seattle. I'll get back to it in the new year. There won't be new condos going on the market over the holidays."

"True enough. You're dragging your feet, though."

"I like my apartment! I'm saving up for a bigger down payment. I don't know why you're so keen on me taking on a mortgage and huge debt."

Mum sighed. "I know, I know—times have changed. We'd just like to see you settled down."

"So you want me to leap into settling down."

"It's bloody rude to point out your mother's logical inconsistencies."

19

I grinned. "I was also going to mention—"

"No more of your cheek! But yes. Something like that. We only want you to be happy, love. You hardly mention seeing your old pals anymore. It feels like something's missing."

It was unnerving how she could sense that. "It doesn't have anything to do with me being single. I *am* happy. They're busy. We're all busy. Relationships evolve."

"Aye, that's true. I always thought Michael fancied you, but I suppose not. You were two peas in a pod last time we visited."

My laugh brayed out like a strangled goat's. "Me and *Michael*? We're friends, Mum. Nothing more." Were we even friends these days? Barely. "I'm straight, remember?"

"Oh, it's the twenty-first century. It's all much looser now."

I knew she was kidding. After all, she'd called me a "ladies' man" only a moment ago. Mum didn't know. There was no way she could know. *No one* knew. It was fine. 'Course it was.

Knuckles white on the steering wheel and heart thumping, I exited the freeway. Sure, I'd fantasized about men occasionally, but I'd certainly never confessed my curiosity to my *mum*. Or anyone else. There was no need.

I'd been bored and missing Michael one night last year and stumbled down a rabbit hole of male/male videos. So, sometimes now I wanked to videos of anonymous blokes. It wasn't anything to make a fuss over.

It wasn't something I needed to discuss with anyone. I'd never acted on it and didn't plan to. It was fine for Michael to date different genders, and it would surely be fine for me too, but...

I was straight. I'd just said it to Mum, hadn't I? I'd always been straight. If I wasn't, surely I'd have known as a teenager? And honestly, I hadn't been interested in dating anyone lately. It felt like going through the motions.

Aside from my girlfriend in freshman year of uni, Amelia—who I'd been quite keen on—my other relationships had been rather...lukewarm. People thought I was such a player, but more often than not, I'd rather stay home and wank than hook up. Or hang with Michael, but that option had disappeared.

As if he fancied me!

My throat was suddenly dry, and I drained my coffee as Mum said, "Are you there?"

I snapped back to attention. "Sorry, you cut out. What were you saying?"

"Your cousin Fiona is making waves again."

As she regaled me with tales of my cousin's lamentably bad choices, I drove on, my head strangely light and stomach full of butterflies. I didn't think about Michael much nowadays. What was the point? He was in love with Jared, and he had a new life that was too busy for me. Aside from occasional likes on social media, we hadn't interacted in ages.

Our friendship had become a decidedly one-way street, and I'd gotten the hint after what was likely an embarrassingly long time. I supposed Michael outgrew me.

Fancied me? I laughed sharply. No chance.

"Sweetie, don't be unkind. You know Fiona means well."

"You're right, Mum. Sorry. It's, uh, jet lag. I flew back to Albany from Seattle today, and now I'm heading straight out to this retreat. I'm tired." I realized my mistake immediately and cut off what I knew she was about to say. "But not too tired to drive. I'll be there soon."

Honestly, I'd much rather be headed home to my apartment instead of out to this weekend of festivities. Attendance wasn't technically mandatory, but everyone knew it was an excellent way to get face time with the boss.

Angela Barker visited several of her offices in December and hosted these family weekends, cycling through the list every few years. It was our turn in Albany, and I couldn't miss it.

I glanced at the time. "Mum, what are you doing up so late?

Must be gone eleven over there."

She grumbled. "Can't sleep with these bloody hot flashes. Your father's out like a light as usual."

Normally I'd tease, but she really did sound tired. Worry tugged, and I reminded myself I'd just seen her a couple of months ago and she was fine. Sometimes I hated the distance as much as she did.

I said, "Sorry. Hope it eases up soon."

"Me too, love. At least I've got Netflix to keep me company."

I chuckled. "You know true crime programs won't help you sleep."

"Did you watch the new four-parter about that awful incident in Kansas? Those poor people never saw it coming."

Of course I'd seen it, and we discussed the case for a few minutes. True crime really was strangely addictive. I listened to spooky podcasts and audiobooks more than music in the car these days.

I wondered if Michael had seen this latest series. Maybe I should send him the link. But what was the sense in bothering him? I'd finally gotten the hint.

Mum said, "All right, I'd better get to bed." She sighed heavily. "And I'm sorry, love. I don't mean to nag. I just worry. Life can pass you by if you're not careful."

"I know. I need to leap—but not out of a plane. Only the right amount of leaping."

"Precisely."

Her philosophy was precise in her own mind, if nowhere else. "Will do, Mum."

"The retreat must be starting soon? You really should get a wiggle on. No speeding, though."

"Wouldn't dream of it." I eased off the gas pedal guiltily.

"Sure, Dario Franchitti. Now don't forget—"

An incoming call beeped, and I glanced at the screen.

I blinked.

Blinked again.

Did it really say *Michael Davis*? Were his ears burning? Was he actually ringing me?

"Mum, I've got another call. Sleep well! Love-you-bye." We always rushed our standard three-word sign-off, the words squished together. As she responded in kind, I jabbed the screen, bracing to hear nothing but the muffled sounds of a pocket dial.

Still, I said, "Hello?" and held my breath.

"Hey. It's me." His tenor voice was incredibly familiar even though I hadn't actually heard it in two years.

"Michael?" I cleared my scratchy throat. "I was just talking about you with Mum." Why the hell did I say *that* of all things? Especially given Mum had put forth her mad theory that Michael fancied me. I shifted uncomfortably and fumbled for the dial to turn down the heat.

After a hesitation, Michael said, "Really?" His voice sounded strange even as familiar as it was. Tense and thin, and there was a loud noise in the background that came and went. A vehicle? It sounded like he was outside.

"She, er, sends her love and says merry Christmas to you and Jared."

His "Thanks" sounded choked. After a moment, he added, "Sorry to bug you. I know it's been a while."

Resentment pinched me sharply. "It has, yeah."

I ordered myself not to fill the awkward silence that followed. Michael was the one who'd ghosted me. I probably should have let him go to voicemail. But Christ, it was wonderful to hear his voice again.

Giving in, I cautiously asked, "What's up?" No sense in getting ahead of myself. Maybe he'd hit my number by accident. I cringed at how happy it made me to hear from him.

He laughed hollowly. "Not having the greatest day. But if

you're busy, I don't want to keep you. I'm waiting for roadside assistance to show up, and it's a little freaky out here."

"What? Did you have an accident?" I sat up straighter, looking at the console screen as if it would display an answer. "Where are you?"

"I'm fine. The engine died, and I'm in the middle of nowhere."

My stomach tightened. "It's freezing. What's their ETA?"

"It's a busy day, apparently. Could be three or four hours."

"Fuckin' hell!"

"You sound so much like your parents when you say that. Your accent really comes out."

"Aye, lad. Och awa and beil yer head, ya wee prick." My smile vanished. "Where are you? I'm coming to get you."

"*What?* You can't. I'm at least an hour outside Albany. Probably more. It's my own stupid fault. I just thought if you're not busy, we could talk. Catch up. But I don't want to keep you. I shouldn't have bugged you."

Something rumbled loudly in the background, and I realized it was a passing vehicle. It was dangerous to be stranded on the side of a road. There were stories on the news about people being hit. Not to mention kidnappings and mysterious disappearances.

"Where are you?" I repeated.

"Uh... I was heading south. Toward Hudson, I guess. I'm not on the main road, though."

"Must be fate because I'm on my way to the Berkshires right now. Give me your coordinates."

"*Seriously?*" Michael's voice rose with obvious hope. He sighed. "But you must have plans. I don't want to—"

"Give me the location. I'm coming to get you whether you like it or not."

"But..." He exhaled loudly. "Okay. Thank you so much, man."

It really must have been fate because it turned out Michael was stranded only twenty minutes away. I kept him on the line as I went full Dario Franchitti. I could hear vehicles passing by him occasionally. It was a black night—no moonlight or stars, and I hated to think of anyone stranded out here. As angry as he'd made me, to think of Michael alone in the darkness had me stepping on the gas even harder.

Michael said, "Of course every true crime story that involves car trouble is running through my head."

I tried to make him laugh. "Well, you are a golden-haired ingenue."

He chuckled. "Can I still be an ingenue when I'm thirty?"

"With that baby face? Of course."

"We all can't be as naturally hairy as you."

I rubbed a hand over my cultivated layer of dark stubble. "I really should grow a hipster beard."

"It would only take a week tops. You already have one on your chest."

Here we were talking shite as my dad would say. Like no time had passed. Making him laugh felt more important than demanding an answer as to why he'd ditched me.

"The women love it." Christ, what a lame thing to say.

"That they do." His laugh was thin. "Kara must."

"Kara? I don't see her anymore."

"Oh. You guys seemed so into each other."

"Not for long. It fizzled out. Not enough in common once I got to know her."

"Sorry." He asked, "Who are you seeing these days?"

"No one at the moment." I felt the strange need to come up with an excuse for why I was single. "Busy with work."

"Yeah. I get it. What are you doing in the Berkshires?"

"Going to some kind of hotel. My boss said something about it being glam. One of those eco resorts, perhaps. She's on a green kick these days, making all sorts of environment-friendly changes to the office."

"Cool. That's for the new job?"

"Not new anymore, but yes." I tamped down the flare of resentment at how long it had been since we'd spoken. "It's a holiday weekend retreat. All expenses paid for staff and their partners and kids."

"Whoa. Um, where do you work again?"

"BRK Sync. It used to be Greenware Sync, but it was only a matter of time after Angela bought the company that it transitioned to BRK branding. Took several years."

My GPS, which I'd named Martha, told me to turn right, and I slowed to follow the road, dark forest looming all around. My headlights automatically flipped to the brights.

"Oh, right. Pretty big company."

"We're the northeast hub now in Albany. I just flew back from Seattle earlier today after helping them set up the northwest hub. Did a systems update."

"Is your boss that woman from Texas who's a little...eccentric?"

I chuckled. "Yep. Angela Barker. She's one of a kind. A genius at making money but she gives amazing benefits and prioritizes people and family. She's the most generous CEO in America while being one of the most profitable."

"Are you sure you should be detouring to get me? I can just wait for the tow. Assuming it'll be a tow since the engine made some truly alarming noises. Not to mention the smoke."

"I'm almost there."

"Yeah, but you're going to this retreat."

"I can be late. I already am. Most staff traveled earlier on the buses Angela hired. Oh, I think I see you!" I vibrated with a strange mix of relief and anticipation.

I checked my rear-view mirror to make sure no vehicles were

approaching and pulled in front of the hatchback with its hood raised and hazard lights flashing in the darkness. I flipped on my own hazards and climbed out of the SUV.

Backlit by flashing lights, Michael waved. He wore the same dark peacoat I remembered, his silhouette incredibly familiar. I'd known I missed him. 'Course I had. It didn't prepare me for the punch of emotion that made it impossible to breathe.

I couldn't just stand there staring at him, so I forced my feet to move. Salt crunched under my boots, and I tensed as the icy wind whipped. Should I hug him? Why not? We'd hugged plenty of times before. A normal, back-slapping—

"Bloody hell, what happened to your face?" I stopped an arm's length from Michael, squinting in the eerie flashing lights. "I thought you didn't crash?" The car seemed intact, but those were nasty wounds on Michael's smooth cheek.

"No, I got scratched earlier. It looks worse than it is. I think I'm having an allergic reaction or something."

Were those fingernail marks? The hair on the back of my neck stood up. "Did someone hurt you?" I could barely ask through my clenched jaw. "Jared?"

Michael shook his head. "It wasn't Jared." But his gaze flicked away.

He was hiding something. What the hell was he doing out here in the middle of nowhere? A fist squeezed in my belly as a terrible thought occurred. If Jared was abusive, did that explain why Michael had distanced himself? I'd read about how abusers isolated their victims. Was that what had been going on?

Shame at my silly hurt feelings flooded me. I should have tried harder to stay in touch. Had Michael been suffering all this time?

I was trying to think of the right question to ask when he shook his head again. "Seriously, it wasn't Jared." He laughed half-heartedly. "I wrestled a Christmas tree and lost."

"Honestly? Look, I know we—" I cleared my throat. "You can

tell me."

Head down, Michael mumbled, "I know. You're always there. *Here.*" He motioned around us. "I don't deserve it." He gave me a sad little smile. "But really, it was a tree. Christmas is dangerous. Hurts like a son of a bitch."

Before I knew what I was doing, I had his face in my hands. I hadn't stopped to put on gloves when I arrived, and his skin was icy beneath my fingers. I peered close at the scratches as if I had a shred of first aid knowledge.

Michael had a slimmer build, but we were both a little over six feet tall, so I didn't have to bend to get a good look at his injuries. I gently examined his cheek. The marks did seem consistent with spiky pine needles.

Michael exhaled in a rush, a cloud pluming between us in the freezing air. He whispered, "God, it's so good to see you."

Our eyes met in the creepy red light, sincerity shining from his. Questions crowded my tongue: *Is it? Then why did you forget about me? Was I just the only person left to call?*

I took a nervous step back, dropping my hands, and joked, "Certainly better than a serial killer showing up."

Looking away, he laughed awkwardly. "Definitely. Um, anyway..." He motioned to the car. "It started smoking and made a bang that sounded like it was about to explode."

"Christ." I joined him by the engine and caught a whiff of smoke still lingering despite the lash of wind. "I can change oil, but this is way above my pay grade. Any word from roadside assistance?"

"Nope. They basically said the truck will show up when it does and not to call in the meantime because it won't make a difference."

"Wonderful." The shoulder of the road was cleared, but claustrophobic and narrower than it would be without the snowbanks. Beyond was only the impenetrable darkness of the forest. "We can't wait here. Come on—I'll take you to wherever you were heading."

"It's okay. I'll be fine. I was freaking out and needed to talk to someone. Thanks for answering. I wouldn't have blamed you if you hadn't. Sorry, I got busy, and..." He trailed off.

Here was the opportunity to clear the air, but I didn't know what to say. That it hurt my feelings? It was stupid for me to make a big deal out of it. It was what it was—we were in our thirties now, and it's not as though we'd be hanging out daily the way we used to. I was probably being a baby. Cutting yer ain nose aff, as my dad would say.

It had also occurred to me more than once that it'd been my pushiness that had caused Michael to stop talking to me. When there was a problem, I wanted to attack it head-on and fix it. Something had been troubling Michael a couple of years ago, and he'd persistently laughed it off when I'd tried to find out what was wrong.

Something sure as hell was troubling him now. This wasn't the time or place to get into it. I shrugged and said, "We've both been busy. Time flies and all that shite."

Before I could say anything else, a large truck approached, speeding as it blinded us with its headlights. I yanked Michael back to the packed snowbank, both of us bracing against the gale of wind as the truck blew past. The hatchback shook.

I shouted uselessly, "Slow down, you reckless prick!" I was still holding Michael's arm, and I felt the tremor that ran through him. I tugged his elbow. "It's not safe here."

"I... Yeah, okay." Michael followed me to the SUV and climbed in.

That was when I noticed the dark stain on his leg. His jeans were a midtone, like classic Levi's, and whatever liquid had splattered his thigh was suspiciously red.

"What the fuck happened?" I exclaimed. Everything was off-kilter, from the scratches on his cheek to being out in the middle of nowhere to him actually calling me.

"Oh! It's wine. Probably looks like blood or something, huh?" Michael tried to laugh and failed miserably.

"It does. Why is there wine all over you?" A terrible thought occurred, and I had to ask, "You haven't been drinking, have you?" The Michael I'd known would never drive drunk, and I hadn't smelled alcohol on his breath.

"No!" He shook his head vigorously. "Not a drop. It's all on my jeans. And the stoop of my—well, not mine. The townhouse. Jared's townhouse." He rubbed his face, wincing and jerking his hand away from the scratches on his cheek.

As much as I burned to find out exactly what'd happened so I could fix it, I forced myself not to push. "You know, if you were a stranger, I might think there's a victim in your trunk and *you're* the serial killer. If I didn't know better."

A gleaming smile transformed his face for only a moment, like opening the curtains on a sunny morning. A dimple creased his left cheek. "Maybe I've been killing all these years. Biding my time to lure you into my trap."

"The car works fine, right? Part of the ruse?"

"Yep. My evil plan is all coming together."

"Honestly, you're damn convincing if that's the case. I almost wouldn't begrudge you."

He chuckled. "Almost. Actually, I just watched a doc on a case in Washington State where the killer didn't fit the usual profile at all."

"Oh, with the hitchhiker and the missing red knapsack?"

"Wasn't that wild?"

"I know everyone always says, 'He was so polite and quiet—we never suspected a thing!' But he really put on a bloody convincing show."

"Yeah, that was a good one." Michael grimaced. "I mean, not

good. What happened was horrible."

"Of course, of course." I had to laugh ruefully. "It's all rather macabre, but I'm still addicted."

"Me too. Jared—" He broke off and inhaled deeply. "Never mind. Maybe it's weird, but at least we're not alone in enjoying it."

"We certainly aren't." I resisted asking one of the many Jared-related questions circling my brain like sharks. "All right, where to?"

"Oh. Really, it's fine. I can just wait here for the truck after all."

I groaned. "Can we just agree that I'm not leaving you out here? Either I wait with you, or I drop you off, or you come with me."

"To your work thing?" He seemed dubious.

"Sure. I don't have to be in a relationship to bring a guest. Angela's big on family, but she actually issued a memo about valuing single people. I guess she caught wind of the rumors that she only promoted married employees."

He frowned. "Isn't that illegal?"

"Depends on the state, but that's irrelevant. It's freezing outside—not to mention dangerous being stuck on that narrow shoulder. I'm on my way to a resort or an inn. It's not far. I'm sure roadside assistance can pick you up there. Do you have any valuables? Shouldn't leave anything in the car."

"There's stuff in the trunk, but I guess I don't need it any-more." He laughed bitterly. "It's just me." He patted his pocket. "I've got my phone. That's all I need."

"We're off, then." I put on a smile and turned on the engine. I had no clue what was going on with Michael, but I'd find out in due time. Step one was getting him somewhere safe and warm.

The narrator's gravelly voice filled the vehicle again. The killer eased open the bedroom door...

"Poised on the threshold, he watched Shirley and Edward sleeping for long minutes, delighting in their vulnerability."

Michael said, "Oh, I haven't heard this one. Is it good? Like, awful-but-good?"

"It is. Fucking creepy. At least it takes place in a city and not the woods."

He peered around uneasily. "Yeah. How is it *this* dark out here? Stupid of me to go so far out of Albany. I didn't think about where I was going."

Hmm. "You were just driving around? No destination?"

"Yeah. I needed to clear my head. Stupid, like I said. We're practically in the Berkshires, I think."

"We are." Pausing the book, I checked the GPS. "Says I'll arrive at my destination in... Oh, only seventeen minutes."

"Really? Cool." He adjusted a vent and rubbed his hands in front of the warm air.

I flipped on his seat warmer before my own. After pressing *play* on the book, we settled into listening, making the odd comment as the narrator described the gruesome scene.

I could almost believe no time had passed and everything was the same as it ever was with Michael.

Almost.

The book paused automatically as the GPS intoned, *"Turn right on Millpond Road."*

"Thanks, Martha," I said.

"You still talk to the GPS, I see. Why is this one a 'Martha'? At least I know that's not your mother's name."

I had to laugh as I braked for the turn and stopped the audiobook. Books were great on the highway, but I couldn't pay attention once the GPS kept interrupting. "No, I don't have an unhealthy fascination with my mum—or a tortured, too-close relationship. None of the serial killer staples, as you know. She just sounded like a Martha. No idea why."

"Of course that's what you'd say to throw me off the scent...
Uh, as you take me deep into the woods to your murder hut?"

I slowed almost to a stop, both of us squinting into the darkness. The snow brightened the forest, but with the moon and stars covered by clouds, the headlights didn't penetrate far.

"Turn right on Millpond Road," Martha repeated.

I asked, "Can you see a sign?" The narrow road was neatly plowed, and the address I'd been given was a seventy-five Millpond Road, so this seemed to be the right place? Aside from the fact that it was the middle of nowhere with no resort, hotel, inn—or anything at all—in sight.

"There—the snowbank's hiding it," Michael said. He squinted. "It says 'Whispering Pines'—nothing about a road."

I pulled up to the tree line so I could see the sign, which was professionally made with an evergreen-shaped logo and gentle script. "This must be it."

"Continue one mile on Millpond Road. Your destination will be on the left," Martha told us.

"Well, Martha seems certain," I said. "Guess there's only one way to find out."

"Let's hope those aren't famous last words." Michael frowned. "I don't know if roadside assistance will be able to pick me up here?"

"Oh. Right." Martha seemed to be leading us even farther into the middle of nowhere. "There does seem to be cell service, at least."

The bottom line was that I didn't want Michael to go. To actually see him again—to have him beside me joking around about serial killers like no time had passed—was the greatest Christmas gift I could have imagined.

I had no idea why he hadn't talked to me in two years, but I'd find out. Whatever was wrong, I'd fix it. My bruised feelings didn't matter.

Reluctantly, I asked, "Do you want me to take you to the nearest town instead?"

For a long moment, Michael looked at me. Then he said, "Nah. I'm sure it'll be fine."

Exhaling, I stepped on the gas.

Chapter Three
Michael

HOW DID I end up here?

Not that I knew exactly where *here* was, but it could've been anywhere for all I cared. Siberia. Antarctica. Transylvania. I was with *Will*. He hadn't hesitated to ride in and rescue my dumb ass, though I didn't deserve it even a little.

It was one of the reasons I loved him.

And yeah, fuck me. I still loved him.

Hearing his deep voice again—his Scottish accent that he insisted had faded but still sounded to me like he'd wandered over from the set of *Outlander*—was everything. Hearing my name on his lips made me shiver.

How had I thought I'd be able to get over him? Or that freezing him out would make any difference? What a joke. My careful plan had unraveled spectacularly.

Jared dumped me, and I couldn't even make it more than a few hours without calling Will for help. I'd almost burst into tears and told him everything, but I'd managed to hang onto a shred of dignity.

It was selfish as hell to be crashing Will's work party, but I wasn't strong enough to insist he take me somewhere else. Not when we were warm and safe in his SUV, and I could hear his low, rough voice so close to me that it gave me goosebumps. I'd always loved how he sounded like he'd just woken up or smoked even though he hated cigarettes and didn't do pot.

We wound deeper into the forest, the SUV's headlights passing over hulking evergreens. The road was plowed, reassuring us it wasn't some abandoned trail that would end with us being stranded and stuck in the snow, huddling for warmth—

Nope. Don't go down that *road.*

It had been disgustingly selfish to call him in the first place, but when I was trapped on the side of the two-lane highway in the middle of nowhere, his was the only voice I'd wanted to hear. I thought if he'd just talk to me for a bit while I waited, I could get through it.

I'd woken up beside Jared this morning. Was that right? Yeah, it was still Friday. But he hadn't even been an option when I'd pulled out my phone. Wow, it was epically *over*. How sad. I'd been kidding myself for a pathetically long time. Even bugging poor Zoe again had been a preferable option to Jared, or calling my parents and disrupting their evening swim.

In the end, I'd had to do it. I needed Will, god help me, and I knew he'd answer even though I didn't deserve it. I'd told myself it was only a phone call. It was safe.

Now here we were. Will was back in arm's reach and just as forbidden as ever. Worst—best?—of all, it felt like the two years of distance had evaporated in a blink. He was so familiar and awesome—generous and caring.

I ached for him. Will still owned my heart, and he didn't have a clue. I couldn't choke down a laugh that sounded awfully manic.

Will glanced at me with a leery half-smile. "What?"

His uncertainty reminded me that, actually, two years of distance *hadn't* completely evaporated. As kind and generous as he was, he clearly still didn't quite know what to make of me dropping back into his life without warning, or finding me looking like hell on the side of a road.

"I can't believe I'm here. This is just so weird. In a good way."

I poked my injured cheek and winced. "Mostly good." Another laugh bubbled up. What was wrong with me?

The truth was undeniable: I was happy. Joyfully, deliriously *happy*. I wished Will could keep driving all night. I wanted to escape with him and go... Anywhere. Everywhere.

"You're sure you didn't hit your head?"

"I swear."

"Middle finger swear?"

A laugh punched out of me. I couldn't remember why we'd created our own rude version of a pinky swear in college, but it still made me giggle. Solemnly, I gave him the finger and intoned, "Middle finger swear."

With a serious nod, Will lifted his right hand from the steering wheel and gave me the finger too. Then our hands met, and we awkwardly hooked our middle fingers.

His skin was warm, and a smile tugged at his lips. I could have held his finger all night, but I pulled my hand back. He was driving, after all.

Will drummed restlessly on the wheel. After a few moments, he asked, "What happened tonight?"

"Can we talk about it later? It's been a long day."

As if on cue, a text from Zoe popped up on the console screen, and Martha asked if Will wanted her to read it. Gripping the arm rests, I almost shouted, *"No!"* in the most melodramatic way possible.

With his brows drawn close, a cute little furrow where they almost touched, Will said, "That's funny. I haven't talked to her in a while." He reached for the screen.

Before I could say anything, Martha relayed the message in her stilted voice.

"Hey. How are you doing? I'm good except my folks are here for the holidays, and I wish it was January already. Kind of, LOL. Anyway, have you talked to Mike? He came by the house before, and it was weird. His face was all cut up. He kind of took off, and we're

worried about him. I've texted, but no reply."

I squirmed at the guilty weight of my phone in my pocket. Both Zoe and Jared had texted, but I hadn't read the messages yet. Martha asked if he wanted to dictate a reply, and Will said no.

Then he said to me, "Something happened with Jared." His jaw was clenched, his blue eyes flashing.

It shouldn't have sent sparks down my spine, but I'd always loved his protectiveness. It made me feel good. Special.

Shit, it was why I'd called him today, wasn't it? Because I knew he'd take care of me, even if I'd honestly only hoped he'd keep me company on the phone while I waited for help. I hadn't dared expect more. Or even that much. More than I deserved.

I said, "Yeah. We broke up." I motioned to my face. "This really was from the Christmas tree and me being a dumbass. He didn't, like, try to scratch my eyes out. I'll tell you the whole story later." Okay, maybe not the *whole* story.

After a tense nod, Will said, "I'm not sure why it's number seventy-five when we've only passed trees." He squinted through the windshield. "I guess addresses don't always make sense."

I exhaled. He wasn't going to push right now. He was so *good.* My chest ached with a ragged swell of affection. How did I ever think I could get by without Will in my life? My plan had been doomed from the start. Even if he'd never love me back the way I wanted, I'd take everything I could get. It would have to be enough.

Realizing I should reply, I said, "Yeah." I checked the console screen. "Martha still thinks we're going the right way." I leaned forward, squinting through the windshield. "Actually, there might be something coming up? I think I see light." A golden glow in the distance grew stronger.

"You've arrived at your destination," Martha announced.

"Is this...a hotel?" I asked.

The trees gave way to a few small buildings, one with a wall of bright windows that looked like a restaurant, and a clearing with a huge bonfire in the middle. Small rectangular structures with rounded roofs fanned out in the distance, set back among the trees. Multicolored Christmas lights were strung around the arched glass-walled front of each little cabin.

Will said, "*Glam*. That's what Angela meant. It's glamping."

Dozens of people congregated by the bonfire, with small fire pits sprinkled around, kids holding sticks in the tamer fires, surely with gooey marshmallows on the ends. The clearing was lined with gold-lit, sparkling Christmas trees.

"Now *this* is Insta-ready," I muttered. Talk about a winter wonderland.

Will parked, and we climbed down from the SUV. Music and laughter carried on the breeze, the wind far less biting here with protective trees all around. Like a little oasis of Christmas cheer and happy families.

The vibe was what I'd imagined for me and Jared and the townhouse—classy and luxurious but festive. Ugh. I cringed as my brain replayed the whole humiliating incident.

Where was I going to go this weekend? There was no way I could stay even one more night at Jared's townhouse. The thought of stepping foot in it again to get my stuff had my stomach churning.

"There you are!" a hot redhead called. She approached with a broad smile for Will. She wore a cute woolen hat, a red coat, and carried a clipboard. "We were—" She noticed me as I came around the vehicle and jolted to a stop. "Oh! Hello."

"Hey!" Shit, this was so awkward crashing Will's work event. The woman stared at me in obvious confusion, and my nervous, embarrassed energy spewed out of my mouth. In words, at least. Not puke. "I'm Michael. Nice to meet you!"

"Uh, hi. I'm Wendy." She smiled and looked between me and Will. "Sorry, I didn't know you were bringing a plus-one."

"Right, this is my—er, Michael," Will said, his words tangling. "It's okay, isn't it?"

"Oh." Her eyebrows shot up. "Oh! Of course! I'll just mark that down." Wendy scrawled on her clipboard with a nervous little laugh. I thought I heard paper rip with the force of her pen. "Okay, super! Welcome to the BRK Sync family, Michael. Terrific to meet you!"

Wendy spun so fast snow flew up around her boots. She didn't even mention my injured face before racing off.

Will said, "That was odd. Usually I can't get rid of her." He grimaced. "That sounds awful. She's a lovely woman. It's just that I've been trying to let her down gently. She knows I'm single, and she's... Very interested."

"Um..." Did he not get what just happened? "Seems like she'll back off now that she thinks we're a couple."

That sure got his attention. "Huh?" Will stared at me.

Honestly, straight guys could be so adorably clueless. "Dude, I'm your plus-one. She clearly thinks we're together. Like, *together*."

Eyes widening, Will practically shouted, "But that's insane!"

It really shouldn't have hurt. It *was* insane. Of course it was! Still...*oof.* I tried to laugh it off, but there was a lump against my windpipe.

Blinking, Will seemed shocked at his own response. He lowered his voice. "What I mean is... I'll clarify with Wendy."

I cleared my throat and joked, "Too late. I'm your boyfriend now. Wendy'll just have to accept you're off the market."

Will smiled weakly, and we made our way out of the parking lot toward the main area of campfires, laughter, and holiday spirit.

Why did I say that?? Being kidnapped by a serial killer might be better than this.

But the thought of being back out there freezing my ass off alone made me shudder. At least I could be safe with Will for a few hours. Surely the tow truck could swing by here and pick me up? Was that a thing? I'd actually never needed roadside assistance before.

I pulled my blood-stained gloves out of my pocket, hoping it was too dark for anyone to notice what a mess I was. The left side of my jeans were stiff from the spilled wine, and I tugged down the hem of my coat.

We approached two men standing by one of the smaller fires roasting marshmallows. Most people were bundled in winter gear, but one of these guys wore a black leather jacket. They were both white and had brown hair, but the one in leather looked as though he'd be more at home on a motorcycle or in the boxing ring.

He was laughing as the other man, who wore dark-framed glasses, tried to feed him a sticky, charred mess. They leaned into each other intimately and were clearly a couple. I watched them and tried to ignore a pang of jealousy.

The guy in glasses noticed us and waved, grimacing at the white goo on his fingers. "There you are!" he called to Will. "We thought perhaps your flight was delayed." He looked to me. "Hello. Goodness, what happened to your face?"

I wished I could wear a sign around my neck that read: *Life and a Christmas tree kicked my ass. I won't be taking questions at this time.*

Will said, "This is my friend Michael. He got scratched by pine needles. Also, his car broke down not too far from here. Michael, this is my colleague Seth and his husband Logan."

I shook with Logan in the leather jacket, and Seth held out his marshmallow-streaked hand before stopping short and waving instead. He pushed up his glasses, then grimaced as he clearly realized he now had marshmallow on his nose. Without a word, Logan swiped at Seth's nose.

"Are you guys hungry? Dinner was delicious. I'm sure they could make something for you." Seth nodded to the restaurant.

Through the floor-to-ceiling windows, staff were visible stacking chairs and mopping.

"Thanks, but I can just grab something later," I said before pulling out my phone. Ignoring the texts from Jared and Zoe, I jabbed the new message from my roadside assistance company.

Apparently, the jazzy recording of "Joy to the World" being piped in around the clearing was loud enough that I'd missed my phone dinging. "I don't want to imp—" I broke off as I read.

"What is it?" Will asked.

I scanned the text again. This couldn't be right. Shit. *Shit.*

"Michael?" Will took hold of my shoulder, his gloved hand strong and secure.

"They can't send anyone to get my car until tomorrow."

"That's all right." He squeezed gently. "You can stay here."

Honestly, staying in this winter wonderland with Will sounded like a fever dream come true, but I'd already made him miss dinner, and I was a mess, and—

A breathless, grinning woman appeared. "There you are!" She focused on me and exclaimed, "Whoa! Did a cat attack you?"

I mumbled, "Christmas tree accident." God, was it really that bad? I squirmed, my face burning.

"Ouch." She looked concerned, but then was fighting a smile again. The hair sticking out from under her woolen hat looked freshly dyed blonde.

Logan narrowed his gaze at her. "What's up with you?"

Seth laughed. "Clearly your sister has gossip to share." He lowered his voice. "Is Angela giving our office the new client group from the Boston acquisition?"

"No. Well, maybe—she hasn't said either way. She's still making the rounds and meeting kids. We had our turn, so Jun took the boys on the sleigh ride." She motioned vaguely at the woods, where apparently sleigh rides were happening.

Then she smiled at me. *Beamed* at me. "I'm Jenna. Will and I are on the People Development Committee together."

I wasn't sure I understood what that meant, but it didn't matter. "Nice to meet you. I'm—"

"Will's boyfriend!" She turned her glowing smile on Will. "Congrats! I'm really happy for you. Everyone thought you didn't want to settle down, but clearly, you just hadn't found the right person."

"What?" Will gaped at her before looking at me and dropping his hand from my shoulder like he'd been burned. Which was a perfectly fair response and shouldn't have made me wince internally. He groaned. "You heard that from Wendy already? It's been less than five minutes."

"No, from Matt. Oh, here he is."

Wearing fuzzy red earmuffs over shaggy blond hair, Matt joined us. He slapped Will's shoulder. "Hey, heartbreaker. So you're gay, huh? Awesome."

Will sputtered. "Why do you think that?"

Matt tilted his head, reminding me of a golden retriever. "Oh, are you bi or pan? That's awesome too."

"I..." Will shook his head, even more flustered now. "Michael's bi, but we're only friends. What did Wendy tell you?"

"Actually, Becky heard Michael say he's your boyfriend and that Wendy'll have to deal with it. I think she had plans to make her big move on you this weekend."

Will gaped. "Becky? I didn't see Becky. Was she hiding behind parked cars eavesdropping?" He inhaled deeply, raising his gloved hands. "It doesn't matter. What matters is that it wasn't—it was a *joke*. Wendy jumped to conclusions, and Michael joked about it."

Great. Me and my stupid joke. How much more could I mess up today? I'd probably get Will fired in a minute.

Seth and Logan shared a glance, and Seth asked, "Why would Wendy think you're a couple if you're not?"

Will explained about the plus-one, and I added, "I'm only

here because my car broke down, and Will came to get me."

"Where were you heading?" the woman—Jenna?—asked. Yes, her name was Jenna. She was Logan's sister, and she worked with Will and Seth, who was Logan's husband. And Logan wore the leather jacket. There were so many new people and names flying at me, and if I didn't repeat info to myself, I'd go blank and not remember anyone's names.

Jenna added, "There's not much around here."

Everyone was looking at me, including Will, and I could practically hear his unanswered questions about Jared filling his head again. I hoped the firelight was orangey enough that they all couldn't tell how hard I was blushing.

I fidgeted and motioned vaguely with my hand. "I was going to a thing. But anyway, I shouldn't even be here. I'm sure I can call a cab." I pulled out my phone. "Uber probably isn't out this far, but…"

Seth said, "I'm not sure there are any taxi companies in this area. Perhaps if we were in the Berkshires proper, but this is a bit of a no-man's land."

"You're not going anywhere tonight." Will's tone was firm and final, but not sharp or pissed off even though I deserved it. He was reassuring and in control, and I could breathe again, my racing heart calming.

I nodded. "Okay. Sorry to cause all this confusion. I can explain to everyone that it was a joke."

Matt said to Will, "Bro, you should just roll with it. Angela *loves* promoting LGBTQ-plus people. I mean, not like you don't also have to be good at your job, but she has a hard-on for disproving Texas-related assumptions about her being bigoted. It'll make you stand out."

Scoffing, Will said, "I'm not going to tell Angela of all people and lie to everyone."

Matt winced. "What if I guarantee she already knows? I mean,

Becky told me because I'm her fiancé. But Christopher was nearby, and you know he's pals with Dale, Angela's assistant. I swear Christopher's her inside man for intel on our branch. Anyway, you know people wonder how a guy as hot as you is single. Our jobs are boring. We need something to gossip about."

My head spun as Matt rattled on. Hadn't it only been *minutes* since we'd arrived?

I refocused when he frowned at me. "Dude, what happened to your face?"

Ignoring the question, Will said, "Becky needs to tell Christopher or Dale or Angela herself if necessary that she was mistaken."

Jenna said, "You know, pretending to be boyfriends worked out for these two." She shot Seth and Logan a grin.

Hold on—they were pretending? Weren't they married? This was getting weirder and weirder. I had so many questions, and my face really did hurt, and my relationship was over, and where was I going to live? God, I'd have to call my parents in Florida and make them worry about me right before Christmas...

Will stared at Logan and Seth. "But you're married."

Seth smiled sheepishly and raised his hands. "Now, yes. But at the beginning, we were strangers. Angela's track record on promoting single people has improved, but she does seem to feel that staff with families are more reliable, even if it's subconscious. Anyway, it's a long story."

Will had just gotten the job at BRK when I'd had my epiphany about needing to grow up and get over him, so this was all new to me. Apparently this aspect was new to Will too.

"Give me the short version," Will whispered.

Logan shoved his hands in his leather jacket pockets and shared a guilty glance with Seth. Seth cleared his throat, keeping his voice low. "Logan and I pretended to be dating when we met to give me a better chance at a promotion I really deserved."

"Which you got!" Jenna added. "You're welcome. Also, you

and my brother fell in love, so again I say *you're welcome.*" She winked at them.

"Caper, caper, caper!" Matt chanted under his breath and raised his palm to Jenna for a high five.

Seth rolled his eyes. "Yes, it was Jenna's impulsive idea, and Matt was our enabler. It was completely harebrained." He gazed at Logan with a tenderness that brought another lump to my throat before saying, "But it changed my life."

"Yeah, now you're stuck with me and Connor," Logan joked, but he leaned into Seth, their fingers brushing. I had the feeling that they would kiss right now if we weren't all standing here. I assumed Connor was their kid? I was never going to keep all these names straight.

Jealously and longing filled me like a balloon about to burst.

Matt said, "Awww. And you *did* get that promotion." He gave Will a pointed look. "You should consider it."

"I'm not going to appropriate an identity that isn't mine," Will said.

"Fair enough," Jenna agreed.

"But everyone's a little bi, right?" Matt elbowed Will. "Come on, it's been way too long since we had a caper. Don't you think, like, Chris Hemsworth is hot?"

Crossing his arms, Will laughed awkwardly. Was he blushing? He shrugged. "Who doesn't? I do have eyes. That doesn't prove anything."

"See?" Matt held up his fists triumphantly. "Be bi for the weekend. It'll be fun! Plus, it'll keep Wendy off the scent. She's been stuck crushing on you for way too long." He put on an announcer voice. "*Operation Fake Boyfriend Two: The Reboyfriending.*"

Will being bi like me *and* my boyfriend would be my greatest Christmas wish come true, and obviously it was never happening, even if it was only pretend.

"Shh!" Jenna hissed at Matt, putting a finger to her lips before motioning with her head to a group of people approaching.

A petite white woman with aggressively blonde hair curling out from under a pink woolen pom-pom hat and wearing a pink ski outfit—including snow pants—marched toward us. She was with a slim, brown-skinned man with designer glasses wearing a sleek black ski outfit that also looked very expensive.

Judging by the way everyone watched her with a mix of awe, respect, and a dash of fear, I assumed this was Angela Barker. Seth and Logan were closest when we widened our circle for her, and to my surprise, she pulled them both into fierce, familiar hugs.

"How *are* you?" she demanded more than asked in a nasal tone mixed with a warm Texas drawl. "Nice glasses, Seth."

"Thank you. The joys of aging."

Angela swatted his arm in his puffy parka. "You're still a spring chicken, trust me. Speaking of which, where's Connor?"

"Finishing up a late exam before he comes home next week for Christmas," Seth said. "He's sorry to miss you."

She clucked her tongue. "Well, I suppose I'll forgive him. Gettin' good grades at Harvard is important. Is he still studying economics? I have a pal opening a company in Boston. I was thinking Connor would be perfect for a summer internship. Fully paid, of course."

Logan smiled. "That's so generous of you. Actually, Connor's switched to pre-med."

She gasped in delight. "That's wonderful! Hmm." Her gaze went distant for a moment, and she seemed to be running through a list in her head. "Lemme know where's he's thinking of applying for med school. I have some connections."

Logan and Seth thanked her again, and Angela waved them off. Was she wearing rings on the *outside* of her leather gloves? "It's my absolute pleasure. And you know I can't resist being nosy. Does Connor have a girlfriend yet?"

Logan shrugged. "Not that he's told us. Too busy studying. He's working damn hard."

"I'm sure you're both so proud. Logan, how's work going for you? Must be tons of contracting jobs these days. Albany's really spreading. Lots of new buildings. My friend Susan was thrilled with the work you did on her new office."

I could almost see Logan puff up with pride. "Thank you for recommending us. Yeah, things are great. I hired three new full-time workers for my crew."

Okay, I could *definitely* see how Angela Barker was a valuable person to know. Especially if you caught her attention and were in her good books.

Angela said, "You know I don't recommend anyone I don't fully believe in." She turned her laser focus on Will with a grin. "Now, Will, I haven't seen you since your interview. I hear you were out in Seattle this week helping them get off to a strong start. I've loved team players since my daddy took me to my first Rangers game. Great work. And I hear you've got a new boy-friend!"

She shifted her gaze to me, and of course this was the part when Will and I would explain the misunderstanding and—

"Sugar!" Angela gasped. "What in heavens happened to your pretty face?"

"Oh, I'm fine! I was carrying a Christmas tree, and I fell, and—"

She grasped my wrist and tugged with surprising strength. "Let's get you cleaned up. Dale, where's the first aid?"

"Really, I'm okay!" I had no choice as Angela marched me over to an outbuilding, Dale somehow walking even faster across the clearing and leading the way. Will scrambled after us, mouthing, *"Sorry!"*

We climbed the few steps to the little one-room building, which sat at the edge of the clearing closest to the restaurant.

Inside, there were pallets of water bottles and piles of boxes—probably corporate gifts judging by the words written in black marker on the cardboard: *T-shirts, hats, blankets, mousepads.*

A table and four chairs sat in the middle, and Dale hefted a large plastic container marked with a red cross onto the table.

Angela had me in a chair prodding my cheek in record time. "Sugar, are you allergic? These scratches sure puffed up. Was it a pine tree?"

"I don't know. Maybe? I mean, yes, the tree was scotch pine. I didn't think I was allergic? But I guess I might be."

I glanced at Will, who hovered nearby looking worried and also devastatingly handsome. I'd muted him on my socials, aside from the few times I'd broken down and looked at his posts. It wasn't like I'd forgotten how gorgeous he was, but that furrowed brow of concern over blue eyes made me feel weak.

I added, "This isn't blood," motioning to my stained jeans before she noticed and had me on the way to the ER before I could get a word in.

Hands on hips, Angela whistled as she shook her head. "Well, I'm sure glad to hear that! I have some over-the-counter antihistamines in my purse if you want. Never leave home without 'em." I nodded, and she added, "And it's wonderful to meet you. Is it Mike?"

"Michael," I said. "But you can call me Mike if you want. It's fine." I weirdly wanted to make her happy. "Most people call me Mike. Except Will and my parents."

Angela's very smooth forehead didn't move as she smiled. "If Michael's what you prefer, that's what I'll call you. And if you'd rather be they/them, that's okay too. More than okay! It's great. I'm she/her, just so you know."

"Oh, thank you. I use he/him." I had the feeling Angela was new to the concept of different pronouns, but she was making the effort. "And really, I'm fine. You must have more people to greet."

She looked to Dale, who nodded. She said, "That I do. Will, do you know how to clean him up? My girls are beyond the scraped-knee phase of life now, but I got lots of practice. First, you dab on the antiseptic." She pulled out a bottle from the first aid kit and gave Will a quick rundown. "All right, I'll leave you two lovebirds to it."

Will said, "Oh, well—"

"I hope you know how very, very welcome you are here." Angela took hold of both our arms, peering up at Will and then down at me in the chair with such sweet sincerity. "Bisexual, trisexual, transgender, asexual, and plain ol' gay—or just queer as a three-dollar bill. Whatever your identity, you are welcome and part of the family. Okay? Okay. Oh, and Will, I'd love a debrief on Seattle. You know, I think you might be just the right person to help me with an exciting new secret project. But no more shop talk this weekend! We're just here to have fun. Get patched up now, you hear? Bye-bye!"

Before either of us could reply, Angela Barker whirled away like a pink, supportive hurricane with Dale on her heels.

"Angela, wait!" Will called. He ran a hand over his thick hair, messing it up.

Was his hair still soft? I obviously hadn't had many opportunities to touch it, but once after an unfortunate incident at a party in junior year, I'd slowly picked gum from the soft waves. I'd been on the couch, and Will had sat on the floor between my legs, his eyes closed, leaning back into my touch. He'd been hungover, though. It hadn't meant anything.

"Michael?"

"Huh?" I jerked back to the present. "Yep. Um, that was a little nuts."

"A little? What just happened?" He dropped his hands to his sides. "I'm sorry. I'll talk to Angela in the morning."

"It's fine. I mean..." I shrugged, my heart skipping as a wild idea crashed into my brain and right out of my mouth. "You heard what she just said about a special project. This could help your career. I don't mind being your boyfriend." *What am I saying?* "Pretending on this retreat, I mean. But I get it if you don't want to be bi for the weekend."

Picking up the antiseptic bottle, Will unscrewed the cap with jerky motions. "I..." He read the label, then screwed the cap back on. Then he twisted it back off before digging through the first aid kit. "Of course it wouldn't bother me, but... You don't feel like I'm appropriating your identity?"

I had to laugh. "No. Sexuality is fluid. I thought I was straight until I wasn't. It doesn't bother me at all." *In fact, it's my deepest fantasy that you'll realize you're not actually straight.* "The truth is, I could use a place to crash this weekend. If it's okay with you, I could stay?"

Will did look at me then, his blue eyes shining with concern. "Yeah. They can tow your car tomorrow. You're staying here with me."

A shiver ran down my spine at his no-arguments tone. Mouth dry, I nodded.

He smiled tentatively. "Maybe a caper is just the distraction you need?"

"Can't hurt, right?" *Don't answer that.*

Will dabbed a cotton ball with antiseptic and sat on the edge of the table, leaning down to take my chin with his fingers. His breath tickled my cheek, his dry fingertips gentle but firm. Desire curled lazily through my belly. I closed my eyes, imagining a brush of his lips on my hot skin...

He murmured, "This is going to sting."

He wasn't wrong. In fact, this would hurt a hell of a lot more than that. Pretending to be Will's boyfriend would break my heart all over again.

Chapter Four
Will

H ADN'T MUM NAGGED me about taking a leap?
    Bi for the weekend.

Well, this was certainly a leap. It wasn't hurting anyone, was it? Not that it felt good to lie to Angela or Wendy or other colleagues. And I was sure this wasn't at all what Mum had had in mind, but…

Is it really a lie? Does wanking to blokes qualify me?

Leaning over Michael, I held his chin with my fingers and dabbed at the cuts on his cheek. He didn't move a muscle even though it had to hurt. Clearly it did since his hands were clenched into tight fists, his shallow breath ragged.

"Sorry. My mum used to let me squeeze her," I said with a smile.

"Huh?" Michael stared up at me, his body so tense he might snap in two.

"Here." I took his right hand, urging his fingers wide over my knee where I perched on the side of the table. "Go on and squeeze."

Adam's apple bobbing, Michael dug his fingers into the flesh around my knee, his palm warm through my jeans.

"There you go," I murmured as I dabbed another cut. "Helps, doesn't it?" Michael was of course stronger than a child, but I didn't mind the bruising pressure. I liked the idea that I was absorbing some of his pain.

He was still my best friend. That remained true without a doubt. It wasn't that I was over him ghosting me with no hard feelings. But I hadn't been prepared for how wonderful it was to see him again. I was going to find out what happened with Jared and get to the bottom of Michael's distance. I wasn't a violent man, but if Jared had laid a finger on Michael…

Patience was key. Tonight, Michael needed bandaging up, food in his belly, and a good night's sleep. I eyed his stained jeans, the fabric clinging to his lean thigh. It was probably sticky as hell.

"Want to take a shower?"

Michael blinked up at me, his hand ready to crush my knee. "Yeah. I'm such a mess. I assume there are real bathrooms and not just outhouses?"

"If there are bloody outhouses, this is *not* fucking glamping."

"I promise there are no outhouses!" a chipper young woman with a dark pixie cut said as she entered. "Hi!"

Michael whipped his hand back to his lap. "Hi," he croaked.

"I'm Abby. I heard we had latecomers and that you might need first aid?" She was short, chubby, and wore a Whispering Pines jacket with a pinned nametag reading: *Abigail Lee.*

"Hello." I stood and nodded to Michael. "Christmas tree mishap earlier."

"A danger of the season!" Abby winced. "Ouch. I'm afraid there's not much to do for it other than the antiseptic and applying a bandage."

"Any chance of a shower?" I asked.

Abby said, "Of course. Every pod has a complete en suite. We provide wash-and-fold laundry service as well."

"This really is glam," I said. "How about a late supper?"

"I'm afraid the kitchen's closed, but we have delicious gourmet sandwiches and snacks available at all hours." Abby pulled out a packet of waterproof bandages. "We'll make up a picnic basket for you."

"You don't have to go to any trouble," I said, but Abby insisted. I got out of the way as she expertly finished with the first aid and led us outside.

"Any food allergies?" She dutifully tapped out a note on her mini tablet that I was allergic to kiwi. "Where's your luggage? The system says you haven't checked into your pod yet."

"Right. My suitcase is in the car, and—bugger. Michael, er... There was a bit of a mix-up, and he doesn't have his things."

A quizzical smile touched Abby's lips for only a moment. "No problem at all." She typed rapidly on her tablet.

Before I knew it, Abby had the keys to my SUV, and she and her team leapt into action. While they handled the luggage, we checked into our pod, which was one of the farthest from the clearing. The little snow-dusted buildings reminded me of Yule logs and were roofed with thick, bark-like brown shingles.

Thick evergreens grew between each pod, and the rows were angled in such a way that each had privacy through the arched, glassed-wall front. The colored Christmas lights strung around the window cast a warm glow as Abby led us inside and turned on the overhead recessed lighting with a remote control.

"We have a small seating area just to the right." She motioned to two chairs with a slim table between them at the foot of the bed. "Along the left wall is shelving for clothing and a small kitchenette with bar fridge and coffee station. The en suite bathroom is beyond the sliding barn door at the back. Of course, most of the space is taken by the bed, as you can see."

"Indeed," I said. The queen-sized bed against the right curving wall was neatly made with pristine linens and looked soft and inviting.

And it was only the one bed.

Which made perfect sense, but still somehow surprised me. Not that it *mattered*. It was perfectly fine.

Michael said, "Yep, that's a bed!" and laughed slightly hysterically. He really must have been tired.

As Abby went on about the Scandinavian-farmhouse design inspiration, featuring pale pine wood and white granite accents on the counter over the bar fridge and into the bathroom, I couldn't stop staring at the bed for some reason.

"You're probably wondering why we didn't go for a folding bed design, but we decided comfort was king." Abby patted the end of the snow-white duvet. "Firm yet soft. It's amazing, honestly."

Well, if there was only going to be one bed, at least it was an amazing one.

"And though you have privacy with the design and spacing of the pods and pathways, there's a custom-shaped blind that can be lowered." She picked up the shiny remote control from the counter and pressed the button. The cream-colored blind lowered with a soft *whir*. "Of course, it must be raised to use the front door," she added, pressing another button and sending the blind back up.

Another staff member arrived with my small suitcase, SUV keys, and a Whispering Pines sweatsuit and pouch of toiletries for Michael. Abby assured us food was on its way, gave us the Wi-Fi password, and left.

"Do you want to go first?" Michael asked, nodding toward the bathroom.

"No, go ahead."

"Cool, thanks." Michael hung up his coat on one of the hooks positioned on the wall by the door just under the curve of the roof. In the middle of the pod, the ceiling was a few feet over us, but the headroom decreased on the sides.

I hung up my coat as well, and why was there suddenly a strained silence? Distant carols were barely audible, and I could hear the thud of my own heart. Michael and I had undressed in front of each other a thousand unthinking times.

The only difference was we'd never pretended to be dating before. That and the fact that we had barely spoken in two years.

Still, there was no reason for nervousness. This was *Michael.*

"I missed you," I blurted.

Michael jerked up straight from where he'd bent to put his boots on the tucked-away mat—and bashed his head on the low curve of the ceiling. "Ow, fuck!" He rubbed the crown of his head.

"Are you okay?" In a stride, I reached him.

He gritted his teeth. "Uh-huh. Yep. Come on, this is the part where you make fun of me for being a dumbass."

Historically, that was true. but it didn't feel right to rib him right now. All I did was take his head in my hands. "Let me see." Whatever had happened today, he'd been battered enough.

Michael lowered his head, and I gently probed to make sure he hadn't done any damage. "I'm fine," he murmured.

The red, green, pink, yellow, and blue lights from outside reflected in his golden hair, which was fine beneath my fingers. He raised his head, and I dropped my hands. His unbandaged cheek was flushed pink.

I forced a careless tone. "Might have a bump in the morning, dumbass." I slugged his arm like we were back in uni at a frat party. It was like squeezing my feet into shoes I'd long outgrown.

Michael slugged me back, though not hard. "That's me. Remember that time I got wasted and jumped off the roof into the pool at that party?"

"Christ, you were lucky it was deep." The memory of watching his reckless leap made my gut twist. I shook my head. "That feels like another lifetime."

"Yeah. I guess we really did grow up. Or I tried, at least. Now…" He ran a hand through his hair, wincing.

"Now?" I prompted after the silence went on.

Not meeting my gaze, he said, "Now I really need to get out of these jeans. I'll just…" He hooked a thumb toward the barn door and disappeared inside the bathroom.

I blew out a long breath. This morning, I'd woken alone in a hotel room in Seattle. Tonight, I was sharing a bed with my MIA best friend in a cabin in the woods. Scratch that, a *pod* in the woods.

Oh, and I was bisexual for the weekend, and said MIA—or *formerly* MIA—best friend was my boyfriend. Not a problem! This wasn't real. It didn't mean anything.

I gulped down a bottle of water from the mini fridge. Maybe a mad caper was the distraction we *both* needed. Why not have fun with it? Put everything else aside and take the weekend to reconnect and relax. It was Christmas, after all.

The shower turned on, and the soothing sound filled the pod. I took a deep breath through my nose and exhaled.

Right, here we go. Relaxation time. Caper time. Fun time.

Easier said than done. There wasn't much room to pace, yet I managed quite a few narrow laps before opening my suitcase and rooting around for my toiletries and the baggy shorts and tee I lounged in before bed. I didn't typically wear anything to sleep, but I would tonight.

I found myself staring at the bed again. Why was I so… I didn't even know. What was this jumbled mix of emotions? Mum would call it a "tizzy."

It was wonderful to finally see Michael again in person, yet questions nagged, and hurt lingered, along with anger that popped up without warning.

The knock at the glass was barely a tap, yet I jumped a mile. An apologetic staff member delivered the basket of food and asked for the laundry he'd been told to collect. I tapped lightly on the barn door and told Michael I needed his clothes.

The water turned off, and as I was about to say I could just grab them, wet feet slapped on the tile. With a white towel snug around his waist, Michael slid back the door and held out a bundle. Steam wafted out, and Michael's pale chest was faintly pink from the hot shower. Water clung to his red nipples.

I snatched the clothing, dropping Michael's black boxer briefs. Laughing nervously, I bent and grabbed the soft cotton. "Here you go!" I said far too loudly and merrily to the young man waiting.

He opened a black tote marked *Laundry* in white. I'd noticed *Coffee* and *Sugar* on the counter. What was with this farmhouse trend of labeling everything as though we'd struggle to identify basic household items otherwise? At least Whispering Pines was too posh for reminders to *Live, laugh, love.*

"Anything else I can do for you this evening?" the boy asked. His gaze slid to Michael and back to me. There was no judgment evident—his polite smile didn't falter. But I was very aware that he surely thought Michael and I were lovers.

A strange sensation rippled through me, and I practically yelped, "No, thank you!" before closing the door after him. What was that reaction? It wasn't embarrassment or shame. I supposed it was a bit of a thrill. This was the first time I'd been perceived as anything but straight.

"What's so funny?" Michael asked. He picked up the sweatsuit from the bed and unfolded it.

"Hmm?" I blinked at him.

"You're smiling."

"Oh!" I grabbed the food basket and brought it to the counter. "I'm hungry. Let's hope there's something good." From the corner of my eye, I could see Michael retreat into the bathroom. The sliding door was still open, and I spotted the white movement of his towel.

Channeling all my focus on the covered basket, I opened it and announced, "Turkey and Havarti on multigrain, corned beef on rye, club on white—you'll want that. Mmm, these cookies are still warm." I took out the peanut butter for Michael.

"I'm done with the bathroom if you want it. Oh, are those peanut butter?"

I handed him the two cookies half-wrapped in white paper, and he bit into one eagerly and mumbled, "Oh my god."

Along with the other peanut butter cookie, I put the club sandwich on a plate for him. The picnic basket also included utensils and cloth napkins. "I'm going to clean up, but don't wait for me." I handed him the plate. "Crack on."

A smile tugged at his lips. "I love how you say that but you insist you hardly sound Scottish anymore."

"Trust me, I don't."

"Sure, I believe you. Cheerio, guv'nor?"

"Oi! I'm not *English*." I grabbed his wet towel from the floor and snapped it at him as he laughed and dodged.

In the compact bathroom, the tile floor was so warm under my bare feet that it had to be heated. After traveling all day, I really did need a wash. Michael had left the towel bathmat in front of the glass-walled shower. There was just enough room for a toilet and sink on either side of the barn door.

There was still plenty of hot water, and though I'd only planned on a quick rinse, I stayed in the shower's cocoon for a good ten minutes. Afterward, standing on the damp bathmat and toweling off, I listened to Michael putter around. Still had to pinch myself that he was here with me.

And everyone thinks we're boyfriends.

Almost everyone, at least. They were going to look at me the way the kid who collected the laundry did. Not that he did anything but smile. Shaking my head, I swiped at the condensation on the mirror above the sink. I was being daft. It wasn't a big deal. Who cared what anyone thought—whether they fancied me a "ladies' man" or not. No skin off my nose.

"Hey, um… Did you want to go back out and socialize?"

Michael's voice came from just on the other side of the barn door, which should have seemed thicker somehow.

I rubbed the towel over my hair. "Frankly, no. It's getting late anyway."

"Yeah, I can't hear the music anymore."

"I'll socialize plenty tomorrow."

After pulling on my shorts and tee over damp skin, I slid open the door. Michael glanced up from where he crouched in front of the mini fridge, then sprang to his feet. Belatedly, he winced and put his hand up as if he was about to bonk his head again.

"You're good this time," I said, squeezing past him to grab my phone from the white bedspread. "I should reply to Zoe. Not right to leave her worrying."

Michael's shoulders slumped. "Shit, yeah."

"I'll just tell her you're with me and you're safe."

"Thanks. I'm sorry to be such a pain in the ass." He rubbed his face, apparently forgetting about the bandage. "Ow! Shit."

"Don't be sorry. You're helping me potentially advance my career, so it all works out."

"Never been a beard before."

"Not with that peach fuzz."

"I'd throw this cookie at you, but it's too good."

Chuckling, I texted a quick response to Zoe. At the same time, Michael looked at his phone and groaned. "Fuck me," he muttered. "Jared must have talked to my mom."

"Okay," I said cautiously.

Michael's parents were a bit strange. He'd been a surprise baby and his siblings were substantially older. Honestly, I'd always felt like his parents were rather over the job by the time he came along. Not that they didn't love him, but he used to stress about handling everything himself and not asking them for help unless he absolutely had to.

"Why would he—" Michael scrubbed a hand through his

damp hair. "Fuck. I guess he really was worried when I didn't reply."

Michael's thumbs flew over the screen of his phone, and then he groaned again. "I texted Jared, but I have to call my mom for a minute. Is that okay? She'll worry too much. Sorry."

"Of course. I can…" I glanced around. This pod was definitely not designed for privacy.

"No, you stay here." Michael shoved his feet into his boots and ducked outside, the phone to his ear.

Fat snowflakes had begun to drift down, and they caught in his hair and landed on his shoulders, white on the navy sweatshirt. He faced the trees. I wanted to tell him to put on a hat so he didn't catch cold.

His voice was muffled, but I could still make out most of what he was saying. I should have popped in my earbuds or run the tap, but I listened to snatches of Michael's half of the conversation.

"I'm sorry he worried you. I'm fine."

"Yes, of course."

"No! I'm not in trouble! Honestly."

"Mom, we just had a fight. Jared's being a drama queen."

So they didn't break up? Hmm. I wasn't sure I believed that. I also wasn't sure why I was so disappointed to hear it. I'd never even met fucking Jared.

There was that resentment ballooning up. I should've been glad if he and Jared had only had a fight. Except it had been around the time he got together with Jared that he'd ghosted me, so maybe it was okay that I didn't jump for joy if they were going to patch it up.

Outside, Michael had one arm wrapped around his middle, and he shifted from foot to foot. It was too cold to be standing out there, but before I could bring him his coat, he hung up and hurried back inside, stamping his boots on the mat.

"Everything okay?" I asked.

"Yeah. Thanks. Brr." He shook like a dog.

I poked at the coffee machine. "Want a hot drink? Or there's wine and beer in the fridge." I examined a bar selection on the counter. "They have those little bottled cocktails as well. How about a Manhattan?"

"Sure, I'm not picky. Thanks. I'll pay for it."

I scoffed. "Angela's paying for it, remember? I'm sure she won't mind, *sugar*." I poured the cocktail for Michael into a glass over ice since I'd never known him not to want booze on the rocks.

We adjusted the chairs and low, narrow table so they were right in front of the glass. I fiddled with the remote and turned off the lights overhead. With the colored outdoor lights reflecting off the snowy evergreens, it was bright enough to see.

"Weird to have a hotel room without a TV," Michael said. "It's kind of nice though."

I glanced around. "I hadn't thought about it. I fell asleep watching terrible crime shows on cable in my room in Seattle this week."

That it was somehow still the same day that I'd left Seattle was surreal. Here I was in the middle of the woods with Michael of all people? Pretending he was my boyfriend? I took a long swallow of Merlot.

"Oh, what did you watch? The ones with the cheesy narration?"

"You'll have to narrow down that field by a large margin."

"True. There's a series all about murders in Orange County. Crappy narration, but the crimes were interesting. They were all solved too."

We chatted about true crime, movies, and the Mets off-season trades. It was all so blissfully normal, as if the past two years of near silence hadn't happened at all.

Then it was time for bed.

Why was it so awkward to crash together? We'd slept where

we fell plenty of times back in the day, including in the same bed. Now, we hemmed and hawed. I asked, "Which side do you fancy? I don't mind."

Michael fiddled with the bandage on his cheek. "Jared likes the left side, so I'm used to the right."

I hesitated. "But which side do *you* prefer?" Was Jared some kind of control freak? A million questions flooded onto my tongue, but I held it. Michael didn't need an interrogation tonight.

"The left if it's cool?"

Putting on an exaggeratedly flat American accent, I said, "It's cool AF, bro."

He chuckled and crawled across the mattress since the left side of the bed was under the pod's curving roof. "Thanks, *Brett*. You going to that kegger later?"

"Fuckin'-A."

We laughed. I hadn't thought about "Brett Yankface," my frat boy alter ego, in ages. I couldn't remember how we'd dreamed up the character, but it had become a running joke between us.

I'd lowered the shade, but the Christmas lights shone through faintly. "Should I switch off the outside lights?"

"Nah. Unless they bug you? It's nice for a change. I don't need pitch black to sleep."

Presumably, Jared did? I reminded myself that it wasn't a character flaw to prefer a dark room for sleeping as I slipped under the fluffy duvet and adjusted my pillows. With the shade down, it was much darker than it had been, and the string of colored lights was faint.

"It is nice," I murmured.

"Mmm."

My body didn't have a clue what time it was, and despite the awkwardness earlier, I found myself relaxing into the very soft— yet firm—mattress. As I drifted off, the lyrics of one of the holiday songs that had been playing in the clearing echoed through my head.

It came upon a midnight clear
That glorious song of old…

Chapter Five
Michael

WHY WAS IT light? Stretched out on my back, I tried to make sense of the pale glow through a cream-colored blind over a huge window and the pillowy mattress under me. In a rush, everything flooded back, and I sucked in a breath, fully awake in a thump of my heart.

"'Morning," Will rasped beside me, his blue eyes watching me. "It's all right," he murmured. "You're with me."

Perhaps he thought I'd jolted with fear. "Yeah. Thanks."

Oh my god, here I was. Safe with Will. Waking up next to Will. Here *we* were, the duvet rumpled, Will yawning and arching his back as he stretched his arms overhead.

I tried not to stare at the dark thatch of hair in his armpit and failed epically. His white undershirt was also thin enough to see the circles of his nipples and his chest hair.

As I forced myself to look at the ceiling, I became extremely aware of how close our legs might be under the duvet. I inched my right foot over, wondering how near I could get because I guess I liked torturing myself? The brush of my skin against his would only make me want to press him back into the soft mattress more.

Also, bless whoever had picked out the extra-thick duvet, because my dick was embarrassingly hard. I could laugh it off as morning wood, but I'd rather not have to. The heat of Will's body was so close, and his unique scent filled my nose, along with Head and Shoulders, the shampoo he'd always used though I don't think he'd ever had dandruff. Maybe that was *because* of the Head and Shoulders?

"Michael?"

"Uh-huh?" I lay rigid as I focused on Will's frown.

"Did Jared hurt you?"

I wanted to roll over and face the low, curving wall of the pod, go back to sleep, and not have to think about Jared or where I was going to live. But Will had been patient, and I recognized the determination in that brow furrow.

"Yes." As Will inhaled sharply, I shook my head. "Not like that. I swear."

Will shifted onto his left side, propping up his head with his hand. Raising an eyebrow, he gave me the finger. I had to laugh as I wrapped my middle finger around his.

Also, I was right about the effect of skin-on-skin.

I let go of his finger and tugged the duvet up around my neck, burrowing underneath. My bandaged cheek was itchy, but I tucked my hands in the pockets of the borrowed sweatpants. Oh wait, too close to my dick. I clasped my hands over my stomach. As I fidgeted, Will waited patiently.

Why was this bandage so itchy? Squirming, I snaked out a hand and peeled a corner loose.

"Oi. Should you be doing that?"

"It's driving me nuts."

"Here." He batted my hand away and sat up.

I held my breath as Will leaned over and took my face in his hands. His thumbs were warm and a little dry, and as he angled my chin, I remembered that moment on the side of the road when he'd first noticed the wounds and had touched me similarly. I'd wanted to throw myself into his arms and never let go.

Wait, had I done that? We'd hugged but I couldn't remember who'd moved first. My memory was a mess of fantasy and reality.

Now I was in bed with Will, and if this was a dream, I'd happily sleep forever.

His exhalation tickled my nose. My heart hammered. Will slowly, slowly peeled off the bandage and tape. He brushed the scratches with his fingertip.

"How is it?" I whispered. There was no reason to be whispering, but in the slowly brightening dawn and the silence of the pod surrounded by the snowy forest, it felt necessary.

"Better. I think the antihistamines helped a lot. Not all red and puffy now."

"Cool. Thanks."

Will relaxed back under the duvet. "No problem."

Pull off the other Band-Aid already.

"So, it turns out Jared has wanted to break up with me for months. It all came out yesterday."

"That prick. Right before Christmas?"

I squirmed, humiliation washing through me. "He was going to wait until January, but I overheard him on the phone. The Christmas tree I was bringing home attacked me. I fell and broke a bottle of wine." And surely had a massive bruise on my ass. The left side ached dully, but the pain was manageable and hadn't kept me awake. I added, "I ran away. And you know the rest."

"Mmm. You went to Zoe's?" He asked it carefully, weird tension in his voice.

"Oh, right. It wasn't on purpose. I was driving around, and I ended up there. She spotted me and came outside." I groaned. "And her mom was there, and then her fiancé came home. It was a whole thing."

Will chuckled. "I can imagine." He rolled onto his back and was quiet a few moments before saying, "I didn't think you were seeing Zoe much these days."

"I'm not!" Ugh, that sounded way too defensive. But I knew he was pissed about the way I'd basically disappeared. Understandably! I cleared my throat. "I know I kind of dropped off the map for a while."

Basically. Kind of. I cringed at my own...what? Weakness? Lack of accountability? I needed to take responsibility for ghosting my best friend. Will deserved a real explanation and apology.

Before I could say more, Will was out of bed and about to slide the bathroom door shut. He said, "Don't worry about it. You want to piss before I shower?"

Now he didn't seem to want to hear it? At least not at the moment. "Nah, I'm good," I lied, ordering my full bladder to simmer down. Not to mention my erection. At least the guilt was taking care of that.

"LAST CHANCE TO back out," Will said as we tugged on our boots.

I straightened to button my coat. "I'm good. Unless *you* want to back out?"

He fiddled with his laces. "I don't like lying. At the same time, it would be so bloody awkward now to say, 'Just kidding! We're only mates.'"

"It seriously would. And will Angela still consider you for that project she mentioned? I wouldn't if I were her."

"Nor would I." Will zipped his coat and pulled down a woolen hat over his head. "This is quite a ridiculous situation we've gotten ourselves into."

"It is. But, I mean, it's two days. It's not a big deal. I need to pay my way, after all."

He scoffed. "You don't. It's good to have you here."

This was why I loved him. One of the reasons, at least. If only I could tell him how amazing he really was... I ran a hand through my still-damp hair, my fingers brushing the tender spot where I'd bonked my head.

I stiffened as it occurred to me that when he'd said he missed me I might not have said it back? Did I? All I could remember was his sweet concern and big, warm hands on my head.

"Michael?" There was that concern again as Will's brows met.

"I missed you too. In case I didn't say that before. It's so good to see you again."

Will looked away to pull on his gloves. Was he blushing? "Cheers. We'd better get to breakfast."

"Okay." I added, "Honey."

Will laughed. "That's right, we need to sell this. What shall I call you? Dearest? Darling? Pookie?"

Giggling, I led the way out of the pod. "Does anyone actually call their significant other 'pookie'?"

"I once dated a woman who called me 'snuggle-wuggle-puss.' It was the first and very much the last time."

"Oof. And I thought 'cupcake' was bad."

Snow crunched under our boots as we made our way to the clearing past cozy pods. We kept our voices low, though no one was close by. Kids shouted distantly, and there was a general buzz of activity coming from the main area.

Will asked, "Is that what he called you?"

"Jared? Hell no. He kept to the standard 'babe' kind of thing."

"Mmm."

I'd put on a gray BRK Sync beanie Will had from a previous event, but the ends of my damp hair were already crispy in the cold. "Pookie-wookie?" I joked, not wanting to think of Jared.

"Maybe we should keep it simple. Shall I call you 'sweetheart.'?"

God, the way my heart soared high into the brilliant blue sky at those words. I nodded and said, "Sure" instead of *I'm begging you to call me that and only that forever and ever.*

Breakfast in the glass-fronted restaurant was a buffet that smelled overwhelmingly of bacon in the best way possible. The

delicious scent distracted me for a few seconds as I stamped my
boots on the mat. Then I realized everyone—and I meant
everyone—was staring at me and Will. The chatter had died down
too.

The restaurant was half-full, but I didn't see Angela. Clearly,
the gossip that Will had a boyfriend had made the rounds since
almost everyone but a group of kids playing cornhole stopped to
watch us.

At a big round table for eight by the farthest window, Jenna
stood and waved us over. I tugged at my scarf as we made our way,
my skin itching with all the attention. At least my cheek looked
less like I'd been mauled by a pissed-off cat.

Jenna introduced me to her husband, Jun, and pointed out
their two kids amid the loud group of children devouring
pancakes. Seth and Logan were there too, and Matt and his
fiancée, Becky—who had overheard us in the parking lot—arrived
right after us.

"How'd you two lovebirds sleep?" Becky asked with a wink.

"It was a great night," I answered honestly. I realized how that
sounded as soon as the words were out of my mouth. "I just mean
that bed is really comfy."

There were a few smirks, and Will was smiling tightly. Even if
he was down with pretending I was his boyfriend, he probably
didn't want me acting like we'd had some amazing night of sex.

Oh, nope! That train of thought is not happening. No thank you.

Matt winked broadly. "Sure, sure, we believe you. Mmm, that
bacon smells incredible."

I stood in front of Will in the buffet line, and when I offered
to put a croissant on his plate because I was already holding the
tongs, I swore to god I heard an actual *"Awww"* from someone. It
was a little creepy how excited Will's coworkers seemed to be
about him having a boyfriend.

Back at the table, I dug into my scrambled eggs, bacon, and

sausage. I admit, I was really curious about Seth and Logan. As they ate their breakfast, I listened to Seth chatting with Jenna and Jun about family Christmas plans.

Jenna said, "You know Pop won't want anything but the same turkey and stuffing we always have. I'm not saying game hens wouldn't be delicious, but we have to do the usual stuff as well."

As they debated it, Seth speared one of the sausages on his plate and wordlessly dropped it onto Logan's, where only eggs remained. Logan ate the sausage eagerly.

So, they had pretended to be boyfriends too? And had ended up getting married for real? If only I could be that lucky.

"Ready for your big performance?" Seth asked me and Will quietly.

Will nodded, and I said, "Yep." Little did they know I'd had years of practice. This time, I'd just have to override my usual pretending-not-to-be-desperately-in-love-with-my-best-friend routine and turn on my pretending-my-best-friend-is-desperately-in-love-with-me charms. Piece of cake.

"Our very own throwback Adam Sandler movie for the holidays," Matt joked.

Logan frowned. "*Happy Gilmore?*"

Becky said, "No, the one where he pretends to be gay for the health insurance benefits or something like that. I think he was a firefighter."

"Oh, right," Jun said. "That was a terrible movie. I'm sure the performances today will be far superior."

I chuckled. "I haven't seen that movie, but I'll take your word for it. Also, I'm not straight. I'm bi."

"Like Logan." Seth gave Logan's muscled forearm an affectionate squeeze.

"Cool." I smiled.

Logan took another bite of toast. He brushed crumbs from his chin and mumbled, "What?" at Seth's pointed look. Logan added,

"Mike and I can do the secret handshake later."

"Michael," Will corrected.

I waved a hand. "It's fine."

"It's not, though." Will sliced through a pancake, giving me a quizzical smile. "Why do you do that?"

"I don't want to make people feel bad."

"But what about *your* feelings? It's *your* name."

Everyone was watching us, and I laughed awkwardly. "It's not that big a deal."

"Wow, you guys are really good at playing a couple," Becky whispered.

Laughter rippled around the table, and I elbowed Will. "Stop nagging, pookie-wookie."

This got a real laugh out of Will—and everyone else. I wasn't sure why Will was so on edge. Yeah, having so much attention from his coworkers probably made him feel weird. But was it so bad to pretend he wasn't straight? Maybe it was the *me* part.

"Okay, time to spill everything about Will that he doesn't want us to know," Becky said with a wicked grin before sipping her fresh-squeezed OJ.

"I'm technically his supervisor," Seth said. "I'm not sure I should be hearing this."

Jenna scoffed. "You're my actual supervisor and you know way too much about me."

"Yes, it's a cautionary tale," Seth replied.

Everyone was looking at me, and Will seemed…curious about what I'd say? I shrugged. "We met in college and eventually became roommates off-campus."

"Aww, that's nice," Becky said. "And you've been BFF ever since?"

Guilt joined the party, but I managed to nod as I chewed a mouthful of extremely sweet and sticky pancake. Would Will mention that I hadn't talked to him in two years before calling him out of the blue for a roadside rescue?

He didn't, because of course he didn't. He was too generous for that, and it would have been awkward and weird for everyone else.

"He must have been beating off girls with a stick in college," Jenna said. "That face, that accent, that—" She seemed to remember this was a work event. "Personality," she finished.

"As if," Will muttered, shaking his head with a smile.

I said, "Oh yeah. He was extremely popular. There was a new girl all the time."

The table laughed and teased Will. His jaw clenched as he smiled, a vein beating on his temple. "Come on, mate. That's not true."

I swirled the black coffee in my mug. "Um, it is. You dated a new girl almost every week back then. They just didn't usually stick around long."

"Love 'em and leave 'em, huh?" Jun said.

Now Will really was bristling. "*No.*"

"I didn't mean it like that!" I insisted. "Will's not a jerk. Not at all. He's amazing. He's sweet and generous and loyal and—" I broke off. "What I mean is he's not a player."

"Of course not," Seth said, the others murmuring agreement.

"Sorry," Jun added sheepishly, pushing up his round glasses.

Will laughed. It was *almost* genuine, but I wasn't sure the others could tell the difference. "It's all right." He glanced around and kept his voice low. "I have this reputation, but the truth of it is I just haven't met the right person yet."

"But you *have*." Becky winked. "It was your best friend right under your nose all along. Swooooon."

A.K.A. my dream come true. I laughed along. Ha, ha, *ha*.

Fortunately, Seth changed the subject. "Matt, do you know anything about the video game that's really popular these days?" He asked Logan, "What's it called?"

Logan mumbled the name through a bite of food and added, "Trying to come up with a surprise for Connor. Little shit guesses everything." He smiled fondly.

Seth said to him, "Well, we could always surprise him with that motorcycle he's been saving up for."

Logan glared. "No goddamned way."

Honestly, I'd have expected Logan to be the one who was pro-motorcycle given his leather jacket and rougher vibe.

Seth raised his hands. "You know I don't like it either, but... Video game it is. We'll have to think of a few more gifts too."

I was so curious about Logan and Seth's son and how he played into the fact that they'd initially been pretending to be in a relationship. But it seemed rude to ask. I stayed quiet as Matt practically bounced in his chair and talked a mile a minute about the video game.

My phone chimed with a text, and I read the message with a sigh. At Will's raised eyebrow, I said, "They towed my car to the garage. The mechanic said it'll be after Christmas until he can even look at it."

"Don't worry." He lowered his voice, leaning closer and making my heart skip. "You'll be with me."

I wanted to argue that he didn't need to be my chauffeur, but...I only nodded and whispered, "Thank you." Letting Will take charge was comforting in ways I didn't need to examine right this second.

Soon enough, breakfast was over and it was time to...do whatever people did at corporate retreats. Honestly, I wasn't sure, especially since this was a family event. Wendy, the woman from the parking lot, called out instructions as we were herded from the restaurant. She looked away as we approached.

Grinning, Matt leaned close as we got outside and asked, "Ready for Operation Fake Boyfriend Two: Bigger, Badder, and—" He paused. "Something I still need to come up with?"

Will laughed while I stupidly said, "How hard can it be?"

Chapter Six
Will

I'D NEVER BEEN much of an actor. Aside from my stirring turn as a kitchen rat in the Cinderella Christmas panto when I was eleven, I'd never had any need to perform. Well, I supposed we all performed in some ways at the office or in our lives, but this was no time to get philosophical.

Because Michael was holding my hand.

And I was holding his hand. We were mutually grasping hands, which was something couples did.

We were bundled up and crossing the clearing under cloudy skies, and a minute earlier, Michael had tugged my wrist and whispered, "Should we hold hands or whatever?" He'd leaned in, his breath tickling my ear.

Right, this was what couples did. "Absolutely." I clumsily entwined our gloved fingers, the leather squeaking.

Michael squeezed my palm. "Um, is this good?"

"Totally. Isn't it?" Was this how people held hands? Surely it was. There was no special queer way to hold hands.

Why was I being a numpty and overthinking this? Yes, this was a perfectly acceptable manner in which to hold hands. With a man. With Michael.

Fresh snow crunched under our boots as we followed Seth and Logan to a hut where people queued for cross-country skis. They were also holding hands.

Logan had to be freezing in his leather jacket, but he seemed perfectly comfortable as they walked along, talking and laughing about something.

I'd been to their house for a summer barbecue, and it was warm and welcoming and very much a *home*. I'd never suspected for a moment that their relationship started as a fake arrangement.

"You sure you're okay?" Michael murmured.

"What? Yes. Why?"

"You just seem really quiet."

"Just thinking."

"Ahh." He nodded seriously. "I thought I smelled smoke."

Laughing, I nudged his shoulder with mine. "Bugger off."

Michael nudged me back. "But are you sure you're okay with this?" He squeezed my palm. "Because it's not like we have to be all cozy or whatever. Some couples aren't into PDA. You don't need to prove anything."

This was my chance to let go of Michael's hand, but it wasn't as though it was a hardship, was it? "Nah, it's fine. If I'm only going to be bi for the weekend, I should go all in."

"Right." He nodded, looking down at his boots. "Uh-huh."

"Okay, no. I'm not skiing," Seth said to Logan. "I'm going to fall."

We'd reached the ski shack and benches where families strapped into equipment. The trail with two grooves carved into the snow with some kind of machine disappeared into the forest.

"I'll catch you," Logan said simply.

Seth rolled his eyes. "With poles in your hands? That'll be a great trick."

As Seth and Logan went back and forth, I eyed the people on skis dubiously. Some were clearly experienced, striding off confidently on the trail with smooth motions, their limbs working in concert.

Michael and I shared a look. "Maybe we should try something

else," Michael said. "I have enough bruises."

"Yes!" Seth agreed. "Because this is clearly a bad idea. Why are all winter activities so darn risky?"

"Darlin', you read my mind!" a familiar voice exclaimed.

We turned to find Angela in her pink snowsuit. "Seth, these Northerners are real daredevils, ain't they? Now, there is one activity here that's smack dab in my wheelhouse. You fellas want to try it with me?"

Naturally, the four of us agreed and followed Angela down another trail. Seth asked hopefully, "Is it sitting in a lodge drinking hot cocoa by a fire?"

I could only laugh as we rounded a bend and the stable and horses came into view. Logan said, "Hold your fucking horses."

"That's the idea!" Angela chirped.

"How is this less risky than skiing?" Logan demanded and rightfully so. He didn't seem to have any compunction about swearing in front of Angela and spoke to her in a way that made it clear they had familiarity. She seemed to like it.

"Oh, horseback riding!" Seth said. "I did it all the time at bible camp as a kid. It's easy."

As Logan and Seth bickered, I asked Michael, "Are you up for riding? I haven't done it in years, but they don't look like wild stallions."

Michael eyed the horses. "Um, yeah. Why not? I rode a camel at the zoo once."

This prompted Angela to sing a song about a camel named Alice, and some of the nearby children joined in.

As we waited to saddle up, Michael whispered, "This is all extremely wholesome."

"It really is."

Also, we were still holding hands, and I was in no rush to let go. It had been a while since I'd dated anyone long enough to indulge in PDA. Joanne from marketing passed by on horseback and gave us a wave and an encouraging thumbs-up, which was quite unnecessary but sweet all the same.

Again, this was the first time—to my knowledge—I'd been perceived as anything but straight. It was... What? I felt oddly giddy, so I supposed it was a bit of fun? A laugh to be pulling the wool over my coworkers' eyes?

My stomach twisted. No, that wasn't it. I didn't enjoy lying. Even as a boy, I'd never been one for telling tales. It was just a relief to not have people asking why I didn't have a girlfriend and when was I going to settle down, etc.

While there were certainly plenty of coworkers that didn't seem to care, it was amazing how often people I didn't know well felt welcome to comment on my relationship status.

On cue, Joel from accounting clapped my shoulder. "Hey, Will!" A fuzzy blue hat covered his balding head. He introduced us to his wife who wore a matching hat and ski jacket. They looked to Michael expectantly, and I realized it was my turn.

"This is my...Michael. Boyfriend." Wow, smoothly done.

"Hi!" Michael shook their hands with a smile.

"Great to meet you, Mike. It all makes sense now!" Joel gave me a quizzical smile before I could correct him on Michael's name. "Should've just told us you were gay!"

As Joel's wife elbowed him and glared, I replied automatically, "I'm not." Since I wasn't. "What I mean is, I'm..." All I had to say was, *"I'm bisexual."* Yet my gut tightened, which didn't make sense. If I enjoyed being perceived as bi, why shouldn't I be able to say it?

"We're not sure about labels," Michael said. That wasn't true in his case, and he'd said it for my benefit. He squeezed my hand reassuringly, and I took a deep breath.

"Oh!" Joel slapped his forehead. "Right, okay. Sorry." His face reddened.

Now I'd made Joel feel bad when the deception was all my

doing. I shook my head. "No need to be sorry! I'm just—er, this is all new to me." That was certainly the truth.

Joel's wife gave an encouraging smile. "I'm sure you'll figure it all out in due time. All that matters is you're happy! Everyone can see you two are crazy about each other."

A few more colleagues appeared, eager to get in a word. Dana from communications exclaimed, "I never would have guessed!"

I smiled and nodded, and Angela was saying something about horses, and Michael was gripping my hand, and I guess I was a better actor than I thought if "everyone" was buying into the idea Michael and I were together? It was the whole point of having a fake boyfriend, so I wasn't sure why it threw me.

Maybe I really should just come clean to Angela and everyone. But Michael was holding my hand, and we were so deep into it now. If being bi for the weekend could potentially help my career with Angela, confessing it had all been pretend would undermine her confidence in me as a person and damage my reputation with my colleagues. How would they trust anything I said?

It was too late. I was all in, and I had to accept it.

"Will?"

I focused on Michael. "Sorry, I was miles away."

He tugged on my hand. "It's my turn. You have to let go."

"Right!" Laughing awkwardly, I released him. He buckled on a helmet and followed the young woman's instructions on pulling himself up and over the saddle.

From my vantage point, I could see the faint red stain that remained on the left side of his jeans, although the laundry department had made a commendable effort. The denim clung to his lean thigh, his coat riding up to his hips as he got settled—and turned pale.

"Michael?" I stepped closer. "Are you all right? Is your arse sore?" How had it not even occurred to me? He'd had that fall last night—horseback riding was a terrible idea.

He flushed pink and glanced around, and I realized too late the implication of my words if we were meant to be lovers.

I had to clear my dry throat before adding loudly—possibly too loudly?—"Is your arse sore from that fall you took?"

Michael shrugged tightly. "A little, but it's fine as long as we're not, like, galloping." He clutched the reins and sucked in a sharp breath when the horse fidgeted.

"Come on, now. Something's wrong."

"I'm fine!" He nodded too vigorously.

I sighed and raised my eyebrows.

He relented and mumbled, "It feels higher up here than I expected."

"But you've jumped off two-story roofs."

"One time! And I was very young and drunk!" He gripped the leather reins. "It's fine. I know it's weird, but I've developed this little vertigo thing. I don't even like being on stepladders these days."

"What?" I reached for his knee. "Why didn't you say so? We don't have to ride! Come on, I'll help you down."

That Michael apparently had a new condition I didn't know about was very unsettling. I'd known everything about him before. Or thought I had.

"Sir? It's your turn."

"Oh, we're not riding after all," I told the woman.

"We are! I'm up here already!" Michael patted my hand where it rested on his knee. "I'm fine. Honestly. Saddle up." He slapped my shoulder playfully.

Reluctantly, I stepped back and put on my helmet. Boot in the stirrup, I mounted my own horse, a mare named Stella. She barely moved a muscle as I got comfortable in the saddle. The leather was cold under me, but it would surely warm up soon.

As we were led out of the stable at a sedate pace, Stella swaying easily beneath me, I watched Michael's straight back in front of me. Beyond him, Logan was complaining, and Seth was laughing and telling him how brave he was. The way they teased each other reminded me of my parents, and I could imagine Mum praising Logan for taking a leap.

Michael glanced behind, and I asked, "Okay?" He gave me a real, crinkling smile and nodded.

The horses obediently followed the trail, our group riding single file behind the guide. The air was cold and crisp, the snow-muffled forest quiet around us.

Even Logan seemed to be enjoying the peacefulness—until, with a rumble, a horse suddenly galloped up from behind us and charged past with a cheering preteen boy on its back.

Amid the shouts for him to stop, another rider passed us, and then another—perhaps one of the parents—brushing too close. Snorting, Stella sidestepped and the low branches of a bare oak or maple scratched my cheek. I jerked away, overcorrecting far too much.

It wasn't that Stella threw me or anything that dramatic. No, I simply leaned past the point of no return and plopped off into the cushion of snow with a *whomp*. Staring up at the gray sky, all I could do was laugh.

There were shouts of concern—quite a cacophony, really—and before I could stop laughing enough to assure everyone I was all right, Michael appeared in my field of vision.

"Guess it was my turn to take a tumble," I said.

Eyes wide, Michael peered at me seriously. "Are you hurt?"

"No, not at all. Don't worry yourself."

But Michael still leaned over me, biting his lip as he peeled off a glove and tenderly touched my cheek. I winced. My skin felt too hot. "Ah, guess I'm cut. We have matching wounds."

Logan was saying, "You see? That could be you, Seth!"

Sitting up, I laughed. "Didn't even knock the wind out of me." Michael knelt in the snow, now gripping my arm with his bare hand. I gave him a smile. "Really, I'm fine." I passed him his glove. "Hey, you got down pretty fast. No vertigo?"

"Oh. Uh, nope! I told you it was nothing." Michael looked around, seeming to realize the rest of our group was staring at us from up on their horses and tugged the leather glove back on his hand.

Angela said, "He's just worried, sugar. You sure you're good?"

The guide was speaking on a walkie-talkie before hopping down and hurrying over with the reins of her horse in hand. "I'm so sorry about that. The medical team is en route."

"Oh, I don't need it!" I pushed to my feet. "Just my pride that's bruised. Did they fetch that kid?"

The guide nodded, seeming to barely resist rolling her eyes. "There's always one."

"At least it wasn't Connor," Seth said wryly.

Angela laughed. "Oh, he's too old for shenanigans now, I'm sure."

Logan snorted. "We'd like to think so, but…"

Michael stood beside me, hovering as if he thought I might faint at any moment. I took his hand and squeezed. "It was way worse when you jumped off the roof into the pool."

"Oh, *this* we have to hear!" Angela said.

Michael obliged and told the story while we waited for two staff with first aid training to ride up and give me a mandatory once-over. I only realized once they arrived that Michael and I were still holding hands. Apparently we were better actors than I'd imagined.

MICHAEL'S CHEST ROSE and fell rhythmically in the soft, distant glow of the Christmas lights through the blind. I'd fallen into a sort of trance counting his breaths.

After a day of riding—and falling—skating on a frozen trail through the forest, a massive buffet dinner, and carol singing around a bonfire, I was beat.

Not to mention a day of introducing Michael as my boyfriend, holding his hand, and even feeding him a sweet, gooey marshmallow at Angela's insistence that it was "romantic."

I'd washed my hands hours ago, but somehow, I could still feel the brush of Michael's lips on my fingertips as he'd taken the marshmallow into his mouth. It had been silly and awkward, and I didn't know why I was still thinking about it when I should have been fast asleep.

I shifted inch by inch, rolling onto my back and trying not to disturb Michael where he stretched out beside me. If I were alone, I'd wank to release any lingering thoughts from the day and slip into dreamland.

I'd always loved wanking. Granted, most people did—at least as far as I could tell. But sometimes I wondered if there was something wrong with me. I didn't think many would choose wanking over a date with a flesh and blood person they had the opportunity to sleep with.

Speaking of sleeping with another person, Michael was snoring very softly, dead to the world and completely unaware he was in bed with a pervert. What the hell was I doing thinking about wanking? I'd be getting hard in a second if I didn't stop.

Shifting again as quietly and gently as possible, I curled on my side away from him. Perhaps I should have showered and taken care of it earlier. My cock throbbed at the idea. I supposed it had been too long. Normally, I wanked every day or two.

Now that I thought back, I couldn't think of many times I'd have been keen to fuck a woman rather than get myself off. There was Amelia in freshman year, of course. Christ, I'd been wild about her.

She'd been my first real love, but she'd called it off right after the start of sophomore year. We'd been long distance over the summer while I'd been in Scotland, and Amelia's heart had not grown fonder. Mine had broken rather dramatically.

I'd been miserable at school and had considered dropping out and going back to Scotland after all. Then I'd met Michael, and Zoe and the whole gang at the house. So it had worked out for the best.

Even when Michael and Zoe were together, he'd always made time for me. I'd gotten over Amelia eventually, but Mum would say I hadn't taken any more leaps after that, and I should have.

But I'd had Michael. Until I suddenly hadn't.

Making a little whimper, Michael kicked and fidgeted in his sleep. In the faint watercolor light, I could see his eyes moving beneath his lids in a dream.

The scratches on his smooth cheek were still visible, though he'd assured me they didn't hurt. My own face was fine, the scratch from the branch much ado about nothing.

The extra-large T-shirt hung low under his collarbones. Fidgeting again, he murmured, and I watched his Adam's apple bob as he swallowed. He snored lightly—a hollow sort of rasp. Was he too hot under the duvet? He kicked at it again, so I eased the fabric down to his waist.

The sweatpants rode low on his hips. The T-shirt was bunched up and askew, exposing his soft, pale skin and the surprisingly dark hair leading down from his belly button.

I fought to breathe. Why was lust tearing through me so powerfully my veins could have been on fire? Clearly it *had* been too long since I'd wanked. Christ almighty, Michael was going to wake up and wonder what the hell I thought I was doing.

After ducking into the bathroom, I inched the barn door closed. There was no window, so I flipped on the light and leaned over the sink, resting my forehead on the cool glass of the mirror. My dick was so hard it was almost painful.

I almost laughed. What a drama queen I was being! Christ, I'd gone a few days without wanking plenty of times. Yet I vibrated with pent-up energy. I'd wake Michael if I wasn't careful—he was right there, only a few feet away in the compact pod.

Spreading my legs and bracing, I pulled my cock out of my shorts. I didn't need lube—I was leaking already. It was a little rough, but oh, that made my toes curl on the lovely warm floor. My cock was full and thrummed in my grasp as I stroked.

I bit my lip, gasping shallowly through my mouth. When I wasn't watching porn as I wanked, there were fantasies I relied on. Images, really. Curved buttocks, breasts, hard cocks. Bodies driving into each other, spread open, surrendering. Kissing, swallowing, moaning.

I'd never sucked a cock, but I imagined what it might be like as I rubbed and tugged my shaft, my balls aching and heavy.

On my knees, lips stretched, spit on my chin, my mouth perfectly full. Licking and tasting, barely breathing, pulse thundering, wet sounds echoing. A hand cupping my head, fingers gentle in my hair, his voice a moan: "Oh, Will."

My back arched as I came, shuddering silently, my body on fire. I jerked as I imagined swallowing his cum. He was no one in particular—an outline. Only a shadow even though—

I focused on the cum as I milked myself, shaking with aftershocks. I reckoned it would be salty and warm in my mouth. Splattered on my face. I'd lick up every drop.

Bending over the sink, I washed up and splashed my cheeks with cool water. When I straightened to face myself in the mirror, my skin was blotchy and red all the way down my neck. My throat was parched, and I filled one of the small glasses, gulping it down and refilling.

Well.

I'd always insisted I had no plans whatsoever to act on my attraction to men. And I hadn't! Yet the excitement and release still buzzing through my body was new. That had been...next-level wanking, and I'd thought myself rather accomplished in the field.

"Will?"

I almost hit the ceiling, spinning around guiltily. "Yes?"

"You okay?" Michael's voice was sleepy and soft.

Not really! Couldn't say that. He'd only worry. So, I checked myself in the mirror, turned off the light, and edged open the door. In the faint colored glow of the Christmas lights, Michael sat up on my side of the bed, the duvet twisted around his waist.

"Sorry I woke you," I murmured. "Go back to sleep." His hair stood up, and my fingers twitched with the need to smooth it down. "Everything's fine."

"You sure, man? Are you sick?"

"Nah, just had to piss. Shove over."

Michael crawled back to his side under the curved roof. He yawned widely as he snuggled back under the duvet. "Okay." Then his voice sharpened. "I wasn't snoring, was I? That can happen after I've been drinking."

I almost lied and said he'd been quiet as a mouse. But I didn't want to lie to Michael. "Only a little. It doesn't bother me at all."

"Okay." He curled on his side away from me, tensed. "Sorry, though."

"I told you—it doesn't bother me." I reached out to squeeze his shoulder, but stopped in midair, pulling my hand back and tucking it under the duvet. "Honestly," I added. "Go back to sleep."

It was true—it didn't bother me. I could sleep through a hurricane. I was being a hundred percent honest. About that much, at least. As for the rest of it... What even was *it*?

I rubbed my damp face. I was being daft, as Mum would tell me—not that I was going to discuss this with her. I could sort it all out in the new year. A fake boyfriend was enough of a leap for now, thank you very much.

Chapter Seven

Michael

WITH OUR ARMS snug around each other's shoulders, Will and I stood hip-to-hip, the sides of our bodies flush as his left ankle was bound to my right. In other circumstances—minus the hundreds of people around and wearing snowshoes—this might have been the beginning of a very satisfying wet dream.

That it was Wendy, the woman who'd apparently had a crush on Will, tying us together only made it more awkward. She'd given us a brittle smile before crouching down. I couldn't see her face now under her beret.

"Cool hat," I said, because I felt like I needed to say something to her. That was the best my brain could do, apparently.

Wendy glanced up, adjusting the beret. "I know it's not very fashionable these days."

"No, I like it!" Had it sounded like I was making fun of her? Shit. As someone with a years-long crush on Will, I hardcore related to this woman.

"Me too," Will said.

"You don't have to say that." She knotted the rope, yanking at it almost desperately. I recognized my own humiliation at unrequited love in her, and I wanted to hug her and say it was okay.

Will seemed genuinely puzzled. "It's a great hat. Wendy, just so you know—"

"No, please!" She sprang to her feet, gripping a spare rope to tie up the next contestants. "You don't have to say anything. I'm very happy for you. All right, bye!" If the snow hadn't been so deep, I think she would have run for it instead of clomping over to Matt and Becky to tie their ankles.

Will sighed. "I just wanted to apologize."

"For not liking her back?" I shuddered. "Don't do that. She's embarrassed enough already. Just act normal with her."

"But she has nothing to be embarrassed about." His brow furrowed under his woolen hat.

"Dude, she's humiliated. Your pity does not help." My skin prickled at the thought of Will finding out that I'd been in love with him for years. Jared's words echoed in my head.

"I just feel so sorry for him."

Will's pity would be *so* much worse. At least with Jared, it was over. But there was no way I could stop seeing Will. Being with him again now made me realize just how lonely and crappy those two years of not talking to him had been. I needed him in my life. He was my best friend no matter what.

Even if I wanted to move my head a few inches, press my face to the strip of stubbly neck where his scarf had slipped, and breathe forever, I'd just have to make do with Will's arm around me, the weight of it perfectly secure.

Our heat of the three-legged snowshoe race also contained Matt and Becky, and Angela and Dale. If it was weird for Dale to be tied up to his boss, he didn't show even a flicker of discomfort. The snowshoes on our outside feet were the big old-fashioned ones that were handmade from wood and...twine? I wasn't sure, but they were large and in charge.

I leaned into Will, soaking up his heat. Sunday had dawned brilliantly sunny but frigid. There would be a morning of activities followed by lunch, and then heading home to Albany. Only a few hours left to be Will's boyfriend.

Home. My gut tightened at the thought. I'd have to get my stuff from the townhouse. I'd have to talk to Jared. Be a grownup and deal with sorting through any shared possessions and bills and all the little things that came with living with someone.

"Okay?" Will asked.

"Yeah. We should come up with a strategy."

"For this race? Isn't it just not to fall down? And go fast?"

"Right." I laughed. "I guess it's not that complicated."

At the starting line, the young man and woman on my left introduced themselves to me, and since Will was talking to Dale on his other side, I said, "I'm Michael. Will's boyfriend."

It was actually the first time I'd said those words since Will had introduced me previously. At the stables, he'd called me "*My Michael,*" with that beautiful Scottish lilt that made my heart sing. I'd be his for every minute I could.

It turned out that three-legged snowshoe racing was exactly as difficult as it looked. Bumping and stumbling, Will and I jerked forward, our boots sinking in the snow on our bound legs while the cumbersome snowshoes didn't sink as far, which was the whole point of snowshoes.

"Left! Left!" Will chanted like he was trying to do some military march.

"But that is *your* left!" I protested.

We pitched forward, sprawling in the snow. I was practically doing the splits with my left leg, the snowshoe clearly having a mind of its own. We were laughing so hard our breath huffed out in cloudy bursts. The assembled crowd howled along with us.

Will and I were practically crawling now, and as the crowd roared, I looked up to see Angela and Dale crossing the finish line. Angela was so small that Dale was practically just carrying her, hitched up against his side.

"The PA/boss relationship in a nutshell," Will said. "Okay, we need to stand up. Ready?"

"Yep."

We pushed to our feet—and took one step before Will tripped and we lurched forward on our bellies, our chins in the snow. I could only wheeze through my laughter. My peacoat and jeans were going to be soaked by the time we got out of this ridiculous situation.

Matt and Becky were having the same issues we were, as well as the other couple I'd spoken to. It felt like Will and I were wrestling even though we were on the same team, one of us pushing or pulling or stumbling at exactly the wrong time.

"How is this so hard?" Will demanded through another grin. "Lean on me. Stop fighting and let me lift you."

Putting more weight on Will to my right, I tried to stay still as Will shoved to his feet with a grunt. I had my arm around his shoulder, and he lowered his to my waist.

"That's it. Keep leaning on me. Okay, I'm walking."

At the finish line, Angela cheered loudly. "Come on! Everyone can finish this race! Teamwork!"

As Will hauled me forward, I had this bananas fantasy of him sweeping me up in his arms like a princess in a fairy tale. Which he couldn't do because our legs were tied—and he wouldn't do anyway because *why would he?*—but just leaning against him made me feel safe and warm and special.

This is going to be over in a few hours. Don't get used to it!

I'd woken that morning and watched Will sleep on his belly, one knee drawn up and his lips parted, drooling a bit on the pillow he'd clutched. His knee had been so close under the duvet. Even though I'd had to piss, I'd remained frozen, knowing it was the last time I'd get to wake up with Will.

Now, we raced forward. I followed Will's rhythm, and we found our groove. I wasn't just leaning on him and letting him haul me across the line. My muscles strained as we ran, the crowd cheering us on. Our boots sank into a divot, and we stumbled.

Sprawling face first into the snow, we sputtered, the snow-shoes on our outside legs making it even more awkward and hilarious, judging by the audience's reaction. Matt and Becky motored past us as we tried to get up.

We were on our knees with the snowshoes sticking up into the air. Will's whole face was dusted in white. "Here," I said, brushing at his stubble. "I think victory's off the table." My gloves weren't helping, so I peeled off one and said, "Close your eyes."

He did, and I lightly brushed the snow from his facial hair and eyebrows. The way he closed his eyes and let me sent a rush of emotion swelling through me.

My fingertips touched his lips, and I murmured, "Sorry. You're good now."

Will opened his eyes, and I swear, my heart just about stopped. A fat, fluffy snowflake sat on the end of his nose, and I caught it with my middle finger. "Make a wish."

"Like an eyelash? I didn't know people did that with snow-flakes."

"Sure, why not?" I shrugged. "My mom always did it. You have to wish before it melts."

Will watched me with a little smile playing on his lips, the creases beside his mouth deepening. He closed his eyes purposeful-ly, then opened them. "Okay. Wish made."

"Just under the wire," I said, and we watched the snowflake dissolve on my pink skin.

"You guys okay?" someone asked. "You need the medics?"

"Not again," Will grumbled. He shouted, "We're fine!"

We made our way to our feet. I realized everyone was watch-ing us, and I imagined from their point of view we must have looked...what? Close? Maybe like a real couple? Maybe...

Nope. Stop that train of thought.

Getting carried away wouldn't do me or Will any favors.

Later, I found myself with Seth as Logan and Will took part in a massive snowball fight. I asked, "So, you and Logan pretended to be together too?"

Seth laughed ruefully. "We did. It was quite a 'caper,' as Matt likes to say. Or chant, to be more accurate. Logan and I were thrust into it like you and Will were, but I can't imagine where I'd be if we hadn't. *Who* I'd be." He gazed at Logan dodging a snowball from the kids. A little smile lifted his lips.

"And it was for Angela's benefit?"

"Yes. I realize that sounds absolutely demented. She had just taken over our company, and there were all these rumors about her only promoting married staff. It's turned out to not be true, although I have to admit she does get very excited about supporting queer couples and families. She's done so much for us, both knowingly and not. Honestly, she gave me my family. Not that she knew it."

Will was packing snowballs with a little girl, shielding her with his body. Meanwhile, one of Jenna's kids shrieked with joy as Logan hefted him over his shoulder. Seth tensed, though I couldn't figure out why.

I asked, "You okay?"

He exhaled in a puff of white air and took off his glasses, cleaning the lenses with his scarf with tight movements. "I'm fine. Logan was injured some years ago, and he should be more careful." He shook his head with a laugh. "I can be a worrywart. Or an 'overthinker' as Connor would put it."

"But you're the one who wants to get him a motorcycle?"

Seth chuckled ruefully. "Not at all, believe me. But I don't like it when he and Logan butt heads. And he's worked so hard at summer jobs saving money, insisting on paying his dorm fees in Boston. It would be such a wonderful surprise for him on Christmas morning, and he's going to get a motorcycle one way or the other."

"I hear you. So your son's at Harvard in pre-med?"

Seth's face lit up. "Yes. It's hard to believe how far he's come. He was Logan's stepson when we met. His mother had recently died, and Connor was really struggling. As was Logan. As was I. We were all…alone."

"Then the caper saved the day?"

He grinned. "It really did." After a few moments, he added, "Who knows? Maybe it'll lead you and Will down an unexpected road too."

I'd been watching Will and the little girl again. Whipping my head back to Seth, my voice raised several octaves. "*Us?*" I cleared my throat. "Oh, no. I'm bi, but Will's straight. And we're just friends! We can't—we're not—it wouldn't—" I'd never be that lucky. It wasn't possible.

Seth raised his gloved hands. "Of course. I was only joking."

Oh. "Right. Yeah!" I tried to laugh. God, was I about to *cry?* What was the matter with me? I'd been scraped raw the past couple of days, and suddenly my eyes burned with tears.

"My goodness." Seth peered at me with concern. "I'm so sorry to upset you."

"I'm not upset!" I practically shouted in an extremely convincing way. Heart racing, I lowered my voice. "I'm not. It's fine. Even if I wanted it, Will doesn't—he'll never feel that for me."

Wait. What did I just say?

Before I could organize my chaotic brain, Seth squeezed my shoulder and said softly, "It's all right. I understand."

"No, wait! I'm not saying *I* feel that for Will either." My pulse raced, and the mascarpone-stuffed French toast I'd had for breakfast threatened to make a dramatic return all over the pristine snow. "That's not what I'm saying. I didn't say that." I wasn't sure now what I *had* said.

Seth patted my shoulder. "Of course not."

The more I protested, the worse I made it, so I forced myself to shut the fuck up and watch the snowball fight. Guilt flooded me as my gaze found Will. He was now piggybacking the little girl while she hurled the snowballs. I was supposed to be helping my best friend, not making this more complicated than it already was.

In our pod a little while later, I stood by the front window, my eyes locked on a snow-dusted pine tree as Will changed into a spare pair of pants after getting his jeans soaked playing with the kids. Mine were still a bit damp from the three-legged race, but I'd live.

Fabric *shushed*, and Will had just started talking about how the little girl had received an expensive new medical treatment that Angela had paid for when Angela herself suddenly appeared outside. She gave me a wave, a bright grin lighting up her face as she approached the pod.

"Dude, she's here." I turned to find Will buttoning a plaid shirt over his slacks, his chest hair exposed. "Katie?" He looked past me. "Oh!" After hurriedly tucking in the ends of his shirt, he did the last buttons as I opened the door.

"G'day, mate!" Angela exclaimed.

I blinked at her. "Uh, okay? I mean hi." Maybe doing a terrible Australian accent was one of her things? I looked to Will, who seemed just as perplexed.

"Hi, Angela. It's…yes, a good day."

She laughed. "I bet you're wondering why I sound like Crocodile Dundee."

I vaguely recalled that was some old movie my parents liked. I closed the door behind her as Will said, "I suppose we are, yes."

Angela grinned. "I know I said no work talk this weekend, but the retreat's almost over and I have a proposition for you. It's about that special project I mentioned."

"Oh!" Will nodded. "Yes, I'd love to discuss it."

"I'll head out to lunch and leave you to it." I grabbed my coat from the hook.

"This might involve you too," Angela said. "If you want it to."

"Uh, okay?" I glanced at Will.

"Do y'all have plans for the holidays?" Angela asked.

Will and I shared another glance. "Nothing in particular."

"No family plans?" she asked. "Because I don't want to get in the way of family time at the holidays. It's sacred."

Will said, "No, I saw my parents when I went to Scotland recently. And Michael visited his parents in Florida for Thanksgiving."

Ugh, of course that made me think of Jared and how he'd been pretending the entire time, and nope, I needed to focus on now and whatever Angela was building up to.

Angela tilted her head. "You didn't want to spend Thanksgiving together? Not that it's any of my beeswax!"

Shit. Right, we were supposed to be a couple. Will was blinking and clearly had nothing, so I blurted, "My work schedule! We couldn't get vacation at the same time to go to both Scotland and Florida. But we're definitely spending Christmas together. I'm off for the next two weeks, actually."

Angela beamed. "Then how do you boys feel about a trip down under?"

Chapter Eight
Will

MUM WOULD HAVE admonished me to close my mouth because I was catching flies. Staring at Angela, I tried to make sense of what she'd said. Australia? She wanted us to go to *Australia*? Beside me, Michael appeared equally dumbfounded.

Angela laughed. "I know, you're wondering what in tarnation I'm going on about. Sit down. Let me explain." She motioned to the two chairs even though this wasn't her pod.

We shifted them around to face her and sat while Angela perched on the end of the bed in her pink snowsuit and earmuffs. I was glad I'd haphazardly pulled up the duvet earlier. It still felt oddly intimate for Angela to be here in our room.

She asked, "What do you know about Australia?"

My mind raced. Australia? The company didn't do any work there to my knowledge. "Uh, there are kangaroos and koala bears?"

"And crocodiles," Michael added.

"Correct!" Angela grinned. "Now, I'm sure you've heard of Sydney and Melbourne. Plenty of companies in our field doing business there. But I've discovered there's an untapped market in Western Australia."

"Oh, Perth?" I asked.

"Yessiree Bob. That whole side of the country seems to get overlooked, and I think there's huge potential for the company.

I've scheduled a few exploratory meetings, and Will, I think you're just the person to come with. You've done a dynamite job coordinating the new hubs in North America. My family will be tagging along, and of course, I'd love it if Michael joined us. The holidays are about family even if we're on the other side of the world throwing shrimp on the barbie or whatever the heck it is they do at Christmas."

"Uh…" I struggled to corral my thoughts. A trip to Australia? Yes, please. Trip to Australia with *Michael*? Yes, yes, *yes*. He was at loose ends with the breakup, so perhaps this was perfect timing? Was there a downside?

"I know!" Angela held up her hands. "I sprang this on you. I was going to go alone, but I got to thinking about how nice it would be to have a partner in crime to talk things over with. Dale usually has to listen to me, but he's off for the holidays. Like I said, no pressure."

I glanced at Michael, who watched me for cues. I said to him, "A trip to Australia sounds like a fun way to spend the holidays?"

He smiled tentatively. "Totally."

Angela added, "And of course, it's all expenses paid. There'll be some meetings for Will and me, but there'll be plenty of time for relaxing too."

I nodded. "Right. It sounds great. I don't think I see a down-side?"

She grinned. "That's because there isn't one, unless you love-birds don't like fun in the sun."

Ah. There it was. Michael and I would have to keep pretend-ing to be a couple. A weekend was one thing—could we keep it up for two weeks? Would Michael want to?

Angela tapped her earmuffs. "I'm ready to trade in this winter gear for sundresses and sandals. Whaddya say, Mike? Sorry—Michael."

"Uh, that does sound great. We just need to…"

Springing up, Angela said, "Say no more. You two hash it out. No hard feelings if it's too last-minute. Did I mention we'd be leaving Tuesday morning? So, you have to have your passports already in order and all that. Regardless, I'm sure there'll be another opportunity before long, Will. Don't let me pressure you. I'm just jazzed up. I think we'd have a lot of fun and hopefully lay the groundwork for an exciting new chapter at BRK Sync. Talk it out and let me know. Bye!"

Before we could say a word, she was gone, only leaving a puddle on the floor where snow had melted off the bottom of her boots.

"What just happened?" Michael asked.

I blew out a breath, puffing my cheeks as I stood and paced. "Bloody hell." My mind raced with the possibilities. Travel overseas and the potential for a promotion. Doing a job I enjoyed for a company and a boss I liked and respected. Excellent for my career.

Yet all that was overshadowed by the opportunity to spend two more weeks with Michael. Sharing a room. Reconnecting. My heart raced. My belly somersaulted like Tom Daley flipping off the diving board.

"There's no way you can pretend to be into me for two weeks," Michael said. His face was flushed pink, and he fidgeted in his chair. "You must hate that idea. Two days was one thing—two weeks would be…"

Exhilarating.

As I struggled to land on an emotion, that was the one that bubbled to the top. After not seeing Michael at all for too long, this seemed too good to be true. "I don't hate it," I said, my voice sounding oddly distant.

Michael smiled hesitantly. "You're not sick of me yet?"

Frustration and hurt elbowed their way past the excitement, and I stepped in the puddle, my sock soaking instantly. "I'm not the one who didn't talk to you for two years."

Michael's face fell, and he dropped his head. "I know. I'm sorry."

Awkward tension stretched between us. Here was my opportunity to get to the bottom of what had happened, yet I found myself saying, "Don't worry about it."

I hated the slump of his shoulders and the discomfort in the room. I wanted the excitement back. I had to let go of the past. What did it matter now anyway?

Ignoring the voice insisting it *did* actually matter because I deserved an explanation, I cracked on. "Think of the fun we'll have. I could do with some sunshine."

"Yeah?" Michael peered up at me hopefully. "Me too. It would be amazing to get away." His smile faded. "Although I really should be apartment hunting over the holidays."

"You know you can stay at mine as long as you need."

"You're not sick of my snoring?"

I chuckled. "You'll have my guest room anyway."

"Right. Of course. Makes no sense to sleep together at your place."

Looking away from him, I peeled off my wet socks and said, "Exactly. Suppose we might have to in Perth, but it's fine. Right?"

"Right! Totally." He shrugged and lifted his hands in a shaky gesture. "Doesn't matter to me one way or the other. I'll do whatever you want."

Hmm. He'd clearly meant that as a positive, but I shifted uncomfortably, pulling off the other sock too and flexing my toes on the wooden floor. "That's not—I don't want you to do anything you're not into." Did that sound like I was talking about sex? My heart thudded. "What I mean is…" Christ, I had no idea.

"I get it." Michael stood and smiled softly. "I'm saying that if you want to go, I'm all in. It'll be an adventure. We can hold hands and say we're a couple. It's easy. No big deal."

"Right." I nodded. "No big deal." It was true, wasn't it? "Holding hands and whatever. Maybe we should practice kissing just in case."

As Michael's eyes grew so wide they were in danger of popping out of his head and dropping onto the heated floor, I cursed myself. Why on Earth had I said that? What had gotten hold of me?

I watched Michael's throat work, my heart about to hammer free of my chest.

"Just kidding!" I practically shouted.

"Oh!" He laughed, and it sounded too loud in the pod as well. "Good one."

We stood there laughing until I forced myself to turn away. My head was so hot I was afraid it might explode like we were in a sci-fi movie. Practice kissing. I'd actually said that aloud.

After casting about for something—anything—to say, I landed on, "Is your passport up to date?"

"Yep." Michael pulled the clothing he'd been given out of the Whispering Pines tote bag and refolded the T-shirt and sweat-pants. "I'll just have to get it from… Uh, from Jared's place." He sighed. "And my stuff. I don't have any furniture or anything, at least."

"Nothing?" That seemed odd.

He shrugged as he refolded the T-shirt for the third time. "Jared's stuff was way nicer, so I got rid of mine. Do you mind taking me over tomorrow? He should be at work."

"'Course not. I'm sure Angela will give me the day off to pre-pare if we're flying out so soon. That is… If we are? Are we really doing this?"

Michael stuffed the T-shirt and sweatpants back into the tote, making a mess of the careful folding. "I mean, I'm up for it if you are." He frowned, watching me. "You're the one with everything to lose. I get a free trip to Australia with my best friend for

Christmas. But are you comfortable pretending to be my boy-friend for that long? It was only supposed to be for a couple of days. And then in the new year, you could invent a dramatic break-up story."

Why did the thought of breaking up with Michael make my stomach roil? This wasn't a real relationship. Except it was, and at the end of the day, Michael had been the one to break up with me two years ago. Even if we'd only been friends, it had been a break-up nonetheless, and I still didn't know why.

A panicked thought invaded my mind. What if I went to Australia alone and didn't see Michael again for another two years? What if this weekend had been a blip—right place, right time—and then Michael would find a new place and go back to his life? His life without me.

"I'm up for it," I said confidently, sticking out my hand. "Boyfriends for Christmas?"

Michael took my hand, his palm warm against mine as we shook. A smile lifted his lips. "Boyfriends for Christmas."

"WILL!"

I turned at Seth's call and waved as he jogged up to me in the parking lot. "Hey. Glad you caught me. I need to speak with you about Christmas."

He wore a quizzical smile. "Are you about to tell me you're going to Australia with Angela?"

I had to laugh. "That rumor mill really never stops, does it?"

"You've been providing it with some juicy grist this weekend." Seth grimaced. "That sounds indecent."

"It really does." I knew Seth had grown up in a very religious household, and he was charmingly prim and proper, especially in comparison to Logan's blunt, rough-around-the-edges approach.

They'd always seemed to have a wonderful yin/yang connection.

But I was suddenly wondering what it was like between them in the bedroom and whether strait-laced Seth had occasion to get, well, *indecent*. Which was absolutely none of my business! What on earth had gotten into me?

"Are you all right?" Seth asked with a frown.

"Couldn't be better. I'm well chuffed."

Seth chuckled. "You tend to sound even more Scottish when you're nervous."

"Do I?" My cheeks were warm. "No, just excited. We've never been to Australia, and it seems like a wonderful opportunity career-wise."

"Absolutely." Seth hesitated. "So, Michael's going with you?"

"Yes, Angela insisted. Should be lots of fun."

"Right! Although…" He glanced around to make sure we were alone amid the parked vehicles. "It's one thing for you and Michael to pretend to be a couple for a weekend. Are you sure it's a good idea to do it for two weeks?"

"It'll be fine," I insisted, forcing a smile. It would be, wouldn't it? It had to be, because the thought of leaving Michael behind was… No. I didn't like that idea one bit. We'd only just reconnected. I needed more time with him.

Seth nodded. "I'm sure it will be. I'm just wondering about whether it's wise to pretend to be someone you're not for that long."

"I—I" Why was I sputtering? Why did those words punch my sternum like a fist?

Someone you're not.

"It'll be grand. Besides, everyone at the office already thinks I'm queer now." My breath caught, and I cleared my throat. "We're best friends. And Michael's bi. It's not a big deal."

"Right. Of course not. I just wanted to make sure it wouldn't be too difficult for either of you." He smiled ruefully. "Logan and

I know firsthand that pretending can be…intense. Surprisingly so. But of course, we were strangers and both queer. Not that Logan was out. Not even to himself."

Curiosity got the better of me, and after all, Seth had brought it up. "He didn't realize he was bi?" I shifted from foot to foot, glancing around the lot. Janet from HR and her partner were climbing into their SUV but were definitely out of earshot.

Seth shrugged with a smile. "Nope. Even though he'd had sex with men on multiple occasions."

My laugh was an awkward little guffaw. "Wait, what?" My stomach fluttered.

Seth still smiled. "I know, it sounds impossible. And Logan would tell you this himself—it's not a secret. Not that he posts about it on Facebook. To be fair, he refuses to get a Facebook. What I mean is, friends know, and we consider you a friend." He seemed to want to say something else as he frowned and grasped my shoulder. "I just don't want you to get hurt."

"I won't! There's nothing to worry about. I'm sorry I won't be spending Christmas with you. Do you think you could talk Angela into bringing you and Logan along?"

He laughed. "Perhaps, but no. Connor will be home for Christmas with his friend Asher. We'll let you and Michael take the reins on Angela-related capers."

"Fair enough." I found I had to ask, "Back to Logan for a moment—he… Why didn't he…?"

"It's not as uncommon as you might think. Men who have sex with men but still identify as straight. For Logan, there'd been no emotional component." Seth smiled shyly, ducking his head and fiddling with his glasses. "Until he met me, which feels extremely egotistical to say."

I smiled. "True, though. That sounds quite special. And you seem very happy together."

"We are. I never would have imagined it the day Logan and I

met. To say we were opposites is an understatement. We still are in some ways, but it works."

My body hummed with a confusing mix of emotions I couldn't quite identify. Was that envy for Seth and Logan's relationship? Yes, it seemed to be. Sure, I'd been jealous of couples before. Everyone was once in a blue moon.

"I never would have guessed that the start of your relationship was caper-related."

He laughed. "I'm not sure how convincing we were to start. But..." He cleared his throat. "You know, I'd think you and Michael were madly in love." He quickly added, "If I didn't know better, that is."

Laughing and waving a hand, I exclaimed, "Oh! It's because we're mates. For ages. That's all."

"Must be," Seth agreed.

"It'll stand us in good stead for our trip to Australia. I should finish packing up! See you in the new year."

We hugged and said our goodbyes, and I stowed my suitcase in the back of the vehicle, which was the extent of the "packing up" I had to do. More people were leaving, and I waved and nodded and wished happy holidays to all while waiting for Michael. He must have gotten hung up talking to someone.

Pacing, I replayed the conversation with Seth over and over. Had I said the right things? Why was I even concerned? What was that nagging sensation I couldn't quite catch, like a buzzing mosquito out of reach?

My mind returned to what Seth had said: That there had been "no emotional component" to Logan's previous interactions with men. That felt...what? Oddly familiar, I supposed. After all, I wanked to gay porn sometimes. Yet I'd assured myself I didn't want to do those things myself.

But...why? There was nothing wrong with it. Why was I so...*what*? Hesitant? I didn't know. I climbed in the SUV and turned on the engine.

Drumming my fingers on the wheel, I checked the mirrors for Michael's approach. I adjusted the vents and tried to think of anything else.

"Bloody hell," I muttered. "Right. What's the problem?" I had the mad urge to call Mum and talk it through with her. I was a grown man. I could deal with this. Still, I found talking to myself could help, so I kept going.

"Right. I've been 'bi for the weekend,' and I liked being perceived that way. I'm attracted to men and women, even though most of the time I'm happier at home wanking than actually fucking. With some notable exceptions. Just not nearly as many as people think."

I shook my head. Was I getting off track? Was I even on the right train? Was I headed for a collision? Was I torturing this weak metaphor?

"Why can't I be bisexual for real?"

As the question swirled in the heated air blasting from the vents, the passenger door opened, and I jumped a mile.

Michael froze with one boot in. "Sorry! Did I scare you?"

I forced a laugh. "Just gave me a start, yeah. All good."

"I had to run back to the pod to make sure I didn't forget anything." He shut the door and buckled his seatbelt. "Sorry. I get paranoid. Last year, I forgot my jacket hanging in the closet of a hotel and we had to drive back an hour."

We meant Michael and Jared, I presumed. Where had they gone? Had they had fun? Had Jared been a pill about going back for the jacket? "All good," I repeated. "Should we crack on?"

He laughed. "Tally ho? Or something? Oh, were you saying something just now when I opened the door?"

"Why can't I be bisexual for real?"

"Nope! Let's tally ho." I shifted into drive. Figuring out what was real could wait.

Chapter Nine
Will

"ARE YOU SURE I should come in?" I hesitated on the threshold of the townhouse. Though the sun was high in the sky, the townhouse was dark and hushed, the gray blinds drawn.

"Yeah, it's fine. He should be at work." Michael tugged off his boots and left them on the mat. He tossed his gloves on a narrow hall table but didn't remove his coat.

I did the same and followed him into the living room. The fireplace was one of those sleek, modern rectangles in the wall with crystals that might not have been real fire. A huge flat-screen TV hung above it. The white couch was low and straight-backed and curved in a cool shape like a...bean?

"I'd be afraid to sit on that," I said. "How do you keep it so clean?"

"No food or drinks." Michael had bent to unplug a phone charger from the outlet by the couch. He grimaced as he stood. "I know. What's the point of a couch?"

"Remember the one at Zoe's? There must be a happy medium between a massive, stained beanbag in zebra print and this."

Michael chuckled. "I'd like to think."

"Is it always so...dim in here?"

"Yeah. Sunlight fades the furniture and the floors. And the art." He motioned to an abstract painting that was mostly white. I reminded myself there was nothing wrong with being neat, and it was practical to keep out the sun. It was Jared's home, and fair play to him.

I supposed that was the problem—there were no signs of Michael at all.

He led the way through the dining room past a shiny round table and gleaming wooden chairs and into the kitchen. He stood by the island, looking around pensively.

I ran my hand over the flecked gray counter. "Nice. Quartz?"

"Granite." He huffed out a bitter laugh. "I thought it was so grown-up."

"'Tis. Bloody expensive, I imagine."

"Yup." He stuffed his hands in his pockets, gazing around. "I don't think there's anything in here that's really mine. You thirsty?"

"I'll have a glass of water. Thanks."

I waited while Michael opened the fridge and poured two small glasses from a Brita jug. Like the living and dining room, the kitchen was sparse and sleek and neat as a pin, as Mum would say. I could believe it was one of those model homes you toured in a new subdivision.

We drank quickly, and Michael turned to the sink, washing the glasses and flipping them over to dry on a semicircle rack even though there was a dishwasher in the island. He seemed about to speak when he was distracted by something through the small window over the sink. Leaning in, he exhaled sharply.

"What?" I joined him, holding up my hand and squinting, the sun glaring on the fresh snow in the postage-stamp yard.

A Christmas tree bound in twine lay outside to the left. I realized there had to be a sliding door in the dining room behind the drawn blind. The tree was askew, partly covered in snow and half resting on what was likely covered patio furniture. As though it had been tossed outside carelessly.

Michael stared at the tree before he swallowed thickly and reached up and rubbed his healing cheek. Then he shook his head and strode from the kitchen.

I trailed him to the foot of the—of course—gleaming hardwood stairs, then hesitated. Perhaps it would be best if I let him do this alone.

What the *fuck* was wrong with Jared that he didn't want Michael? How could he not appreciate Michael or the tree Michael had bought for Christmas? And maybe there was an explanation, but it was his loss. The prick.

If we weren't jetting off to Australia—a plan that was still surreal—I'd haul that tree out of the yard and take it back to mine. We could go to Target for decorations and when we got back, we'd turn the radio to the Christmas music station and the TV to that channel that showed nothing but cheerfully burning logs in a fireplace for the month of December. We'd flop on the couch and eat and drink and be fucking merry, *Jared*.

To hell with him. I liked that idea for me and Michael. Why not be roommates again in the new year? I wanted to buy a condo with a guest room anyway, so two bedrooms was already in the plans. Or we could just stay in my current place. No rush on moving.

Assuming Michael would be keen to live with me. He'd agreed to come to Australia, and it'd been so much fun spending time with him again. Now that *Jared* was out of the picture, surely *my* Michael was back. He wouldn't ghost me again.

I still stood at the foot of the stairs. Michael was surely packing, but it seemed awfully quiet. I crept up, my socked feet silent on the wood flooring. I stopped on the second-floor landing, listening. Footsteps thudded softly on the third floor.

Feeling like an intruder, I tiptoed up the other flight of stairs, then followed the sound of rustling, stopping in the open door of the master bedroom. Michael was tossing clothing into a pile at his feet. An open suitcase on the floor in front held toiletries, a laptop, and I wasn't sure what else.

"All right?" I whispered. Why was I whispering? We weren't breaking and entering. This had been Michael's home. Though again, the monochromatic bedroom looked barely lived in. The blinds were down in this room too, and Michael had switched on the light in the adjoining bathroom.

"Yep," he said tightly. He yanked a shirt from a hanger, and the end of it bounced off the closet's back wall with a bang. "Can you grab a few garbage bags from under the sink downstairs for my clothes?"

"Sure." My gaze slid over the neat corners of the duvet. I turned away. The sight of the bed they'd shared while Michael hadn't even spoken to me filled me with... It didn't matter. I gritted my teeth against the unpleasant sensation and hurried downstairs. The sooner we left, the better.

Black bin bags in hand, I froze by the kitchen island as a key turned in the front-door lock. I had a perfectly unobstructed view of Jared bustling into the townhouse with cloth grocery bags he deposited on the floor.

Bloody buggery hell.

He kicked the door shut behind him as he straightened and saw me.

I raised my free hand. "Hi. It's all right. I'm here with Michael."

The alarm on his face gave way to suspicion—then a flare of...derision? He snorted. "The famous Will Stewart in the flesh."

All I could do was stare. "I'm sorry?"

He lined up his boots on the mat, unzipped his jacket, and hung it in the hall closet. "You're Will, aren't you?"

"Er... I'm Will, yes." I wasn't too sure about the "famous" bit.

Jared picked up the groceries and marched into the kitchen, brushing past me by the island. "Nice accent. You're even hotter in person. The pics on Mike's phone don't do you justice."

"I…"

Sighing noisily, Jared shook his head and opened the fridge. "Never mind. Sorry. I'm being a dick. That's got nothing to do with anything." Holding a jar of kimchi, he met my gaze. "How's he doing?"

"Fine. As well as can be expected."

Jared's face pinched, and he rolled up the sleeves of his thin black sweater before plugging the sink and turning on the tap. "I feel terrible about how it went down. He's such a sweet guy. We're just not right for each other. I should have told him that a long time ago. Although he already knew it—he had to. Though the denial runs deep with that one. I'm sure you know."

Before I say anything, Michael appeared in the kitchen entry. "Right, I should have gotten the hint when you happily came to my folks' place for Thanksgiving and promised my mom you'd take good care of me. Stupid me," he spat.

Jared faced him. "You're right. That was on me." He winced. "Those scratches are worse than I thought."

Michael shrugged. "No biggie."

Jared unpacked the groceries, stacking cans and boxes in the pantry before filling the fridge with sharp movements.

As much as I didn't want to leave Michael alone, I said, "I should go so you two can talk."

"I don't think we have much to say," Michael muttered.

After tossing leeks into the water filling the sink, Jared said, "It's up to you. But there are a few things we should discuss. The internet's on your account."

Michael rubbed a hand over his hair. "Yeah, okay. Let's talk." He turned to me. "Do you mind going up and packing the clothes on the floor?"

"Sure." I was still gripping the black plastic bags, and I forced myself to head upstairs. Michael had assured me Jared wasn't abusive. It was fine. Everything was fine.

In the bedroom, I shoved clothing into the bags. Why was I "famous"? What had Michael said about me? *Why* had he said much at all when he'd stopped actually speaking *to* me?

Raised voices echoed from downstairs. Crouching on the wood floor, I didn't move a muscle. I couldn't make out what they were saying from two floors up, and I didn't allow myself to creep out to the stairs to eavesdrop.

What if Jared is *abusive? What if Michael needs me? What if he gets hurt?*

I crammed more clothes in the first bag and knotted it shut as I told myself I was letting my imagination run away from me. There were more clothes to bundle, but I found myself pacing restlessly.

How strange to be in Jared and Michael's bedroom. The closed suitcase sat on the bed. I imagined Michael on the right side and Jared on the left.

And I tried not to imagine anything else, banishing memories of gay wank material I'd watched online. Christ, that was the last thing I wanted to think about. Not Michael with *him*.

I paced again. Why was I thinking about any of this? It was none of my business! I was here to support Michael. It didn't matter what their relationship had been like. Especially not in *bed*. Hell, I wanted to be anywhere else.

Yet I couldn't look away from the mattress and its smooth gray coverlet. Jared had been bloody lucky to wake up with Michael every morning. He hadn't even appreciated it. I'd only shared a bed with Michael for a weekend, but I'd felt strangely bereft this morning to wake alone, even though I was home. Even though I'd known Michael was in the guest room next door.

Footsteps sounded on the stairs, and I hurriedly stuffed the rest of the clothes in the other bin bag. Michael returned. His face was flushed, but his eyes were dry. He grabbed his suitcase.

"Thanks. Let's go."

"Are you all right?" I hefted the bags.

He nodded a little too vigorously and led the way downstairs. Jared was mercifully nowhere to be seen. In my SUV, I barely resisted gunning the engine and peeling away from the curb. Michael didn't look back at his former home as we left.

"Is it cool if he forwards my mail to your place? Just until I find an apartment." He fiddled with the air vents.

"Of course. You know you can stay at mine after we get back." From the corner of my eye, I could see Michael unclip his seatbelt, loosen it, and snap it closed again, silencing the alarm that beeped. He was silent, and perhaps he didn't actually know? Had I not made it clear?

Before I could ask, he said, "You've already done too much for me. I'm sure I can find a motel."

Frustration flared. "Fuck off—you're not staying in a bloody motel." I wasn't sure why I was so bothered. We were quiet as I braked for a red light, the air thick with tension. I forced a laugh. "You're doing me a massive favor, remember?"

He scoffed. "An all-expenses paid trip to Australia?" He tried to joke. "Gee, such a hardship!"

I smiled more genuinely this time. "Good point." Relaxing my grip on the wheel, I adjusted the rear mirror even though it hadn't moved. "But really, it's not a bother at all for you to stay at mine. You can do the dishes and clean if it makes you feel better."

"Um, you do remember living with me before, right? Cleaning isn't exactly my best event."

"The townhouse was spotless."

He shrugged tightly. "That's the way Jared likes it." He quickly added, "Obviously I won't be messy at your place either."

"It's not a worry. You can be yourself."

After a long moment, Michael cleared his throat. "Cool. Thanks. I guess we need to pack when we get back. The flight's tonight."

"No, it's actually tomorrow after all. Tuesday."

"Uh, Tuesday at zero-twenty-five. That's twenty-five minutes after midnight. That's tonight."

"Bloody hell!" I gaped as my mind did the calculations. "I had it all wrong in my head. Good thing you're here or I would've stood up Angela. So much for advancing my career."

"Glad to be of service. You don't need to speed, though. We have all day."

I eased my foot off the gas pedal. Mum would be pleased there was someone else to keep an eye on the speedometer. The frustration and tension disappeared. If I wasn't driving, I might have hugged Michael and told him again how much I'd missed him.

"You need to give me a primer on anything I should know before we meet up with Angela again."

"Right." Guilt nagged. Lying didn't sit right for so many reasons. "The trip down under is great, but are you sure about the rest of it? Being my boyfriend. Pretending to be my boyfriend, I mean."

Eyes on the road, Michael nodded. "It's just what I need, actually. A chance to be someone else for a while, even if it's only for Christmas. Real life will be waiting in January, but for the next couple of weeks, we don't have to be ourselves."

I shifted uncomfortably. I was already uneasy with deceiving Angela and my colleagues. I still wanted to be *myself*.

Whoever the hell that was.

A few days ago, I'd had it all under control. Now, I wasn't sure if I was coming or going.

Michael met my gaze, giving me a crooked smile. "It'll be fun." He imitated Matt, punching his fist and chanting, "Caper, caper, caper."

No need to overthink it, was there? Why not enjoy the holidays together in the sunshine and possibly further my career? "Suppose we all need a good caper sometimes, don't we?"

I thought of Mum and her leaps. Grinning at Michael, I stood on the edge. All I could do was dive in headfirst.

Chapter Ten
Michael

AS AN APPARENTLY endless stream of people filed past us to the economy section of the plane, I sipped the free glass of champagne and stretched out my legs. "I've never been in first class before," I murmured to Will, who was sitting next to me by the window.

"This is actually premium economy," he said. "I bet the bastards in first have beds."

In the window seat ahead of us, Angela turned around. "They do. But I didn't get where I am by spending company money on beds in the sky." Grinning, she sipped her champagne. "Good thing they had these empty spots or you'd be stuck back there."

Will grinned. "Definitely not complaining! Thanks again."

It really did seem luxurious to have two wider seats by the window instead of the usual three. There were only six rows of premium, and when I glanced back at the rest of the plane, it looked like a *lot* of people were crammed in.

Will was tapping on his phone, and Angela went back to hers, soon making a call and firing off orders in the friendliest way possible. Her family was flying from Texas and joining us in Perth in…two days?

We'd flown a quick hop from Albany to JFK, and now we were going to Hong Kong and then onto Perth after a layover. I was pretty sure that because we were crossing the dateline it would take us two days.

Not that it really mattered. It could take a week, and I'd be happy to spend it with Will. Not just *with* him, but as his boyfriend. My two days of fantasy had morphed into two weeks, and it was the greatest Christmas present ever.

Will snorted and showed me his phone screen. It was a text from Seth:

By the way, Angela is very big on mistletoe, so be prepared.

My mouth went dry, and I tried to think of a good joke. I leaned over and whispered right in Will's ear given Angela was so close, though she was still talking on the phone. My lips brushed his skin.

"Maybe we should practice kissing after all."

Oh, my *GOD*. I'd really just said that. Like, out loud. To Will. Of all the jokes, *that* was what my asshole brain coughed up? Awesome.

Will laughed and fiddled with his phone, not looking at me. I gulped the rest of my champagne in one mouthful and wondered if it was bad manners to ask for more. Maybe once we were up in the air. I scrolled through my phone restlessly, crossing my ankle over one knee and then the other. Then back again.

Shit, the plane hadn't even left the ground, and we had almost sixteen hours to go. I needed to calm down. Everything was fine. Will had joked about practicing kissing, and I'd only been bringing up *his* joke.

My phone buzzed in my hand, and I eagerly read the text, desperate for a distraction. Zoe had written:

Glad you're okay. You kind of freaked me out. So you and Jared are done?

I choked down my bitterness and hurt. Oh yeah, Jared and I were done. It had been so freaking weird to be back in the townhouse to get my stuff. "The townhouse" that had been "home" for months. How had I ever believed I belonged there?

That Jared and I belonged together?

I hadn't expected him to get off work early, and I definitely hadn't expected him to narrow his eyes and grit his teeth about Will being there with me. Like, what? He was *jealous*? He didn't want me in the first place! And there was obviously nothing between me and Will. It was all pretend, and Jared didn't even know about that.

Now Jared was free to sit on his pristine couch and joylessly celebrate the holidays without any food or drinks or inconvenient Christmas trees messing up his plans. The sight of my tree tossed outside and forgotten, almost completely snowed over, really summed up the whole thing.

I wrote back to Zoe, tapping out:

Definitely done. We should never have been together.

Fidgeting, I crossed and uncrossed my legs. It was honestly humiliating that I'd moved in with a man who was such a terrible fit. I reminded myself he wasn't a bad person, even if I felt bitter at the moment.

"Okay?" Will's warm breath tickled my cheek as he leaned close and put his hand on my knee.

Aside from fighting an instant, massive boner, I was swell. "Uh-huh!"

He arched an eyebrow. "You're jiggling your knee so much they can probably feel the vibrations in coach."

"Oh!" That explained his big hand resting on my knee. "Sorry. Just, you know." I tried to think of an excuse. "Nervous to fly," I blurted even though I'd always been fine on planes.

"Are you?" Both his thick eyebrows shot up. "I didn't realize. I guess we've never flown anywhere together before. Don't worry. You're far more likely to be..." He waved his free hand. "Trampled by elephants than die in a plane crash."

"Am I though? How about if I never go to Africa."

"Hmm." Will seemed to ponder it, and while he did, he

stroked my knee with his thumb. Did he realize he was doing that? Angela was still on the phone and not paying any attention. Will said, "There could be a stampede at the zoo."

I tried to breathe and act normal. His hand felt so heavy and huge on my knee, and I could barely look away from him. I was legit going to be visibly hard if I didn't get a grip. "Seems unlikely, though. And it's easy to avoid zoos."

"What if they escaped from the circus?"

"Do circuses still have elephants?"

Will made a face. "I'm not sure. They really shouldn't."

"Honestly, I think I'm safe from the threat of rampaging elephants."

He squeezed my knee gently. "You're safe here too. The odds are very much in our favor."

Even though I wasn't afraid to fly, I still felt soothed and safer—as if Will could protect me from a plane crash. I believed he'd try, and that felt better than it had any right to. This was exactly why I'd called him from the side of the road.

This was exactly why I was in love with him.

"Welcome aboard," a smooth voice said over the speakers. "Please remove your headphones and turn your attention to the safety demonstration."

Will's hand slipped from my knee, and he sat up straighter, dutifully watching the flight attendant a few rows up as she pointed out the exits. Honestly, it wouldn't have surprised me if he examined the laminated safety info in the seat pocket as requested.

He glanced at me and whispered, "What?"

"Huh?" I hadn't said anything.

"What are you smiling at?"

"Oh! Nothing. Just, um, thinking about elephants. They're so—" *Think of a word! Any word.* "Cute," I managed.

Will chuckled. "Probably not so much if they're trampling you to death, but yeah. They are."

My ears burned as I forced my attention back to my phone. There was another text from Zoe.

Sorry it didn't work out. Glad you're hanging with Will again.

We had to put our electronics in airplane mode for takeoff, so I didn't have time to over-analyze why exactly Zoe was glad I was with Will. I quickly tapped out:

Yeah, it's great. We're on our way to Australia for Christmas for his work. Long story—I'll fill you in later. Sorry I freaked you out, and say hi to your parents. Especially your mom.

I ended the text with the little heart/winking/blowing a kiss emoji and switched off my phone.

We'd been in the air an hour or so when the flight attendants served more drinks and directed us to the printed menu in our seat pockets. I whistled under my breath. "Nice. This food actually sounds good. Short ribs? Although it's weird having dinner at, like, two o'clock in the morning or whatever."

"Totally," Will agreed. "I've never flown this far. I guess we eat dinner, then try to sleep." He tapped his screen on the back of Angela's chair. "Plenty to watch, at least."

I could see that Angela had her headphones on and was watching what looked to be old episodes of *Sex and the City*, which felt very on-brand.

Soon, dinner was served, and the short ribs were delicious. I sipped my glass—actual glass, not plastic!—of Australian Shiraz. "Not that the egg salad sandwich and Coke I had on Delta weren't great, but this is next level."

Will swallowed a bite of roasted root vegetables. "But have you had United's ham and Swiss and 7-Up? Not to be missed."

"A fine vintage, I'm sure."

"Only the best."

I had to admit this all did feel wonderfully grown-up even though I knew it was more about having the money for premium. Still, sitting up front on a business trip with my partner gave me a rush.

I scooped up garlic mashed potatoes on my fork and internally rolled my eyes. Will wasn't even my actual boyfriend, and now I was thinking of him as my partner? *Dial it down there, my guy.*

We idly scrolled the entertainment options, swiping our screens. Will asked, "Have you watched this doc? A wild murder story, that one." He pointed to a movie thumbnail on his screen.

I shook my head. "What's it about? I mean aside from murder."

"I don't want to spoil it. Can't say too much."

"Okay, I'm intrigued. Thanks." I took another sip of wine. "By the way, are you sure I don't need a suit?"

"Positive. I'm bringing one for meetings if I need it, but it'll probably be business casual anyway."

"Yeah." Still, it was cringey I didn't own a suit that actually fit me anymore. "I should have one though. For weddings and funerals if nothing else."

"Not a bad idea. We can go shopping for one when we get home."

Boy, did I like the sound of that word. *"Home."* Not "shopping." Shopping was fine and all, but the thought of *home* with Will—and making plans together for the new year—made me want to jump up and dance down the aisles as we flew over the North Pole.

Watching the flight path on the screen, I said, "I had no idea flights went up this way. I always pictured everything going left and right."

"Me too! It's wild, isn't it? Wouldn't want to crash in Siberia. Or anywhere, for the record."

"Not so much, no." I grimaced. "My mother's worst fear would come true."

"That you'd die in a plane crash?"

"Me or any of her kids. She's always been paranoid about

flying."

"Makes sense it would rub off on you. You're feeling all right, though?"

Ugh, I didn't want to continue the lie. "I'm good. It's more just before the plane takes off. Then I'm totally fine."

Will peeled the lid off a small container of chocolate ice cream that had been frozen very solid and was now thawing in time for us to eat it. He said, "Not so for your mum?"

"Nope. She hates it with a passion."

"Even though it's far more dangerous to drive?"

"Yep. No logic works." I peeled the lid from my ice cream tub.

"I get it. We all have those fears."

"I guess. At least this time there was no need for me to tell my mom I'm flying. I'll let them know when we arrive, but no sense in making her worry in the meantime."

"Mum would skin me alive if I pulled that."

I laughed. "Yeah, but you and your mom are tight." After swallowing a creamy, sweet, and impressively cold mouthful of ice cream, I asked, "What did you tell her about me?"

Will frowned and looked pointedly toward Angela, who still wore her headphones as she ate dinner and watched TV. Oh, right. I leaned close and whispered in Will's ear, "My bad."

He mouthed, *"It's okay."* Then he murmured in my ear, "We need to be careful, though. We should really try to pretend all the time if we can. Except for when we're truly alone."

Nodding, I tried not to let my imagination take off running.

We finished dinner, and the cabin lights dimmed. Both Will and I picked a movie to watch and tried to get comfortable to sleep.

While I was tempted to watch the true crime doc Will had recommended, for the moment I went with *Almost Famous*, which had been one of my favorites as a kid. I knew it practically by heart, so I could close my eyes and doze and still know what was happening. It was weirdly comforting.

If only I could get *comfortable*. I shifted every few minutes even though the seat and legroom weren't bad at all. The guy sitting beside Angela had his seat back a few inches, and I followed suit, adjusting the pitch of the screen.

Will reclined the same amount—and slipped his arm around my shoulders, urging me wordlessly to lean on his shoulder as my heart thumped. Right—we were a couple. This was what couples did.

I adjusted my headphones and found the right angle to relax against Will without jamming my headphones against him. He squeezed my arm in a way that said this was a good spot.

At least, I was pretty sure that's what the squeeze meant. Asking would mean moving, and he'd nudge me if he wasn't comfortable. I closed my eyes, listening to the movie as I drifted off, Will's warmth and the weight of his arm just as comforting as the familiar songs on the soundtrack.

Chapter Eleven

Will

"ARE YOU TOGETHER?"

I blinked at the airport worker waiting expectantly. It took a moment to realize she was asking if Michael and I were a couple. "Oh! Er, yes."

"Step up to number three and wait at the line." She announced this emotionlessly, and I wasn't sure why I was bracing for judgment.

Michael and I shuffled forward to the assigned customs booth to wait. It hadn't occurred to me that couples typically went through customs together, and I shifted nervously. Which was ridiculous—it wasn't as if the customs agent would grill us on our relationship and declare us a fraud.

Michael groaned softly, stretching his arms overhead. He wore sweatpants, and his hoodie and T-shirt rode up, exposing a few inches of pale skin at his belly.

He said, "God, it's been a long day. Days? I'm ready for bed. And another shower."

We'd been fortunate that Angela had sprung for one of the lounges at the Hong Kong airport for our ten-hour layover. We'd been able to shower and change and enjoy the constantly replenished buffet.

Still, the flight to Perth had been another seven hours, and now it was just past eleven p.m. local time.

"Did you sleep at all?" Michael asked.

"Hmm? Here and there," I lied. Well, I had slept a bit on the first flight, though eventually my arm had gone numb where Michael had leaned into me. I hadn't the heart to wake him, so I'd flexed my fingers as unobtrusively as possible and watched the latest fast cars action movie with Vin Diesel.

I knew he was asking about the second flight. He'd dozed after the first meal around four p.m., but I'd hit overtired. Hopefully I'd be out like a light once we reached the hotel.

The customs agent waved us up to the booth. Taking our passports with a serious expression, she scanned them and asked, "What's the purpose of your visit?"

I cleared my throat. "I'm here on business with my boss."

She eyed Michael. "And you?"

"Um, I'm just coming along. With my boyfriend."

"Any alcohol or tobacco?"

We shook our heads and answered a few more questions before being released. We'd officially entered Australia as a couple. Impulsively, I took Michael's hand as we fetched our luggage and waited for Angela and her family.

Michael laced his fingers with mine and smiled absently before saying, "Oh, I see your blue hardshell."

For a few moments, I could hardly breathe. It all felt so natural and normal. Like Michael and I really *were* a couple. Again, I was being perceived as something other than straight—by the customs agent and airport employee—and it felt...ordinary in the best, most thrilling way.

Michael tugged my hand, giving me a quizzical smile. "We should probably grab that suitcase."

"Right!" I let go to circle the carousel and fetch the suitcase before it did another loop. I really did need some sleep.

Angela, her husband Paul, and their two daughters approached. Even Angela appeared exhausted, only giving us a wan smile. She said to Paul, "Honey, I'm gonna use the little girls' room."

Her teenaged daughters, Olivia and Makayla, followed her. Paul yawned widely. "Hoo boy, is it good to have solid feet under my ground again." He shook his head. "What the heck did I just say? Y'all know what I meant."

Michael said, "Yeah, we get it. That was a long trip."

Paul ran a hand over his shiny, bald head. He was white, stocky, and wearing a purple golf polo, Levi's, and actual cowboy boots. We'd all had lunch in Hong Kong, but Angela had done most of the talking about the business opportunity in Perth. Paul had seemed content to listen while the girls had been busy with their phones.

He pointed to the carousel. "Oh, there's one of Rosie's suitcases." He squeezed through the growing crowd to snatch the massive pink hardshell.

"Rosie?" Michael asked. "Sorry, I thought it was Olivia and Makayla?" He bit his lip. "Did I get that wrong?"

"No, no! Angela and I met in Rosebud, Texas. Rosie's my little pet name for her."

I smiled. "That's sweet."

"Where'd you two meet?"

"Albany," Michael said. To me he added, "You can call me Al."

"Like the song!" Paul chuckled. "Good one."

Michael and I frowned at each other, not getting the reference, but we didn't ask.

Just as we picked up the last suitcases, Angela and the girls returned. Olivia was nineteen and in her freshman year at Columbia, while Makayla was fourteen. They were both Asian and slim with long dark hair, while Olivia was almost my height and Makayla smaller than even Angela. Makayla also had braces that she sadly seemed self-conscious of given how often she covered her mouth when she spoke.

The terminal was small, and it was easy to spot a driver holding a sign bearing Angela's name amid the groups of people hugging and kissing.

I'd always enjoyed airport reunions. I watched an older couple run to an adult woman who was probably their daughter, and I missed Mum and Dad with a fierce pang.

The driver called, "Merry Christmas!" as we approached. He checked his watch. "In about twenty minutes, that is."

"Wait, is it?" Michael asked.

"Too right," the driver replied. "It's Christmas Eve right now. Santa's on his way for biccies and milk. Though he'd probably prefer a fry-up and a tinny."

Outside, we all exclaimed at the warm summer night air. After the frigid damp of Albany, it felt luxurious. Pulling his small suitcase, duffel slung over his shoulder, Michael spun around in a circle, his eyes closed and bliss written all over his beautiful face.

His...wait... What had I thought? I laughed to myself. I was really getting into character, apparently.

The driver led us to a black minivan. Olivia sighed loudly. "Couldn't you get a limo, Mom?"

"No, I couldn't. We're not too good for a van, young lady."

Paul said, "It's a Mercedes-Benz, Liv. You'll manage."

We climbed in, Michael and I volunteering to take the back seat. The streets were deserted and tree-lined, and I wished I could open the back window and breathe in the blossoms. Being dropped into summer was magical.

"This is an amazing Christmas present," Michael murmured to me. "Thank you."

"Hey, this is Angela's gift, really," I said.

Paul nodded. "Indeed! Let's all thank her for organizing this wonderful Christmas vacation."

"That she's going to work during," Olivia muttered. At her

dad's glare, she looked abashed. "But yeah, it's awesome. Thanks, Mom."

"It's my pleasure, y'all. Besides, Dale gets all the organizing credit."

"That goes without saying," Makayla added. "Dale is a saint. Why couldn't he come along?"

"He had family plans," Angela said. "But Will's gonna be my partner in crime. Did I tell y'all about the terrific job he did in Seattle last week?"

"No more work talk until after Christmas, Rosie," Paul said gently.

"You're right!" Angela dramatically mimed zipping her lips.

We drove on through the empty residential streets past dark houses, everyone apparently tucked away snugly with dreams of sugarplums in their heads.

Michael muttered to me, "Dude, I'm so tired." He rubbed his face.

"Bro, tell me about it," I drawled with my Brett Yankface flat accent. "That kegger really wiped me out."

Makayla giggled while Olivia shot us a dubious glance. Angela clapped delightedly. "You sound very convincing."

I laughed. "Thanks. It's an old joke with Michael. I know I don't usually sound so American."

Not looking up from her screen, Olivia asked, "Since when do you sound American even a little bit?"

Michael said, "I've been telling him that for years, but he swears his accent has, and I quote, 'dulled significantly.' He's in serious denial."

"I am not! My family all sound much more Scottish than me."

"Oh, aye…captain?" Michael said in a truly terrible brogue.

"Oi!" I pinched Michael's side, and he squirmed away.

"Don't! You know I'm ticklish."

"*Really?*" I wiggled my fingers lightly over his ribs. "Had no idea. Is this bothering you?"

Everyone laughed—even grumpy Olivia. She said, "You guys are disgustingly cute."

And that shouldn't have made me smile so hard, but it did. In the glow of streetlights as we stopped at an intersection, it looked like Michael was blushing. Without thinking, I reached up and brushed his heated cheek with my knuckles before pulling my hand back and looking out the window. His eyes had widened just for a heartbeat before I'd turned away.

It was fine. I was the one who'd suggested we lean into our fake relationship, and clearly it was all going right to plan.

Chapter Twelve

Michael

B EYOND THE STEADY hum of the ceiling fan, cheerful voices drifted on the air. The sun was up, so it was clearly time to open my eyes. I knew where I was—if this was Jared's townhouse in Albany, there'd be no fan or distant laughter through an open window.

It was amazing to open my eyes and see an incredibly blue sky through the big window in our hotel room. To see Will standing on the balcony looking out over the marina and hear birds—seagulls, maybe?—calling.

Dressed in a green polo and a pair of cream linen pants that hugged his round ass and thick thighs spectacularly, Will fit right in with the tropical vibe of the blue room. Wait, was Perth tropical? I thought I'd seen palm trees the night before, but it had been dark.

There was definitely a beachy vibe, and Will matched it. God, he was gorgeous. Inside and out. How did I get so lucky? Here we were on the complete other side of the world, and I got to share a bed with him and hold his hand and—

And it's all pretend.

Right. Sleeping in the same king-sized bed wasn't a big deal. It wasn't like we were fucking. No kissing or touching or cuddling or blow jobs or—

I rocked up to sit on the side of the bed before my morning

wood got any bright ideas. The mattress squeaked, and Will turned. He smiled broadly, teeth gleaming, with his gold aviator sunglasses propped on his head.

"Merry Christmas."

"Oh, right! Yeah, merry Christmas. That's so weird that it's the twenty-fifth now. Although we were on a plane forever, so I guess it makes sense."

Will smiled. "It's discombobulating to be sure. Did you sleep well?"

"Yeah, I guess I did." I'd gone to sleep in a fresh pair of boxers and nothing else because I'd been too tired after a quick shower to paw through my suitcase for a tee.

I spotted a small box on the round breakfast table in front of the window. The box was wrapped in red, green, and gold with a glittery bow on top. "What's that?"

"Merry Christmas." Will passed the box to me.

"Huh? When did you get this?" I held the perfectly wrapped box in my hands, guilt washing through me.

"There's a little gift shop downstairs in the lobby. I was surprised it was open today. Apparently, they do a steady business on Christmas Day for the blokes who forgot to get something for their wives."

"You've been downstairs? What time is it? How long did I sleep?" I grabbed for my phone on the wooden side table, relieved that it was only showing just past ten a.m.

"You're good. I woke up around six and couldn't get back to sleep. Jet lag, I suppose, although I've no clue what time it is in Albany." He motioned to the gift, which was very light. "It's just a little something that made me think of you."

"I didn't get you anything."

"Sure you did. You're here, aren't you?"

"Yeah, it's a real hardship. However will I survive all this luxury?" I peered around Will. "Wow, that balcony looks huge."

His face pinched. "Oh, wait. Does it bother you? The vertigo thing you mentioned? Granted, I was the one who fell off my horse, not you. But if this is too high, I'm sure we can move."

"No, I'm good on balconies as long as I'm not right near the edge. It's weird, I know. A ladder or horse shouldn't be scarier, but... Besides, this room is amazing. How did Angela get this at the last minute at Christmas?"

"Dale's nothing if not a miracle worker."

Sitting on the side of the bed in my boxers with the duvet tangled around my waist, I unwrapped the box. "It's so neat. I feel bad wrecking it."

"I can take zero credit for the wrapping job." He shifted from one bare foot to the other and back again. "As I said, it's just a wee something."

Inside the box, surrounded by tissue paper, sat a koala Christmas tree ornament. On the end of a gold string, the koala wore sunglasses, a red and white Santa hat, and stood on a surfboard. Grinning, I held it up. "Oh my god."

"I know you'd bought that Christmas tree, and it all went wrong, so I thought if you get one next year, you might like a new ornament. It's tacky, I know."

"I *love* it. It's fun." I laughed. "Jared would hate this so much. It's perfect. Thank you."

Hands shoved in his pockets, Will shrugged. "You're welcome. It's just a little bauble. They had some lovely classy ornaments as well, but I tried to imagine which one you'd pick for yourself. I was torn between this and a kangaroo holding a beer."

"That sounds amazing." I hopped up and pulled him into a hug. "Seriously, thank you. I love that you know I'm not classy."

Will hugged me and rubbed my bare back. "I knew you'd want something fun."

"Classy's overrated." I leaned against him, yawning widely "Merry Christmas."

"I'm glad you're here." Will ran his hand up and down, up and down. "I'm glad *we're* here."

It honestly took me a minute to realize we'd been hugging way longer than normal, especially considering I was only wearing underwear and Will's hand seemed glued to my back.

What were we doing? This was all very non-hetero even though we didn't have an audience. We'd never hugged like this in the past. Definitely not. I could have closed my eyes and snuggled closer, pressing my face into Will's stubbly neck to kiss him softly...

Would he let me?

Would he...like it?

Whoa. That morning wood was about to roar back to life, so I gave Will's back a bro-y slap and wriggled away toward the bathroom. I paused to hang the ornament from the lamp sitting on the desk in the corner of the spacious room. The sparkly koala grinned against the smooth cream of the lampshade.

I said, "I should get in the shower. Do we have plans?"

"Not for an hour. Take your time."

I scrubbed under the water in the glass stall shower, setting the jets to cool to wake myself up and get a grip. Will was straight. Of course he wouldn't like it if I kissed his neck.

That had just been a hug. A long, weirdly intimate hug. I couldn't get carried away. It was the jet lag. I was imagining things.

But seriously—since when did Will tenderly stroke my back? My shirtless back at that.

I twisted the knob on the shower and ran the water as cold as it would go. Which wasn't very cold given how hot Perth was. Tepid would have to do.

After my shower, I stood on the plush bathmat in front of the sink with a towel around my hips and leaned close to the mirror, inspecting a zit growing on my chin. I guess I shouldn't have been surprised given we'd just spent two days traveling.

Still, I wished I had some stubble to cover it up. On my pasty face, it stood out like a…really red thing. Oh well.

I squeezed styling cream into my hair and fiddled with it. Even though I'd just slept more than eight hours, my brain was definitely still in a previous time zone.

When Will knocked softly on the door, I told him to come in. He asked, "Can I brush my teeth? Forgot to do it earlier some-how."

"Jet lag is how." I moved over at the sink and pulled out my toothpaste from the big Ziploc bag I'd thrown my toiletries into. I passed it to Will even though he'd probably brought his own.

My morning breath was probably hellacious, so I pulled out my toothbrush. Will squeezed the paste over his and passed it back. Side by side, we cleaned our teeth, pausing to spit into the sink now and then.

Toothpaste dribbled from the side of Will's mouth, and he mumbled as he bent over and spit, turning on the tap to wet his brush. He muttered, "All I need is to spill toothpaste on my clean shirt." Looking in the mirror, he carefully wiped his mouth.

I laughed and immediately drooled frothy toothpaste onto my right pec. Because of course I did. It just made me laugh more, and around my toothbrush, I mumbled, "Like this?"

Will grinned. "Can't take you anywhere. Good thing you're not dressed yet."

Then, he lifted his hand and swiped up the toothpaste with his finger.

From my bare chest.

With his *finger*.

Also, he brushed my nipple in the process.

Will froze with his finger hovering in midair, the toothpaste drool on his skin. He blinked, looking at his finger and seeming to belatedly realize what he'd done.

We were only inches apart. My dick was hard. My skin tingled. My heart was about to pound right out of my chest. This casual intimacy was going to kill me.

Will's laugh was loud, echoing off the white tiles. "Jet lag!" He bent and scrubbed his hands in the sink while I stood rooted to the spot. Were his ears turning red?

He blurted, "Coffee?"

I'd gone back to brushing even though there was hardly any toothpaste left in my mouth. I spit in the sink and said cheerfully, "Yeah, thanks!"

"I'll figure out the machine. It looks fancy, so it should be pretty good."

"I'm not picky about coffee. Not like—" I needed to stop talking about Jared. Or thinking about him. "I'm not picky," I repeated.

"Great, I'll..." Will jerked his thumb over his shoulder and disappeared into the main area.

Puffing out my cheeks with a big exhale, I looked in the mirror. *Ugh, that zit.* But what I really had to focus on was that it had taken all my self-control to keep from kissing Will.

Not just *kissing* him but shoving him against the pristine white wall and devouring him.

This was all supposed to be pretend, and yeah, I'd known I was still in love with him, but I swear he was acting differently too. What was up with that hug? It wasn't possible that Will could... For me?

Nope. Don't even go there.

I'd been so tired the night before that I'd barely registered sleeping in the same bed with Will again. At least I hadn't been tormented by how close-but-far he'd been.

I had a feeling tonight would be a different story.

"MERRY CHRISTMAS, Y'ALL!" Angela held up her mimosa, and we all clinked our champagne flutes.

Including Makayla, who said, "Happy birthday, Jesus," before gulping.

Paul gave her a pointed look. "Mimosas are a privilege, not a right. And you're only getting one, so I'd sip."

Makayla giggled while Olivia rolled her eyes. We sat at a round table on the huge balcony attached to the Barkers' suite on the top floor of the hotel. The balcony wall was glass, and there was an amazing view of the marina and incredibly blue ocean, with lighter shades closer to shore.

The sun beamed down above a roof of wooden slats with pale fabric woven through. A ceiling fan kept us cool, which was good, because holy shit, it was *hot*.

But I'd put on sunscreen, and I wasn't complaining after the cold, gray December in Albany. "I've never seen a fan on a balcony before," I said. My mimosa tasted a little funny thanks to the toothpaste, but it still went down smoothly.

"Such a good idea, isn't it?" Angela said. To the young blond man serving us, who was already mixing another pitcher of mimosas, she added, "Your hotel is just lovely."

He nodded. "Thank you."

"It's not like he owns it," Olivia muttered. She asked me, "Haven't you ever been to Mexico or the Caribbean?"

She played with a pink pearl necklace. All the Barkers were dressed in summery pastels, and Will fit right in with them. I wore long khaki shorts and a short-sleeved button-up shirt in red and blue plaid. It was my only dressy summer shirt, and it probably needed ironing even though I'd carefully rolled it in my suitcase.

"No, actually," I answered. "My parents live in Florida, though." I cringed. What did that have to do with it? "But it's, uh, cool. The fan."

"Quite literally!" Angela grinned. "Now, tell us all about your family. Are they supportive of you and Will?"

"Um, yeah. They think Will's great." I finished my mimosa and smiled at Will beside me.

It wasn't a lie—my parents had no issues with Will and Zoe and my other friends from college. I mean, they weren't super interested in my friends, but they liked them all fine. They'd said they enjoyed meeting Jared at Thanksgiving. Not that it mattered now.

The Barkers seemed to be waiting for me to say more. I almost wished the girls were allowed to have their phones at the table. Why did I feel like Olivia in particular would spot any inconsistency and roast me? Not that I had any reason to lie about my family. Only my boyfriend.

I was still jittery as I gave them the rundown on my parents and siblings. Another mimosa went down like water, so it was a good thing the food started coming in waves.

It was a pretty fancy brunch, with eggs Benedict and a seafood frittata, amazing warm sourdough bread, grilled prawns—which I discovered were shrimp—and waffles with the best fresh fruit I'd possibly ever tasted. They were all small courses, but soon I was getting full.

Angela may not have sprung for first class on planes, but she didn't seem to rough it when it came to hotels and food. Dishes kept coming, and there were juicy grilled sausages that the server called "snags." I groaned as I took a bite.

Chewing, Will nodded and gave a thumbs-up.

"Ain't this all to die for?" Angela said. "Such a nice change from turkey and stuffing, though I do love those traditions." She asked the server, whose name we'd learned was Lachlan, "Is this a typical Australian Christmas brunch?"

While working off the wire on another bottle of sparkling wine, he said, "It all depends, really. My nan would do a glazed ham and a turkey and all that stuff. But my parents are more into salads and prawn cocktails. Skewers on the barbecue and that sort of thing." He popped the lid on the bottle. "And sparkling shiraz."

Another server—they came in and out with more food, all wearing crisp white shirts and khaki shorts that were embarrassingly similar to mine—gave us clean flutes. I'd never had sparking red wine, though I didn't say that.

Angela took a sip and declared, "Delicious! Now, I've had my fair share of rosé—no comments from the peanut gallery," she added to Paul with an affectionate wink, "But I've never had a bubbly red. Have y'all?" she asked Will and me.

I was relieved when Will said no. It wasn't just me being uncultured.

Makayla asked Lachlan, "Do you have to work all day on Christmas?"

He smiled. "Nah, I'm off in a couple of hours. I'm meeting my folks at the beach. That's an Aussie Christmas tradition for sure."

"Oh yes, there's a famous beach right near here, isn't there?" Angela asked.

Lachlan grinned. "Yep. Barking Beach. It's been called the best beach in Oz. You've got to head down to Barkers once this lot's digested."

"They named the beach after us!" Angela exclaimed.

"Oh my god, we totally have to go!" Makayla grinned.

Olivia said to Lachlan, "Barker's our last name. Well, my sister and I are Barker-Robertson."

"Sweet," Lachlan said. "It's only five or ten minutes on the boardwalk. It'll be hectic today since it's Christmas, though it's hectic most days in the summer. Just be careful and swim between the flags. Mind the lifeguards."

Olivia perked up. "Lifeguards? Yeah, we should go down this afternoon."

"Sounds good," Will said. He glanced to me. "If you're up for a swim?"

"Totally. I might need a nap first though." I shifted in my chair. "This was a lot of food."

"Mmm. A nap," Paul said contentedly, sipping his shiraz.

The sparkling red really was refreshing, and my head buzzed pleasantly. I wasn't close to drunk, but my cheeks felt warmly flushed. A nap sounded awesome.

Angela held up her glass. "Merry Christmas. I know no one wants to say grace these days, but I'm so grateful to be happy and healthy and here with y'all." She beamed at Paul and then the girls. "With my beautiful family." She turned her smile to me and Will. "And new friends. Such a beautiful couple. Love is love. I believe that so firmly. I remember once when my daddy—"

"*Mom*, please don't tell that story!" Olivia exclaimed. "You're so extra, oh my god."

"I know, I know." Angela shrugged with a smile, not seeming bothered. To me and Will, she said, "If you boys have kids one day, be prepared for them to find you very embarrassing. Do you want to have kids?"

"Don't grill them!" Olivia shook her head and muttered something under her breath.

I took another swig of bubbly wine as Will said, "It's okay. We haven't gotten that far yet. But I'm sure my mum and dad would be thrilled."

"Family really is life's greatest joy," Angela said solemnly. "Everyone should get to experience it."

"I think Mom's getting drunk," Makayla whispered, though she didn't seem bothered.

Olivia muttered something again that I couldn't make out and swatted at a buzzing fly.

Angela only laughed. Her cheeks were pink, and she very well might have been buzzed. She leaned over and took Olivia's chin to kiss her cheek. Olivia let her.

Angela said, "You're in college now, baby. You're too old to be embarrassed by your parents."

Olivia raised a sleek eyebrow. "I didn't say anything about Dad."

We all laughed as Paul reached up a hand and mimed patting himself on the back.

Unfazed, Angela said, "Christmas is a time for family and traditions, and even though we're here in the sunshine on the other side of the world and we can't have a tree, that's okay." She winked at me. "Trees can be dangerous anyway." Reaching into her pocket, she pulled out a green plastic sprig with white berries and held it over her head.

As Paul leaned over to plant a kiss on her, the girls cried with laughter, Olivia repeating how embarrassing it was. Angela tossed her the mistletoe, and Olivia batted it toward Makayla, and somehow, we were suddenly playing a game of hot potato.

It was probably a combination of jet lag and wine, but we couldn't stop laughing as we tossed the plastic sprig around the table. Then Lachlan appeared and snatched it out of the air before holding it over his golden head. He waggled his eyebrows at another server who'd arrived pushing a cart of desserts.

The older woman, who had to be nearing retirement, sighed wearily, trying not to smile. It was silly and *fun*, and we clapped as she pressed a kiss to Lachlan's cheek in what was probably an HR violation, but no one seemed to mind.

Then the mistletoe flew wildly in my direction, and I reached up to grab it before it sailed too far and went over the side of the balcony. "Got it!" There was more applause, and I kept my arm raised triumphantly.

And Will leaned toward me.

And Will kissed me.

We were both smiling, and our lips only met for a moment. An endless, perfect Christmas moment under plastic mistletoe on a warm Australian balcony with people we hardly knew, who hooted and laughed and clapped joyfully.

Will *kissed* me, and I wanted to pause that moment like it was a movie and take a screencap I could keep on my camera roll.

But life wasn't a movie, and it was over in a few thudding beats of my heart. Our eyes met as Will leaned away, and all I could do was grin, giddy laughter bubbling up. I'd never loved anyone as much as I loved Will, and I couldn't imagine how I ever would.

Will would never be mine, but I'd always have our kiss under plastic mistletoe in the sunshine.

Chapter Thirteen

Will

I HADN'T MEANT to kiss Michael.

Not that it was a *problem* or anything of the sort. I simply hadn't planned it. It wasn't choreographed for Angela's benefit. He'd lifted the mistletoe, and we were all laughing, and kissing him had felt like the most natural thing in the world.

Now, we left the elevator and strolled back to our room for a snooze before we met up with the Barkers again in a few hours to visit the beach. Correction: I attempted to "stroll," which proved a challenge given I was having an out-of-body experience.

I'd kissed Michael, and I had to do it again.

Did he feel the same? It'd likely been nothing to him. A Christmas kiss between friends at a boozy brunch. It had only been a peck. Not a deep, sexy, tender, rough, wet, dirty—

Stumbling, I caught myself on the door frame outside our room. I forced a laugh. "Oops. I'm cut off." In reality, I could drink a fair sight more before I got stocious, as they said back home.

Michael chuckled, resting his hand on my shoulder. "Okay?"

Christ, no. I'm not okay.

I managed to nod and fit the key card into the slot. We'd left the Do Not Disturb sign on the door, so the bed was still a rumpled tangle of sheets. How had I slept beside Michael without having him? I'd die if I didn't have him.

Before I could do anything profoundly unwise, I escaped into the loo to splash my face. Leaning over the sink, I breathed deeply as water dripped from my chin. A splodge of toothpaste stained the side of the basin, and I shivered thinking of touching Michael's chest.

It truly hadn't been intentional. Again, it had simply felt…natural. I'd missed him so much the past two years when he'd cut me off—*no, don't think about that!*—but it hadn't been like this. My curiosity about men and new wanking material hadn't been about Michael.

Fuck me. *Had* it been about Michael?

Lifting my head, I gave myself a good hard look in the mirror. It didn't matter. What mattered was that now, in a hotel room on the far side of the world, I wanted Michael desperately.

Heart hammering, I flung open the door. Michael turned from the sliding balcony door, a little crease between his eyebrows. Before he could ask, I blurted, "Can I kiss you again?"

His blue eyes widened. His mouth opened and closed—Christ, his *mouth*—and he glanced around with a tentative smile, as if he thought I'd made a joke and was waiting for the punchline.

He said, "Sure?"

"Oh, thank god," I muttered as I strode to him and claimed his mouth, gripping his face as I kissed him properly. Not a sweet wee peck, but like I meant it this time, pressing our lips together powerfully.

Michael startled against me before pressing back, whimpering and grasping at my sides with his hands. There was still a hint of sweet meringue from the Pavlova on his lips, and I wanted to lick inside his mouth. I wanted to suck his tongue and tear off his clothes. I wanted to—

His palm flat against my chest, Michael stepped back. He regarded me warily and whispered, "What are you doing?"

I was panting already, my cock swollen in my linen trousers. "Er... I don't know." What *was* I doing? I'd kissed women before. Was I crap at kissing a man?

"You don't know?" Michael's brows met. Something flickered in his eyes. Hurt? He dropped his hand.

I laughed, sounding unhinged. "I'm drunk." I backed away, panic taking over.

"You're drunk?" Michael peered at me dubiously.

That he apparently still knew me well enough to know I wasn't drunk made my belly flip. Which was ludicrous because I was being dramatic. It had only been a couple of years—of course he could still tell. Yet it made me happier than it had any right to.

"I'm not drunk," I confessed. "I'm... I was kissing you." Not that there was actually any doubt. Michael's lips were shiny with spit. I looked between his eyes and his lips, caught in a helpless loop.

"Why? For...practice?" Michael watched me warily.

Here was the perfect excuse. Well, it was remotely plausible at least. But I couldn't look into his eyes and lie. "No," I rasped. I cleared my throat. Sweat prickled my palms, and the hair on the back of my neck stood. "No," I repeated. "Not for practice. Just...for us."

Michael's lips parted. "Us?" he whispered.

"If you want? I'm—I'm...curious."

"Curious?"

"Are you just going to repeat everything I say?" I tried to laugh.

"Sorry." Michael's cheeks flushed red, and he still watched me uncertainly.

My mouth was dry. My heart pounded. I was hard. I tore my gaze up to his eyes—which were dark with desire. His chest rose and fell, his harsh little breaths filling the sleepy, sunny quiet of the room.

"I want to know what it's like to be with a man," I said, my voice rough. "I've wondered for a long time."

Michael's eyes widened at that, his fingers twitching.

Before he could reply, I blurted, "Not just any man. That's not why I—" I ran a hand through my hair, laughing rather hysterically. "I'm making a right mess of this, aren't I? What I'm trying to say is that, yes, I've wondered what it would be like with a bloke, but I haven't done anything about it because I didn't want to until now. And now, I really, really want to know what it's like. With you."

"With me," he repeated slowly.

"Will you show me?"

There was no time to dangle on the end of the hook waiting for his answer since Michael didn't so much kiss me as leap against my mouth. With Michael in my arms, we crashed back against the bed so forcefully we were lucky the whole thing didn't collapse.

There was no more hesitation or confusion. This wasn't a sweet, curious, gentle kiss. This wasn't indecision and tentative exploration. This was tongues and teeth and spit, and I was gasping for every touch.

He was hard in his shorts on top of me, and I thrust up, desperate for friction, full stomach be damned. Michael pulled back suddenly, his teeth almost bringing my lower lip along.

Before I could worry he was having second thoughts, he tore at his shirt, struggling with the buttons, and I went to work on mine, my fingers clumsy. Between us, we got our shirts off, and Michael straddled me, which had every right to be strange yet wasn't.

He laughed—in delight, I hoped—those gorgeous dimples creasing his cheeks. I had to kiss him again, taking his face in his hands, both of us smiling as we'd been on the balcony under the mistletoe.

He slid his palms over my stomach and up to my chest, his

rough fingers teasing my nipples. Electricity shot straight to my dick—still achingly hard in my linen trousers—and I groaned.

It was like Michael drank in my noises. He kissed me deeply, touching me and rocking our hips together. I strangely remembered being tossed about in the ocean in Mexico on holiday once—that feeling of the tide and the sea's power, of being helpless to do anything but ride the sensations until I landed on the sand.

My spinning head managed to focus on the sensation of Michael's tongue sweeping through my mouth. I didn't want to be carried along in the tide. I was finally getting my chance to be with a man. With *Michael*. Christ, *had* I wanted this all along?

All I knew was that I needed to grab this opportunity with both hands.

Or at least one.

Michael moaned as I fumbled for him. Suddenly all I cared about was feeling him all over, skin to skin. Knowing this was real. I managed to get his shorts open and shoved my hand inside and—

"Oh, *fuck*," I groaned. "You're hard." *For me.*

My best friend was hard for me. I could feel the proof right there, hot against my palm. I wrapped my fingers around Michael's thick, curving shaft, teasing and gripping the way I'd do to myself, albeit with a different angle.

I'd imagined this countless times. Not with Michael, but various random men, typically faceless. Now, there was a real cock throbbing in my hand, and I wanted every inch of it. I wanted everything.

He tasted like the meringue and berries and sweet cream, but with a perfectly sharp edge of the cappuccino he'd had with dessert. I moaned into his kisses, squeezing his shaft. It should have been bizarre to get off with my best friend, but it felt like puzzle pieces slotting into place.

Coarse hair tickled my fingers, and I explored his heavy balls. It was different than sex with a woman in obvious ways, but I supposed it was all the same principle at the end of the day: touching and rubbing and delighting.

When Michael cried out through parted lips, his eyes wild, my own balls drew up. That I was giving him pleasure—that I could make him happy—filled me with a rush of joy and purpose.

Michael was hard for me, and I was going to make him come.

He braced a hand on my chest, digging his blunt nails into my flesh as I stroked him with more confidence. He whimpered, his face flushed and eyes wide. I'd always loved knowing my partner was genuinely getting off, and feeling his excitement build against my hand was everything.

"*Will*," he moaned helplessly.

"It's all right," I told him, thumbing drops of precum from the head of his hot cock.

I wanted to roll him under me and sink down to swallow his cock whole. Make him come and take every drop. I wanted to spread his legs and drive into his body and come inside him until neither of us could walk.

He was supposed to be showing me how it all worked, but I wanted to take care of him. He shook and gasped, clearly right at the edge, and even though he was on top of me, I felt totally in control.

"It's all right," I repeated. "I'm going to make you come."

With another gasp, Michael rutted into my hand, his spine arching. His face and neck were flushed red down to the middle of his chest, his mouth open and eyes closed as he sprayed cum over my stomach. He curled over me, trembling with a few final drops.

Dazed, I whispered, "Mission accomplished."

Michael shook again. Was he cold? Our skin was slick with sweat, and the sun was beaming through the window. I wrapped my arms around him, his breath hot on my neck, and I realized he was laughing.

Then I was too, but I was so hard it turned into whimpers as I rubbed myself through my trousers. I hadn't come in my pants in years, but I was dangerously close to it now.

"It's okay, baby. I've got you."

My best friend just called me *baby,* and somehow it was exactly what I wanted to hear. Michael tugged my trousers and white boxer briefs down mid-thigh, and nestled between my legs in a blink, my cock in his mouth.

I'd been sucked plenty of times but this was different. Even though Michael barely had any facial hair, I could feel the faintest tickle of it against my balls, and though his golden waves were soft under my fingers, there was a hardness to his jaw. A maleness I'd never experienced and that I'd wondered about for too long.

And of all men, it was *Michael.* I'd missed him so fucking much. Much more than I'd let myself acknowledge. But he was here now, and he was bringing me off with fingers against my taint and the sweetest suction on my cock.

I let go, the pleasure crashing over me, that wild ocean ride returning. I could only gasp as Michael swallowed around me. I watched him milk me, and there were white splashes on his rosy lips as he pulled off. All I could do was take his face in my trembling hands and kiss him, tasting myself, a thrill rippling through me.

When I could talk—but likely shouldn't have—I said, "So, it's like that? Being with a man, I mean."

Michael's eyes searched my face, the crease returning between his brows. He was heavy on me, but I liked it. He murmured, "Not always. But, um, yeah."

I didn't know what to say, so I went with, "Thank you," because I was a bloody idiot.

But Michael smiled, that dimple appearing. "You're welcome." He pressed his face into the side of my neck, kissing my damp skin. I tugged the sheets over us even though we were sticky and half-dressed. I wasn't about to let go of him yet.

Chapter Fourteen

Michael

UH, YEAH, IT was *never* like that.

At least not for a long time. I'd had good sex with Zoe and a few other people, but it hadn't been like that with anyone. Maybe the sex with Jared had been so unsatisfying that getting a hand job from Will blew my entire mind in comparison?

Or maybe love was the difference. Laying tangled with Will— on top of him, hiding my face against his neck—I loved him so much that tears burned my eyes. I was afraid to look up. Was this real or some fucked-up dream fueled by jet lag and years of wanting him?

Will traced my spine with his fingertips. His warm breath tickled my shoulder. I could taste his cum and sweat. If this was a dream, it was pretty realistic.

This was the greatest Christmas ever. I'd gone from cherishing one laughing, public mistletoe kiss to *all that.*

What was this though? Aside from sex, did this mean Will...liked me back? I cringed at what a kid I sounded like. But I felt young and stupid and unsure. I'd been in love with Will for so long that even thinking he might feel anything close to the same left me shaking and sweating.

"Michael?" His low voice rumbled beneath me.

He probably wanted me off him. I rolled onto my back beside him and stared at the smooth white ceiling. "Yeah?" My voice came humiliatingly close to cracking.

Nope, I could not start crying. It would freak out Will, and I couldn't do that to him. This wasn't about me. If he was really bi-curious—and, uh, yeah, apparently he was!—I had to be there for him and not make this any weirder than it might already be.

I kept rolling, pushing to my feet and ducking into the bathroom. I ran a washcloth under warm water and tensed to stop my knees from trembling.

"Michael?"

I turned my head to finally look at Will again. He sat up, his dick still hanging out of his open pants, hair sticking up, and was that my jizz stuck in his chest hair? He was *gorgeous*.

"Yeah?" I realized I was smiling.

He smiled back, tilting his head. "Are you... Is it...?" He frowned toward the sink.

Oh shit, had I been standing here too long? I said, "Water took a while to heat up," and squeezed out the cloth. My dick was hanging out too, and I figured I should clean myself while I was standing there.

Will watched.

My skin tingled, goosebumps spreading over my arms that I couldn't blame on the A/C. Will and I just had sex. We gave each other orgasms. We'd *kissed*. I'd wanted this for so long, and now I didn't know what the hell to do with any of it. Was he okay? Had he liked it?

I touched my swollen lips. Anyone would come from being sucked. It didn't really mean anything that he'd shot down my throat. I couldn't get ahead of myself. I'd screwed up our friendship already, and I had to get this right.

Whatever *this* was. I couldn't just hit him with all my bottled-up feelings. He'd had his first bi-curious orgasm. I couldn't spew my *I've-been-in-love-with-you-forever-please-love-me-back* bullshit all over him.

I rinsed the cloth and brought it to him. "Here." He took it, and our fingers brushed. I was standing there with my wet dick still hanging out of my shorts. Will looked away, and I looked away. I had no clue what to say.

To stop myself from saying all the wrong things, I busied myself stripping off my shorts and tugging on the boxers I'd slept in the night before.

"Are you okay?" Will asked.

I turned to face him. He sat on the side of the bed, his boxer briefs and linen pants balled up in his lap. His legs were sprinkled with dark hair, and I wanted to drop to my knees and just rub my cheek against his thigh.

I nodded. "What about you?"

He nodded too, smiling tentatively.

"Cool," I said. "So…" We were adults, and we needed to talk about this. I sat beside him on the bed. Our knees brushed, and more goosebumps spread over my leg. "How long have you been into guys? You never said anything. Which is okay! I'm just kind of confused."

Will laughed under his breath. "You could say I've been confused too. It's been fairly recent. You weren't around."

"Oh." Guilt gurgled in my belly. "I'm sorry."

Will shrugged tightly, not looking at me. That didn't put my mind at ease. Also, I'd pushed him away—no, I'd *run* away like a coward—because I'd had to get over him for my own sanity. It hadn't worked even a little, and now we'd messed around together, and I thought Will had liked it, and maybe we…

I was dizzy. There were a shit-ton of maybes.

Will asked quietly, "Can we get under the covers?"

"Totally." The wet cloth sat on top of Will's bundle of clothes, and I stood and grabbed it before hesitating. "You missed a spot." Leaning in, I dragged the cloth over Will's chest, the rough fabric rasping over his hairy skin. I rubbed at the flecks of dried jizz.

He let me, his eyes on me, but it wasn't sexy this time. He suddenly seemed vulnerable in a way I wasn't used to. Will had always been strong and capable and in control, and now I was about to tuck him in and kiss his forehead.

I took his clothes from his lap, dropping them in the corner with mine. We'd deal with laundry or whatever later. Will curled under the top sheet, and I slipped into bed so we faced each other on our sides.

We weren't touching, the king mattress big enough that there were several inches between us. I wanted to pull him into my arms and tell him everything would be okay, but was that for my own benefit?

I wanted to ask him what he needed, and I would have in the past. You know, when we hadn't just had sex. It was hard to say the right thing, and now it was like we were speaking a brand-new language.

I went with, "Do you want to nap?"

He shook his head, his forehead creased, tension radiating from him.

"Okay." I had to get this right, but all I could do was blurt, "Are you freaking out?"

A laugh punched from him, and his frown relaxed. "A little. You?"

"Yeah. It's... We can just talk, right? It doesn't have to be weird."

"Right." Will folded his hands under his head on the pillow. The sheet slipped down, and I pulled it back up to his shoulder. He said, "So... What did you want to talk about?"

His deadpan delivery cracked me up, and we both laughed. I pretended to think about it. "Hmm. Anything new going on? How about this weather? I've never had a tropical Christmas before."

"Me either. It's nice, though. Shit, don't let me forget to ring my parents later. I need to check the time difference again. I looked it up last night, and now I've forgotten completely."

"Were you distracted by something?"

He tapped his chin thoughtfully. "No. It's all been business as usual."

"Same old, same old." God, I itched to reach out and play with his chest hair.

"You know, I'm not sure exactly when I started fancying men as well as women."

Okay, we were doing this talking thing. I made a soft listening sound and gave him an encouraging nod.

"I've never done anything about it. Aside from wanking to gay videos."

Now there was a mental image that threatened to make my dick hard again *really* fast. "That's okay. You don't have to do anything with anyone."

Knowing I really was the first man he'd been with made my head spin. I wanted to beg him, "*Why me?*" but this was about Will.

His forehead furrowed again. "It's odd. There have been a few exceptions—Amelia, especially—but most of the time I find I'd rather just get off with porn or a fantasy."

I'd never met Amelia, but I'd wondered if she regretted letting Will go all those years ago. I couldn't imagine what she'd been thinking. But wait—did that make me an exception?

I tried to focus. "There's nothing wrong with just pleasing yourself. We all jerk off. Or most of us do. I guess some people don't?"

"Yeah, but most of the time I prefer it. I don't think that's the norm."

Most of the time but not today? Was it only curiosity? I cleared my throat. "It's not *abnormal* or anything. Like, some ace people really like masturbating, I think. It all depends on the person."

Will seemed to be considering this. "I do love sex, though. I think about it a lot. And I loved—" He waved a hand over the mattress between us. "What we did."

God, do you love me too?

Okay, no. I could not even hint at that. If Will said it, awesome, but he was clearly confused and working through his stuff.

Still, I had to ask, "You enjoyed it?"

He burst out laughing as he propped up on his elbow. "Was that not abundantly clear?"

Relief flowed through me. "I don't want to assume! This is all new. I mean, obviously I've fucked guys before, but you haven't. And we're—we've never—" My face went hot, and I know I was turning red. "I want to make sure everything's cool." I barely resisted pulling the pillow over my head.

Will smiled sweetly, and my stomach flipped. "It's cool." He hesitated. "I'd like to…explore. We're not really boyfriends, but we are friends."

My joy balloon was punctured with a sad little *hiss*. Right. Okay, not boyfriends. That was fair. I could handle that. Scratch that. I *had* to handle it. There was no other option. I'd ghosted Will once, and I'd never do it again. I'd love him as much as he'd let me, and if all he could give me was friendship, it had to be enough.

I said, "Friends with benefits? It's definitely good practice for being Angela's bisexual wingman."

"I suppose it is. So… While we're here we can have fun? Be bisexual for the holidays?" He quickly added, "You always are, of course. And I'm…"

"You're figuring it out. It's cool. There's nothing wrong with having fun. It's Christmas, after all."

"Yes, Christmas is famous for sexual exploration."

"It's in all the best carols. You know 'We Three Kings' is about a hot poly hookup."

Will laughed, his shoulders shaking. I loved seeing him like this—the tension that had been coming and going vanishing. At least for now.

He said, "'O Come All Ye Faithful' is about a Bethlehem orgy."

"Have you ever noticed how many Christmas songs have an 'O' in the title? I'm just saying."

Still smiling, Will bit his lip. His gaze grew darker, flicking between my face and…my nipple? Slowly, watching me carefully, he reached out and brushed up over my nipple with his knuckle the way he had when I'd drooled toothpaste. Lust tugged low in my belly, my balls tingling.

"You're up for it? Playing?" He'd inched his hand back, and it hovered in the air as he waited for my answer.

Kicking off the sheets and my underwear, I licked my palm and stroked my swelling dick because I was a sucker for puns. "I'm up for it."

Will made a sound that might have been a growl as he rolled half on top of me and latched his mouth onto my nipple. Moaning, I clutched his head—and were my nipples directly connected to my balls? It sure felt like it.

Had he wanted to do this earlier during the Toothpaste Incident? I bet he had, which made my dick even harder.

My nipples were wet and ready to cut glass by the time he was finished with them. Breathing hard, he propped himself up with one hand on the mattress, half hovering over me, his eyes locking on my cock.

His lips were shiny with spit, and *fuck*, I could imagine them closing around my dick with a slurp.

I had the feeling Will was imagining the same thing—but he hesitated. I ran a hand over his deliciously hairy chest as it rose and fell.

"It's okay," I murmured. "No rush."

He seemed embarrassed, nodding but not meeting my eyes. He started to say something else but stopped.

"What?" I smoothed my palm back and forth over his furry pecs. "You can ask me anything."

He seemed to consider this. "Can I look at you?"

"Um, yeah. You already are." I laughed, trying not to fidget. "Go to town. Not much to look at," I joked.

"That's not true." Will met my gaze sharply, his voice firm. "I hate it when you do that. Put yourself down."

"Oh. It's fine! I'm just not—I don't work out as much as you do. I try, but..." Jared loved the gym, and I'd gotten a personal trainer but was still on the skinny side.

"You look great just the way you are."

Will said it so confidently, his gaze dropping down to my chest. I barely stopped myself from sucking in my tummy and puffing up my pecs. Instead, I concentrated on breathing as Will examined me.

This is about him.

I watched him watch me, butterflies flapping all over the place in my stomach. I wanted to make another joke. His gaze might as well have been his fingers or lips or tongue. My whole body tingled, and my dick leaked.

Being on display for Will excited me in a way I hadn't expected. I didn't think numbers went high enough to count the times I'd fantasized about touching Will and kissing him and being fucked by him. But I hadn't pictured this.

Somehow, I said, "Do you want me to jerk off for you?"

Eyes practically bugging out of his head, Will did that growly thing again. "Yes."

I spread my legs wide, and he shifted to sit back on his heels, his big hand like a brand on the inside of my left thigh. Honestly, I wasn't sure why I'd said it. But as I worked myself, spitting into my palm and liking the roughness, my dick getting sore from being jerked again so soon without lube, my instinct was proven right.

Will panted as he watched me, his fingers digging into my thigh. His gaze roamed from my dick to my face to my chest to my dick to my face and back again. Sweat shone in the hollow of his throat, and his cock leaked even though he didn't touch it and we'd come recently.

I'd never been like this with anyone else. A, a—what was the word? Exhibitionist? But knowing he was so turned on by watching me was the greatest rush. I'd fucked up so many things with Will, but I could give him this. I could make him happy and turn him on.

I reached down with my other hand to play with my balls, knowing that would get me there.

The orgasm ripped out of me, and I shouted as I shook with deep, burning pleasure. Gasping as if it was him coming, Will watched me milk my cock. God, I wanted to lift my legs and beg him to fuck me. But we had to take this slow. I laughed on the edge of hysteria. As if this was "taking it slow."

Adam's apple bobbing, Will watched me, probably confused about why I was laughing like that.

I said, "It's okay," and sat up to kiss him. Like before, it only took a few long pulls of my mouth on his cock for him to come. I swallowed as he tangled his fingers in my hair, his jizz dripping from my lips since I was bent over.

We flopped back on the mattress to catch our breath. "Holy shit," I mumbled. Again, the salty, bitter aftertaste of Will in my mouth was proof that, yep, we'd actually just done that.

I wasn't usually a... I tried to think of the right word. Displayer? No. Show-off? That didn't quite fit. Whatever, the point was that I'd jerked off for Will shamelessly, and it felt like he was really *seeing* me.

Aside from being literally naked, it had been like showing him how much I wanted him. It'd been raw and real.

Seemed it was easier to be brave here on the other side of the world. Like we were in a magic bubble or something. Though as I caught my breath, my bravery started to fade, and worry slithered back in. Was it about to get awkward again?

I turned my head to the left. Beside me, Will panted softly, a dazed expression on his flushed face as he stared at the ceiling. Then he looked at me, lighting up with a bright, beautiful smile.

"Promise this won't get weird?" I blurted, even though *I* was the one in love with him and he'd only talked about friends with benefits.

Grinning, Will gave me the finger, and I hooked my middle finger around his before we got lost in slow, lazy kisses. No mistletoe required.

Chapter Fifteen

Will

"Y'ALL HAVE A good nap?" Angela asked as we greeted her in the garland-festooned lobby by a gold, silver, and red-themed Christmas tree towering over several couches. One of the classic carols played overhead, though I wasn't sure if it was one of the ones with an "O" in the title.

Adrenaline shot through me as flashes of what Michael and I had done—no napping involved—cartwheeled though my mind. Desire sizzled through my veins, heat flushing my face as I attempted to formulate a response that involved a recognizable word and not solely the giddy noises eager to burst forth.

Fortunately, Michael apparently recognized my struggle and replied, "Yeah, it was really relaxing." He squeezed my hand, threading our fingers together.

"Nothing like a Christmas Day nap," Paul agreed, patting his stomach under a bright Hawaiian shirt. "Now if only we had football on TV."

"Going to the beach is way better than stupid football," Makayla said, adjusting the brim of her wide woven hat.

"The beach and football are both awesome," Olivia said. "Dad, did you check the score? What time is it at home? I'm all f—messed up."

Bugger, I really had to call my parents. I'd declined a video chat from Mum when Michael and I had just gotten out of the shower. Where we'd made out like teenagers under the spray of hot water. Even if I'd pulled on a robe and sat on the balcony to talk to Mum and Dad, I was sure they'd have known something was up.

Gripping Michael's hand now, I glanced around the lobby. Did we look different? Could everyone *tell*? Christ, I was a grown man, but I felt like a teenager. The rush I'd felt at the glamping retreat at being perceived by people as bisexual, or at least not straight, was amplified by a thousand. By ten thousand. A hundred, a—

"You okay?" Michael whispered.

I nodded. "Just...happy. Thrilled. Delighted."

He laughed softly. "Ecstatic?"

"Yep." I bit my lip to stop myself from grinning madly. I could have danced a jig around the Christmas tree.

After a hotel employee brought us an insulated picnic basket that I offered to carry, we made our way along the crowded boardwalk. Even with sunglasses, I blinked against the glare of the afternoon sun. Our palms quickly became damp where we held hands, but I wouldn't have let go of Michael for anything.

We'd held hands in public several times in the past...week? Must have been a week by now, or almost. Time had lost meaning with the travel and being in our bubble under the sun so far from home.

I'd become comfortable holding Michael's hand more quickly than I would've expected, but now? Oh, now it was magical.

The warm pressure of his fingers made me think of the sensation of those fingers on my body. I thought of watching him wank and the way he used his hands to tease and touch himself. It was all new and thrilling. I'd lost my virginity more than a decade ago, but I hadn't been bisexual then. Well, perhaps I had been if I was now.

Which I certainly seemed to be, didn't I?

Another giddy rush of happiness bubbled through me like champagne, and I nudged Michael's shoulder before pecking his cheek. That brief brush of my lips on his cheek would have to do for now when I'd have loved to drop the basket and haul him into my arms for a proper snog.

Michael laughed, whispering, "How long do we have to stay at the beach? Also, are there any drug stores open today?"

It took me a moment to understand he was talking about buying lube. And likely condoms. A shudder of lust gripped me, nervousness quick on its heels. I wanted to do everything with Michael, but it was daunting at the same time.

Perhaps it would be good if we couldn't buy supplies until Boxing Day. Because waiting until the twenty-sixth would be *plenty* of time, right?

The beach was absolutely chock-a-block with people, as promised. Santa hats and bikinis were the order of the day, and it was a noisy, merry scene. We made our way through the throng to find an empty spot, sand hot and fine between our toes.

The Indian Ocean was spectacular, the water crystal clear as it washed over the pale sand. Even with the crowd, I could see why this was such a popular spot.

We laid down blankets provided by the hotel and got settled next to a family playing Mariah Carey's Christmas album on Wi-Fi speakers.

Angela immediately started speaking with the parents, cooing over a gurgling baby in a holly-and-ivy onesie. Paul cracked open a bottle of sparkling water and settled in while Makayla tried to convince Olivia to swim with her.

The beach was only about a thousand yards or so long, and there had to be thousands of revelers squeezed onto the sand. I hoped this was the busiest day of the year, because I couldn't imagine many more people could fit.

Michael looked around. "Wow. This place is packed."

The woman chatting with Angela bounced her baby on her lap and said, "This is the busiest time of year. School holidays and all that. Be sure to swim between the flags." She pointed to her right and the north end of the beach. "There's a bad rip up there. Stay away from the Croc. It'll drag you out in a blink."

Olivia looked up from her phone sharply. "There are crocodiles here?"

The woman chuckled. "It's just what we call that rip. A dangerous current. Swim between the flags and mind the lifeguards and you'll be right."

I tugged Michael's hand lightly, and he knelt beside me on the blanket. "Okay?" I asked.

He nodded. "It's just a *lot* of people."

"Do you want to go back?" I murmured, sliding my hand behind his neck. I rubbed softly with my thumb. "We don't have to stay." And if we returned to our room…

Makayla had apparently heard my question—and to be fair, quarters were close—and she pleaded, "Please go swimming with me first? Olivia doesn't want to get wet. *At the beach.*" Her sister ignored her, and Makayla added, "My parents don't like swimming unless it's in a shallow pool."

I said to Michael, "Do you want to head back, and I'll be along in forty-five minutes or an hour?"

He gave me a sweet smile. "Nah. Let's go swimming." He pulled up the hem of his Old Navy tee. "Strap on your sunglasses, Makayla. You're about to be blinded."

She giggled as Michael stripped off his shirt, her eyes widening. I followed her gaze and choked as I realized Michael's pale white chest had red beard burns and marks I'd left.

Olivia gave me a thumbs-up, and my face burned with a combination of embarrassment and silly pride. Fortunately, Angela and Paul were now deep in conversation with our neighbors. I didn't need my boss to have that much info about my sex life.

My sex life. With a man. With Michael.

I found myself laughing. Practically *giggling*. I hadn't felt this excited or *young* in years. It was a sort of euphoria, as though I was drunk or high. I likely should have been more embarrassed than I was at the girls seeing the evidence, but Christ, the thrill at marking Michael for my own!

Only meant to be friends with benefits, remember?

Michael smiled quizzically and passed me a bottle of fifty SPF sunscreen. "Can you?" He motioned to his back.

Hell yes. I eagerly squeezed the white cream into my palm, kneeling behind Michael. I smoothed the lotion over his back while he spread it on his chest and arms. I swooped and dipped my hands, following the planes of his slim, firm torso, my fingers sliding around his ribs. Down his spine, across the top of his board shorts, skimming just under the waistband to be sure to get every inch of pale, vulnerable skin...

Michael cleared his throat. "I think you got it."

Blinking, I dragged my hands up to his shoulders. "You sure?"

He looked back at me with a laugh and hissed, "Dude, this is a family show."

Right. Yes. Excellent point.

I stripped down to my swimsuit, and we quickly spread the sunscreen over my bare skin as we tried not to snicker like kids. After promising Angela and Paul we'd stick with Makayla, the three of us made our way through the maze of towels, blankets, drunken pyramids of people, and sun worshippers.

We neared a buggy with two lifeguards, one standing up in the back and the other behind the wheel, both surveying the water closely. They wore blue long-sleeved uniform shirts and long black shorts.

Makayla elbowed me, nodding to the blond lifeguard standing over the buggy's roof. "That guy looks just like Chris Hemsworth! You know, Thor?"

Just how old did she think we were? "He does," I agreed with a smile.

"Maybe he'll have to rescue me." She grinned.

"No, let's not need rescuing today. Cheers."

Michael said, "I mean, I wouldn't mind either, tbh," and gave Makayla a grin.

An acidy, unpleasant sensation stabbed me. I glanced back at the lifeguard as we passed, taking his measure. Was tanned, muscled, and strong-jawed Michael's type? I imagined how I'd compare next to this Hemsworth doppelganger, and—

Why was I *jealous*? How absolutely ridiculous. Even if Michael and I were... He wasn't about to go hook up with a lifeguard. Surely not.

"Will?"

I'd slowed to a crawl, glancing back at the lifeguard in question, who'd pulled out binoculars as he surveyed the water. I looked guiltily to Michael, who frowned back at me.

"Coming!"

The stretch of water between the red and yellow flags planted in the sand teemed with shrieking children and people of all ages rolling about in the surprisingly strong surf. We quickly discovered we needed to time our splashing run into the water properly or risk being flattened by the incoming waves.

Sputtering and wiping salt water from my face, I retreated a few feet, letting another wave crash around my knees. Makayla tumbled onto her butt, but she was laughing as Michael and I pulled her up. She was so small that we almost yanked her right off her feet.

Gulls cried, and the sun bore down as I inhaled the briny air deeply. It had been too long since I'd been to the seaside. Not a typical Christmas, but it was joyous in its own way, especially with Michael at my side.

"We have to get past the break!" Makayla shouted with authority. She straightened the straps of her cute polka-dot two-piece and eyed the incoming waves with steely determination. "I'll tell you when!"

Like runners on the starting line, we waited, letting another wave crash and swirl around our legs. On Makayla's command, we raced forward.

How was running in water so bloody hard? I lifted my feet sideways, eyeing the waves barreling our way. I stumbled, and Michael and Makayla surged ahead.

"Oh shit!" Michael lunged forward into the water, stroking with his arms and riding over the top of the wave just before it broke.

Makayla dove under, and I froze with indecision. Dive? Turn and ride it? Or—

No time! Planting my feet in the sand, I closed my eyes and braced with all my might, fists clenched. The wave scoffed at my attempt to withstand it, tossing me backward arse over teakettle as Mum would say—a perfect back somersault.

I slammed onto the sand on my backside, coughing and sputtering as the wave carried me to shore. Another wave crashed into my face, and I shoved to my feet, stumbling to shore along with a few other people who'd mistimed their entry.

It was already tough to find Michael and Makayla amid the sea of heads, but I spotted them bobbing over another swell. Coughing, I waved and motioned with flat palms, hoping Michael would know I meant to stay there. I wasn't about to be defeated.

This time, I sucked in a huge breath and dove under the incoming wave, water bubbling over me. I came up the other side and narrowly avoided smacking into an old man with his granddaughter. Michael called out, and I paddled over.

"Okay?" he asked, reaching for me and sliding his arm around my back securely. "You can stand here. We found a sand bar."

"Yeah, I'm fine." A swell of water lifted us, but it was mild compared to where the waves broke near the shore. As we found the sandbar again with our feet, I kissed Michael and slipped my arm around his shoulders. "Missed you."

He blinked at me, smiling quizzically but looking pleased. "It was, like, three minutes, tops."

I shrugged as we surged up and down with another passing wave. "I still missed you."

Makayla cooed, "I missed you *tooooo.*"

"Sorry, we're being one of those annoying couples," I said, Michael jerking against my side before we surged up on a stronger wave.

"God, they really weren't joking about how crowded this beach gets," he said.

It really was just a sea of people in the water and on the narrow stretch of sand. A low concrete wall ran across the back of the beach area separating it from the boardwalk and a grassed park with tall evergreen trees beyond. A windowed lifeguard tower sat in the middle of the beach. I couldn't imagine how the lifeguards could spot anyone drowning in this chaos.

As we dropped down the back of another big swell, the sandbar no longer under us, a guy chasing an inflatable ball suddenly appeared. Makayla dodged him, sputtering with a face full of water as he kicked and almost hit her head.

Michael and I shouted, "Hey!" in unison, but it was an older woman around sixty in a bright green one-piece who got the guy's attention.

"Oi!" she snapped. "Rack off, you bogans! I told you it's too crowded to be roughhousing like that."

The guy grumbled but took his ball and swam back to a group of people in their early twenties. I took hold of Makayla's arm gently and made sure she was all right. I wasn't sure what a "bogan" was, but it didn't sound complimentary. We thanked the woman, but she waved us off.

"Just keep an eye out. Some people don't give a stuff about anyone else's enjoyment, especially when they're on the grog. Sometimes I wish Barking had never been named the best beach in Oz. It was never this busy when I was younger." She snorted. "Then again, when I was younger, the Earth was flat, and we thought the sun revolved around us."

Michael laughed. "Sorry, you must hate tourists like us."

"Nah. As long as you can actually swim and you mind the lifeguards, you're good in my books. It's idiots that don't follow the rules that do my head in."

"Why would anyone go in if they can't swim?" Makayla asked, treading water as another big swell lifted us up and down.

"That's the question, isn't it?" the woman laughed. "But they do, in droves. The lifeguards have their work cut out for them, especially today when the drunk backpackers are causing mischief. But I've had a swim in the arvo here on Christmas Day every year since I could walk, and they're not driving me away."

Under the water, as we circled our arms on the surface to stay afloat, I rubbed my foot against Michael's, the need to touch him simmering through me constantly. He shot me a smile and rubbed back, and our fingers entwined as we bobbed up and down on the swells.

I tuned back into the conversation as Makayla said to the woman, "One of the lifeguards looks like Thor with short hair."

The woman laughed heartily. "Ah, that's probably Liam Fox. He was a star footballer. Now he's famous for being gay. It was a big drama. His partner Cody's in the service as well. Good blokes."

"That's so cool!" Makayla grinned at us.

Before I could answer, someone shouted on a megaphone from shore. Michael's grip on my hand tightened and he asked, "Is there a shark?" as he glanced around.

The woman laughed. "Nah, they're moving the flags. There's

a siren for shark sightings."

That there were enough regular sightings to necessitate a siren somehow wasn't reassuring. "Why are they moving the flags?" I asked.

"Currents and conditions change," the woman said as she began stroking confidently, heading south. "Come on or get back to shore. Merry Christmas!"

The wind had whipped up, seemingly in a blink. "Let's go back in," I said. The conditions were getting too rough for my liking.

Michael and Makayla agreed, and I let go of Michael's hand so we could swim. On the crowded shore, lifeguards motioned to their left, shouting on megaphones for us to shift down the beach.

We kicked and stroked with our arms, glancing behind to keep an eye on the waves that never stopped coming.

"Why are we going the wrong way?" Makayla asked, her voice rising.

My stomach sank like a stone. She was right—though we'd been swimming toward shore, it looked farther away. I kicked harder, but the sickening sensation of being dragged backward toward the open sea was unmistakable.

"It's all right!" I shouted even though it felt like invisible tentacles were ensnaring me. It had to be a rip current. I looked to Michael, who kicked vigorously, his eyes wide. I had to stay calm. He needed me. Makayla needed me. Everything was fine.

Except for the fact that we were undeniably being dragged away from safety. Waves swallowed us, our hair plastered to our heads. Makayla pushed her hair from her face, grimacing as she kicked and struggled. In the growing swells of water as we bobbed up and down, the shore appeared and disappeared.

I realized with a start that Michael was out of reach. I opened my mouth to shout for him and choked on saltwater crashing overhead. My heart hammered as I kicked to the surface and coughed.

We'd been happily bobbing along a minute ago! I kicked hard, swimming madly toward Michael and Makayla.

Though the sun was still high in the cloudless sky, I shivered, the current's vicious pull like icy fingers. My head buzzed, pulse racing and my limbs suddenly like lead as I fought to keep my head above water and get back to Michael and land.

Michael and Makayla bobbed in and out of sight. Michael was saying something to me, but I couldn't hear him over the buzzing. We initially hadn't been that far out, but now the beach looked terrifyingly distant.

I'm going to die!

The lifeguard appeared as if from thin air, grabbing my arm and hauling me over the front of his longboard as he sat up and straddled it, his legs in the water. "You right, mate?" He kept an iron grip on my upper arm.

I took a proper breath for the first time in what seemed like hours. It was Thor—no, what had that woman called him? Liam? He said, "I've got ya. No worries."

The few seconds of relief I'd enjoyed evaporated. "Michael!" I squirmed and struggled to sit up and find Michael and Makayla.

Liam's grip didn't waver, but he angled the board and pointed. "Your mates are fine."

The sweet relief flooded back—so strongly this time tears pricked my eyes. "He's my boyfriend," I rasped, even though there was no need to pretend with a lifeguard.

"That's *my* boyfriend picking him up." Liam squeezed my arm reassuringly. "He's safe."

Makayla and Michael hung onto the sides of a female life-guard's board, and I watched as Liam's boyfriend—Cody?—powered over a swell and sat up, grabbing Michael and transferring him onto his board. Cody was fair, compact, and wiry.

Liam manhandled me the same way—pulling me onto my

stomach on his board and settling between my legs to paddle us side-on to the beach before pointing the nose toward shore. He expertly navigated the waves, and I couldn't hold in a whoop as the water surged beneath us and carried us all the way into the shallows.

We rolled off, and Liam tugged me to my feet as I wiped more water from my face. My throat was dry, and I coughed, ignoring it as I reached for Michael. He hugged me tightly, face pinched in concern.

Makayla laughed as she splashed to shore. "That was *awesome!*"

Liam, Cody, and the female lifeguard—a beautiful young Asian woman—laughed too, but as I coughed again, Liam insisted I sit down on the sand just beyond the water's reach.

"Did you swallow much water?" Liam asked.

I shook my head, squirming at all the attention, my skin crawling with all the eyes of the little crowd that had gathered around us.

Kneeling beside me, Michael rubbed my back and said to the lifeguards, "Everything was fine and then it was pulling us out."

"Flash rip," Cody said. "Permanent rips like the Croc happen in the same place, but flash rips can spring up anywhere. That's why we moved the flags. It's getting hectic out there." His accent sounded strangely North American. "Most important thing is not to panic."

A voice on a radio in the nearby buggy crackled to life and said, "Got another head out the back—fourth ramp."

The woman picked up her board and sprinted back out, paddling so fast my head spun. I felt like I'd swallowed concrete. I blinked at the crashing waves, distantly listening as Cody spoke on the radio. Michael's hand sweeping up and down my back was the only thing that felt real.

Crouching on my other side, Michael still anchored to my

right, Liam said, "You're sure you didn't swallow much water?"

I almost joked, "*Just concrete*," but Liam was too busy for that. I croaked, "No. Just a mouthful."

Nodding, Liam stood and shared a glance with Cody, communicating silently. There was quite a size difference between them, and Cody looked a fair bit younger too. I'd have to look up their story online, assuming Liam was as famous as that woman said.

Liam nodded at Cody, apparently signaling the end of their silent conversation, and said to me, "If you start to feel crook, see a doctor right away. The problem is that you might have gotten water in your lungs without realizing it. But I think you should be okay."

I nodded. "I just feel like I ran a marathon."

"Panic does that to you," Cody said. "Sucks all your energy. But you'll be right. Happens to the best of us, believe me."

Shame slammed through me like another wave. I'd panicked. I'd made everything worse. Since when did I panic? I kept a level head in crises. I told other people what to do when they started flapping. Angela wouldn't have brought me on this trip if I was someone who *panicked*.

I wiped my mouth. My lips tingled from the salt, and my head was so hot it was in danger of exploding.

Michael stood and shook the lifeguards' hands. "Thank you so much." Makayla thanked them profusely too.

Cody smiled. "No worries. That's why we're here. You did great."

"More heads out the back—the Croc's waking up!" Liam called to Cody from the buggy. "Fifth gate."

Cody had their boards on the buggy's side rack in a blink before hopping in, Liam leaning on the horn as they sped north along the wet strip of sand at the water's edge, weaving around people to save more lives.

"Wow," Makayla sighed. "That was so hot." She clapped her hand over her mouth adorably, and Michael shook with laughter beside me. He still rubbed my back steadily.

I had to laugh, but it didn't dispel the shame that I'd failed so miserably.

What must he think of me?

"Come on, we have to tell Mom and Dad!" She tugged at my hand.

I groaned. "Can't wait to tell Angela and Paul that I almost drowned their daughter. Merry Christmas!"

"Huh?" Hands on narrow hips, Makayla looked down at me. "It's not your fault there was a—what did they call it? A flash rip?"

I shrugged, knocking Michael's hand away unintentionally. "Still, I was supposed to be watching you."

"I'm fine!" She shook her head. "It's not your fault. It's, like, the whole reason they have lifeguards."

Michael's hand felt cool on the back of my flushed neck. "Makayla's fine. We all are."

"No thanks to me," I muttered. What if the current hadn't pulled me away from them? Would I have been one of those people who drowns their companions in a blind panic in these situations?

"Are you sure you're okay?" Michael squeezed my neck, leaning around to peer into my face with obvious concern. "Is it hard to breathe? We can call an ambulance."

Wonderful, now I was being a drama queen and worrying him on top of my failure in the water. "No, no. I'm fine." And I *was*. I could sleep for days, but there was nothing wrong with my limbs as I forced myself to stand and walk and smile.

Chapter Sixteen

Michael

"H APPY BOXING DAY, Mum. Is Dad there too? Sorry we didn't get a chance to speak properly yesterday."

I'd been half-awake for a while, drifting in and out of sleep as I listened to Will putter. It was a surprise when I opened my eyes now to find that he was on the balcony with the sliding door shut. It sounded like he was sitting beside me. I guessed that it made sense in such a warm place to only have single-glazed glass.

"Yes, it was a lovely Christmas at the beach. We're having a grand time."

Curled on my side, I could see the back of Will's head through the window. He wore a pale blue shirt with cuffed short sleeves that probably had buttons down the front, and most likely his plaid shorts. The sky was a cloudless blue again, and I'd probably slept too late even though we'd crashed early.

"Aye, the weather's gorgeous."

I had to smile. Will's accent really did immediately get thicker as soon as he was talking to his parents. But *were* we having a grand time?

We *had* been—uh, understatement of the year considering all the orgasms we'd shared yesterday. Merry Christmas to me and god bless us everyone and all that stuff.

But Will had withdrawn after we went to the beach. Had our near-death experience made him realize he didn't want me after all? That he wasn't bi, and this experiment was over, and we were going back to being strictly fake boyfriends?

The glittery surfing koala ornament watched me from where it hung against the cream lampshade. "Hey, uh...mate," I whispered. Because now I was talking to Christmas tree ornaments. "What do you think?" The koala didn't answer for obvious reasons.

Rolling onto my back, I stared at the ceiling. I'd slept naked, and so had Will, but we'd barely touched. I'd been ready for round...four? Five? Whatever number it was, I'd been ready.

But Will had been quiet the rest of the day after we were rescued. I'd waited for him to kiss me, but he'd turned off the lights and gone to sleep.

I'd looked up the symptoms of what was often called dry drowning, but he'd insisted he was fine. Maybe it really had only been jet lag, but if something was wrong, I wished he'd just tell me.

That's rich coming from you, mate.

Great. Now a sparkly surfing koala bear was dunking on me in my head. "Shut up..." I pulled a name out of the air. "Kevin. Kevin the koala doesn't get a vote."

Will was making listening noises, and he held the phone to his ear, so there was no risk of me tiptoeing by in the background of a video call. I slipped into the bathroom and had a shower. When I stepped out, I rubbed my head with a towel and wrapped it around my waist.

"Michael?"

I almost groaned out loud hearing Will's low voice. He'd never once called me "Mike," and my name on his tongue was sweet and sexy. I swiped my palm over the steamy mirror and made sure my voice was worry-free. "Come in! Good morning. Afternoon? I'm not sure." Normally, I'd look at my phone before I was out of bed, but who cared what time it was here?

Behind me, Will tentatively opened the door as I winced and poked the bruise on my shoulder where I'd smacked the lifeguard's board. His eyes widened.

"Are you hurt?" He strode forward and examined the top of my shoulder.

I watched his serious intensity in the mirror, my belly flip-flopping. "It's just a bump." His fingers were warm on my wet skin. "Yesterday was scary, huh?" I said quietly. We'd been so tired last night that we hadn't really talked about it. "Did you tell your parents?"

In the mirror, I saw him…clench up and make a face. He dropped his hands and walked back into the bedroom. "No. They'd only fret."

I caught his wrist by the bed, needing to touch him. "What's wrong? And before you say 'nothing,' I know it's something." If anyone should know when someone was trying to hide their feelings, it was me. "Even Kevin can tell something's wrong."

Will's brow creased. "Kevin?"

I motioned to the lamp. "Kevin the koala. He's wise."

Will snorted, then smiled softly. "What's gotten into you?"

"What? I always talk to Christmas tree ornaments. It's totally normal." I wasn't actually sure what was up with me. What I did know was that yesterday was the most amazing, magical day of my life—until Will got quiet and distracted. Maybe what we'd shared had only been a limited-time Christmas miracle.

The thought almost buckled my knees.

Sitting on the end of the bed, I tugged Will down beside me and took a deep breath. If he wanted to go back to only being friends, I had to know. Even if it killed me. Because it might.

In one day, I'd fallen so much deeper in love with Will. It had felt so *right* kissing and touching and coming.

I was still gripping his wrist. I let go and clasped my hands in my lap. "Do you want to stop?" I motioned between us, forcing myself to look at his face. "Having sex, I mean. It's okay if you want to stop. I know it's new, and maybe you decided you're not into it."

"*No.*" Will said that one word with so much conviction and low baritone power that my dick got hard instantly. He squeezed my knee, then hesitated. "Unless you want to stop?"

I shook my head so violently I probably gave myself a concussion. "Nope. I'm good."

A smile tugged at Will's full lips. "Then we're in agreement to keep…experimenting."

"Uh-huh." I pulled his face close and kissed him. We opened our mouths, our tongues meeting.

He hadn't shaved, and I loved the rasp of his stubble as we kissed and kissed. If this really was only an experiment that was going to end after the holidays, my heart was going to shatter into too many pieces to find.

That's future Michael's problem, Kevin said, and that glittery koala was right. After all, we could die tomorrow, so fuck it.

I had Will stretched out on his back and his shirt unbuttoned, and I was about to open the fly of his plaid shorts when I stopped. I'd straddled his hips, and he ran his hands up and down my thighs under the towel, which was barely hanging on.

I'd bitten my tongue so many times with Jared. I'd said nothing to Will when I probably should have told him everything— even though the idea of confessing how much I loved him still made me want to throw up. I had to swallow hard and push away the fear. This wasn't about me.

"Michael?" He frowned up at me.

"So, if it wasn't about what we're doing together, what's wrong?" My heart thudded. Was I going to mess everything up by not letting this drop? Maybe I should have just kept my stupid mouth shut, because Will looked away, his grip on my thighs loosening.

But he didn't let go.

Slowly, I ran my hands over his chest. We were both hard, but that didn't matter right now. I wanted to soothe him and make whatever was wrong okay again.

"Baby, please tell me." I'd never called anyone "baby" before, but it felt right. "Are you upset about what happened at the beach?" It seemed logical since he'd been acting differently after. "It was really scary."

He puffed out his cheeks, still not looking at me, and laughed hollowly. "Yeah, but you and Makayla didn't panic. I made everything worse."

"Wait, what?" I honestly couldn't believe my ears. "Are you shitting me? Dude, I was totally freaking out."

Will looked at me, his gaze narrowed. "Come on. Cody said you and Makayla did great. *I'm* the one who panicked and almost drowned."

"Did he?" I tried to play back the conversation on the beach with the lifeguards. "I don't even know what he said. I was so relieved we were all okay. It would have really impacted your promotion prospects if we lost Angela's daughter on day one."

A laugh burst out of Will, and I swore I could sense a bit of tension easing. He said, "We should really wait a week at least."

"Exactly." I rubbed my thumb over his collarbone. "Believe me, I panicked. But I guess I realized it wouldn't help, so I stopped fighting. I could see the lifeguards coming. Honestly, Makayla was a superstar. She just treaded water and held her breath when waves came. I might have freaked out more if I'd been alone." I shuddered. "One second you were beside me, and then you weren't."

Will nodded, spreading his fingers over my thighs. "I couldn't reach you. I didn't know the lifeguards were coming." His throat seized, and his fingers dug into my flesh. "I couldn't think."

"It's okay, baby. It's not your fault."

He sighed noisily, shaking his head. "It shouldn't happen to me! I'm stable. Reliable. I shouldn't be bloody panicking."

I smiled, affection for Will filling me to the bursting point. "You're still stable and reliable, I promise. That's why I called you that night on the road. I knew you'd answer. You're just like those lifeguards, swooping in to make the rescue."

"Hardly." He scoffed, but I could tell he liked to hear it. Why shouldn't he? It was true.

"It's okay that you panicked. It's over now. It doesn't change who you are, I promise."

Will took a deep breath and lifted his hand—middle finger up. "Swear?"

I wrapped our fingers together. Leaning in, I pressed a kiss to his fingertip before licking across the top. A shudder ran through him that I felt where I straddled him. I sucked our fingers into my mouth, and Will grabbed my hips, thrusting up against me.

Who knew middle fingers could be so sexy?

Chapter Seventeen
Will

MICHAEL PULLED HIS hand free to work on my shorts, keeping my finger firmly between his lips as he sucked. I groaned, thrusting up helplessly as he took out my straining cock. When my finger dripped with saliva, he pulled off with a filthy *pop* that tightened my balls.

The towel's knot had finally given out, and he tossed it aside and said, "We still need to go to the drug store, but that should be enough. For your finger, I mean."

I was apparently supposed to respond to this, which was a challenge given I was already close to the edge. "I... Okay?"

He leaned down to kiss me messily, his breath hot on my mouth. "Will you just, you know. Play with my hole?"

Gulping, I nodded. "I don't really know what I'm doing, though." My laugh sounded erratic and high-pitched. I'd felt so guilty about the incident at the beach, and Michael had soothed those worries away. But now I was all knees and elbows when I should have been able to easily give him what he wanted.

Michael slid off me onto his side, urging me to face him. He gently pushed his leg between mine and slipped his hand under my open shirt to lightly trace my ribs. I held onto his waist, wishing I was better at this.

I said, "You must think I'm..."

He watched me patiently, finally prompting softly, "What?"

"I dunno." I closed my eyes. "I have this ridiculous reputation for being a player, when the truth is, I've never even done...you know."

"Butt stuff?"

Laughing, I opened my eyes. "I suppose that's one way to put it. But no, I haven't really. I realize it's not solely something between men, but..."

"Yeah, women can definitely be into butt stuff. Nonbinary people too, obviously. Butt stuff is for everyone. Only if they're into it."

"I know." I ran my hand up and down his side. "Honestly, even though I've been curious about men, I never thought I'd actually do it. Didn't ever imagine...experimenting."

His gaze dropped. "Right. I totally get it."

"It's embarrassing, really." I wanted to roll away and cover up, but Michael's leg was lodged between mine, our skin hot and getting sweaty in a way I surprisingly enjoyed.

"What is?" He watched me closely.

"That I'm supposed to be a, a—lothario when most of the time I had straightforward sex that was enjoyable enough but nothing to write home about." Not since Amelia, and that was a decade ago now.

"Ohh, 'lothario,' huh? That's a twenty-five-cent word."

I laughed. "More like a dollar at least with inflation these days. A pound-fifty in the UK."

Michael laughed too as he stroked my back and torso before scratching his nails through my wiry chest hair. "It's because you're so gorgeous. Everyone assumes you're getting laid every five minutes."

My heart stuttered. "Gorgeous?"

He rolled his eyes with a smile. "Come on, you know you're extremely good-looking."

I supposed I did know I'd been blessed in the genetics department, but the idea that *Michael* thought I was gorgeous was very pleasing. I squeezed his thigh between mine.

My cock was hanging out of my open shorts. I needed everything off, and I tugged and yanked until I was naked too. I murmured, "There. That's better," and kissed him softly.

"Mmm. It is." With his leg between mine again, he rolled our hips together.

Perhaps it was because we'd known each other for years, but I couldn't recall being this comfortable hanging about naked with someone. Even Amelia, though we'd been young and still settling into our adult bodies.

"You said you usually like jerking off, right?" Michael asked. "Will you show me?"

How was I expected to *breathe* let alone wank? It had been such a turn-on to watch Michael yesterday—was that right? Was it only yesterday? Yes, it had to be.

Christmas Day was yesterday, and that was the first time we'd kissed, and then the first time we'd done all those other wonderful things…

I corralled my disarrayed thoughts. Michael wanted me to show him. I swallowed hard, trying not to overthink it as I took myself in hand. Michael inched back, giving me an encouraging smile, his gaze avid.

"Do you need lube?" He asked. "God, I hope drug stores are open today."

I cupped my right hand and spit a few times. "S'all right. I'm a wanking expert. Years of experience."

He laughed and grabbed my wrist. "Here." Michael leaned over my right palm and spit. He slowly licked across my fingers before spitting again.

The soft, wet sounds were beautifully intimate. Sunlight poured through the windows, and on our tangle of white sheets, we could have been in the clouds. Just the two of us in our world.

Michael lifted his head. "Is that good?"

I groaned and stroked myself. "*Yes.* You did a very good job." I'd meant it as a joke, but his eyes widened briefly, his breath catching. Mmm, so he liked that kind of praise, it seemed. I'd have to remember that—when I wasn't working myself with long, hard strokes.

Honestly, I'd have been embarrassed by how quickly I was on the verge of coming, but Michael was so rapt with the show that I was strangely proud. Panting softly, I squeezed the base of my cock.

Michael ran his thumb over the leaking head. "Seeing this is so hot." He lifted his thumb to his mouth and licked up the drops. "I love cum."

I shuddered. "*Fuck.*"

He grinned and stroked my shaft slowly with his fingertips. "It's like when you slip your fingers inside a girl, and her pussy's wet for you. I love that."

Nodding, I groaned. My whole body pulsed with heat.

Michael tangled his fingers in my hair and kissed me hard. I could faintly taste my own precum, and it had no right to be as hot as it was. Because *Christ*, I was about to explode.

Stroking me again, Michael whispered urgently, "I love feeling how much you want me. Tasting it."

I nodded. "I want to suck you." I wouldn't likely be much good, but I was dying to try. "It feels so good when you do it to me."

Before I could blink, he shimmied down the mattress and swallowed me almost to the root.

"Jesus!" I shouted, arching my back.

Sucking forcefully, Michael pulled off with a loud, wonderfully filthy slurp. "Will you fuck my mouth? Hard. I want to choke on your dick. I want you to come down my throat."

All I could do was nod and make a strangled noise of assent as we scrambled into a new position, both of us almost frantic in our need. I straddled his chest—no, his *neck*, which felt so very kinky and forbidden to me.

I'd never done anything like this before, but Michael was gripping my arse and urging me into his mouth, opening wide and moaning as I filled him.

Bracing my hands on the headboard, I did what he'd asked. I fucked his mouth, pulling back when he choked and coughed, pushing inside when he dug his fingers into my flesh. My cock was slick with his spit, and he gasped around me.

"*Michael*," I moaned. "You feel so good. I'm going to..." Sweat dampened my forehead, and I rocked into Michael's perfect mouth, my balls so tight they were about to—

I shot down his throat, pulling out as he coughed and tried to swallow. The next spurts landed on his red, swollen lips and his flushed cheeks, dripping down his chin. My whole body shook with white-hot pleasure, and I made a sound I barely recognized.

"That's it. Everything," Michael muttered.

I could barely breathe, but I didn't stop to regroup before crawling backward and pushing Michael's thighs wide. As I took his throbbing dick in hand, he moaned, "Oh god, yes. *Baby*."

Hearing him call me that gave me a thrill. Taking his hard cock in my mouth, I sucked the head, boggling at the thought of swallowing the whole thing the way some people could. The way Michael could.

It was earthy and hot and raw, and part of me couldn't believe I was actually sucking a man's cock.

Michael's, which made it all the better. I wanted to bring him off and please him—which I seemed to be accomplishing given his cries and fingers tangling in my hair. He caressed my head as I licked around his shaft, slurping noisily.

Sucking him a little deeper, I swallowed, spit dribbling from between my stretched lips. To feel Michael's desire hot and hard in my mouth gave me a heady burst of confidence. I fumbled for his balls, and it was only a few moments before he flooded my tongue with salty jizz as I swallowed desperately.

Cum dripping out of my mouth, I panted and groaned, muttering unintelligibly. I had no idea what I was trying to say. Michael tugged at my shoulders, and I returned to him, licking my own splatters from his face before kissing him deeply.

Sweaty and sticky, we kissed, moaning into each other's mouths. The rush I'd felt when I'd first pretended to be bi at the work retreat returned, spinning me around joyfully.

Safe to say *pretending* to be bi wasn't necessary and never had been. This was me.

I kissed Michael through a giddy grin. "Thank you," I whispered, holding his face in my hands.

Red-faced, he laughed. "Anytime."

There was so much else to thank him for, wasn't there? The ghosting had cut me to the quick—and I had to breathe through a bolt of hurt—but I was so grateful he was here with me in Australia. In this bed. In my arms.

I couldn't hope to make sense of the whirlwind in my mind, so I kissed him, and kissed him, and kissed him.

Chapter Eighteen

Michael

EET SINKING INTO the wet sand, I waded through the shallows along Barking Beach. Will had gone to meet Angela for a meeting about the meeting they were having tomorrow with one of the companies Angela wanted to partner with.

I chuckled to myself. A meeting about a meeting. Why was that funny to me? Probably because I felt drunk without having anything stronger than coffee.

I turned my face up to the sun under the brim of my Mets cap, breathing the ocean air deeply. I'd slathered any exposed skin with sunscreen and wore a loose T-shirt over my shorts.

Carrying my flip-flops, I walked the length of the beach again, dodging splashing kids and surfers returning to shore at the north end. Grinning to myself, I could have held my arms out and twirled the length of the beach like whatshername at the beginning of *The Sound of Music*. Except on the sand and not in the Alps.

That was my mom's favorite movie, and I found myself humming the song about favorite things, my mind jumping around like pop rocks were fizzing in my head. Will was one of my favorite things. No, my absolute favorite thing. My *favoritist* thing, even though that wasn't a word.

Gulls fought loudly, squawking in outrage over what was left of an ice cream cone. I dodged a frisbee as the next wave washed by, swirling around my ankles. The surf was calmer than it was yesterday. Despite the crowd, it was paradise, except not because Will wasn't with me.

"Dude, it's been, like, two hours. Calm down," I muttered to myself.

A small bodyboard bumped my calf, and I scooped it up to return it to a little girl who'd tumbled off but seemed totally unfazed. I was happy to stay on land today, though the swirling waves were refreshing as they washed by and retreated.

Besides, I'd promised Will I wouldn't swim without him. Because he said he'd "fret" about me all through the meeting.

The hills are alivvvvvve!

Fuck, I was being such a weirdo, but I didn't care. It was hard to believe that everything Will and I had done had actually happened and wasn't just one of my fever-dream fantasies. Thinking now about him sucking my cock was—

Dangerous. This was a family show here at the beach. No thinking about cock sucking or kissing or the amazing feeling of being held down by Will's weight as he'd fucked my mouth...

Nope! Think of the singing nun again!

I dug my toes into the sand, my feet disappearing. Maybe it was a good idea to call my parents. That would definitely get my mind off sex and Will and how even though we'd agreed this was a friends-with-benefits situation... This was way more, right?

That wasn't all in my head. It couldn't be. The connection between us was stronger than it had ever been. I'd loved him for years, and I'd been right all along. He was the one. We fit together. I wasn't imagining it or forcing it the way I had with Jared. I was being myself, and Will wanted me.

Before I actually started doing cartwheels or something, I hit my parents' number on my phone. I'd texted them yesterday on Christmas, but it would be good to talk. They'd been disappointed about the breakup with Jared, but now I had good news.

Oh shit, what time was it in Florida? And wait, I couldn't tell my folks I was screwing Will. I couldn't say a word until we were actually a couple, and I had to stop assuming we would be. It had only been twenty-four hours since we'd first kissed, even though that seemed impossible.

The phone was ringing, so I couldn't hang up, but seriously, what time was it back home? I was trying to do the math when my father gruffly said hello.

"Hey, Dad. Sorry, did I wake you?" Ugh. Great way to start the conversation.

He grunted. "What's wrong?"

"Nothing! I just wanted to say merry Christmas. I guess Christmas Day is over."

"It's…four-thirty."

Shit, so it was definitely way too early. "Sorry. Go back to bed." It had to be thirteen hours behind in Florida.

He said, "I'm up now. Hold on." He mumbled something, and I realized he was talking to my mom—probably telling her everything was fine and to go back to sleep. There was a soft slapping sound that had to be his flip-flops, which had become his slippers of choice in Florida.

The long, low metallic noise of the patio door sliding open followed. I said, "It's warm enough to sit outside so early?"

"I've got my robe. Besides, we're having a winter heat wave. The humidity is ridiculous. At least I can sit by the pool thanks to global warming."

I could imagine him on the flagstone patio in a Costco deck chair in the darkness with his legs crossed and the small in-ground pool lit from under the water. There was a remote control that could change the colors of the lights—red, blue, green, purple—but Dad always kept it on plain white.

He asked, "What's the weather like there?" His voice was familiar and sharp. His questions usually sounded like a cross-examination even when I knew he didn't mean it that way.

"Hot and sunny." I smiled as a wave surged up to my knees as I walked along the shore. "Perfect beach weather. It's beautiful here. The Indian Ocean is incredible. Have you ever seen it?" I took in the endless blue again, breathing the sea air deeply.

"No, I don't think so. You'll have to send us some pictures."

"Sure! I will." I held the phone closer to my ear as I passed a group of teenagers playing hip-hop on wireless speakers.

"You talk to Jared?"

For a second, I thought I heard him wrong. "Um, no. We broke up, remember?"

He sighed. "Well, you argued. Surely you're not giving up on your relationship so easily. The holidays can bring people back together."

"Jared's not into Christmas." I thought of the tree abandoned in the yard. "Besides, I'm all the way over here. I'm not—Jared and I aren't getting back together anyway. We're not right for each other."

"Pity. We liked him. How's Zoe?"

"Good. Engaged to a nurse."

His voice rose in surprise. "A nurse? I didn't realize Zoe liked girls."

"His name's Peter. Men can be nurses too."

Dad laughed. "I suppose they can. Well, that's good for Zoe, then."

"Yeah, I'm not getting back together with her either."

"Of course not. Where are you going to live when you get back?"

"I don't know yet."

He sighed again. "You'd better figure it out soon."

I laughed half-heartedly. "Yeah, I will. It's Christmas. It's fine."

"What's the vacancy rate in Albany now?"

"I don't know."

As my dad talked about leases and how renting long-term was throwing money away, I reached the end of the beach. I turned back, but now the sun on the water glared too much, even with my sunglasses and cap. Kids shrieked, and the number of people around suddenly got to me. I headed up to the closest exit.

The sand was burning in the late-afternoon sun, and I hurried to the grassy area beyond the boardwalk, trying not to yelp. Still holding my flip-flops, I dragged my feet over the shorn grass to dry them as I swatted at a persistent fly. Considering how dry Perth was, their grass was surprisingly green even if it was a strange, spongy texture.

I said, "Yeah, I definitely want to buy something at some point."

"That really would be wise. When we were your age, we had a house and car and two kids already."

"I have a car." Sure, it was a beater that was in the shop after breaking down on the side of a deserted country road, but Dad didn't have to know that. It was fine. And, yeah, Will had to rescue me, but it had all worked out.

Still, I shifted uncomfortably and started pacing. I should have been able to buy a newer car. I added, "Things are different now than when you and Mom were my age."

"True. Young people don't want to work anymore."

I inhaled, pressing my lips together to stop from blurting something defensive. "It's not that people don't want to work. It's that wages are below the poverty line, and so many people have student loans they can never pay off, and—"

"You don't have loans."

"I know. I'm really lucky you guys paid my tuition. I'm just saying in general, it's not easy these days. It took me a long time to find a steady job where I could at least make a decent living." I could admit I hadn't tried as hard as I could have out of college.

I'd felt…lost.

But now I had a good job, and maybe Will and I could actually make it work. I exhaled, remembering his kisses.

"Are you paying rent?"

Blinking, I focused on my dad's voice. "Sorry, can you say that again?"

"Are you paying Will rent while you stay with him?"

"Oh. I… I hadn't thought about it. I was only there one night before we got on a plane."

"Yes, well, you need to think about it, Michael. No one likes a freeloader."

I paced near one of the tall pines, its long, strange needles—leaves?—looking like dried snakes under my feet. "His boss is paying for this trip. I'm his plus-one."

He sounded dubious. "Pretty generous boss to bring along her employee's pal."

"Yeah. She's really generous." Of course Dad didn't have to know she'd brought me along because she thought Will and I were a couple.

But maybe we are now? Maybe it's not a lie.

The buzz of happiness at the thought of Will being my boyfriend—my *partner*—for real evaporated as my dad said, "We don't want to see you floundering again. You were finally settled with Jared. You know, your brother—"

"Dad, I've got to go. It's getting close to dinner time. I should get changed." I didn't even know what we were doing for dinner. It didn't matter. "Tell Mom merry Christmas. Enjoy the heat wave. Or not since global warming sucks." Sweat dampened my forehead under the brim of my cap.

"Merry Christmas to you and Will. Just think about what I said, son. Take care."

We hung up, and my dad would be delighted to know I fucking couldn't think about anything else.

Will had said I could stay with him, but it was probably a bad idea, wasn't it? I'd rushed and forced it with Jared. I couldn't risk messing this up with Will. Whatever *this* actually was. God, maybe I was kidding myself. Was I reading too much into it?

I had to laugh thinking of the things we'd done in the past how-ever-many hours since yesterday. It was a blur of nakedness and coming more times than should be legal. But we'd made an agreement. He was curious, and I was helping him figure out if he liked fucking guys.

The results seemed pretty conclusive, but I had to remember that didn't mean he felt the same way about me. How could he? It hadn't been long enough, right? Orgasms didn't mean he'd ever love me back.

"I just feel so sorry for him."

Jared's voice filled my head as I circled the park, walking blindly, and for a horrible moment, I thought I'd puke all over the grass. Will wasn't Jared. But even though Jared and I hadn't been right for each other at all, the humiliating truth was that I hadn't realized Jared had been wanting to dump me for *months*.

Even if I'd known deep down we didn't fit, I'd been clueless. I'd still been trying so pathetically hard.

My skin prickled, sweat dripping down my spine as I relived standing in the doorway clutching that stupidly huge Christmas tree and hearing Jared complain about having to wait to break up with me.

"Will isn't Jared," I whispered under my breath. Holy shit, I was going to start crying in a second.

"You right, mate?" a woman asked, peering up at me from her yoga mat and shielding her eyes from the sun. She sat cross-legged with her flexed feet up on her knees.

"Uh-huh!" It was funny how Australians seemed to leave out the "all" in "all right." I tried to smile. "I'm good. Thanks." I probably looked sick and desperate and like I was about to star in a true crime story.

I had to get my shit together. Phone gripped in one hand and flip-flops in the other, I escaped her concerned squint and found a spot on the low concrete wall running along the boardwalk.

Facing the ocean, I let my feet dangle above the sand not far below, trying to recapture the joyous peace I'd felt before the phone call.

Okay. I had to be proactive. I could do this. I was not going to fuck up my friendship with Will. I had to do something productive. The question was, what? Sitting around feeling sorry for myself was definitely not productive.

Feet jiggling, I ran through possibilities before settling on apartment hunting. There! That was productive. Will had said I could stay with him, but moving in with Jared too soon had been a huge mistake. Will wasn't Jared, but it still made sense to find my own place. The last thing I wanted to be was a freeloader.

I hooked my sunglasses on the neck of my tee and scrolled the rental listings in Albany. It was weird to be doing it in the sunshine on the other side of the world. Reality had burst in and demanded a seat at the table. That's what I got for calling my parents.

"Hey, you," a familiar voice said right in my ear—and I jerked so violently I almost fell off the wall.

"Jesus!" I shouted as Will wrapped a strong arm around my chest and pulled me back. I found my feet on the boardwalk, and we both laughed.

"What are you so engrossed in?" Will asked. He propped his sunglasses on his head. He'd rolled the sleeves of his navy button-up shirt to his elbows and wore long shorts and loafers without socks. Business casual in eighty-five-degree temps.

"Just looking at apartments back home. How was the meeting with Angela?"

Will blinked, opening and closing his mouth. "It was fine."

"Are you sure?" Another knot of worry tightened in my stomach. "Is there a problem with the pitch or something?"

He shook his head. "No, it went to plan. We have our first meeting tomorrow morning. What was that about apartments?"

"I'm just looking to see if there's anything decent open for January."

"You're staying at mine, though. Unless…you don't want to?"

"It's not that. I just don't want to be a freeloader, you know? Although I'll pay rent, obviously. I should have said that before."

His brows met. "I'm not concerned about money. What's this about?" Rocking back on his heels, he shoved his hands in his pockets, his shoulders hunching.

"Nothing." I put my phone away. "Don't worry about it. What are we doing for dinner? I'm not sure if we're meeting up with the Barkers, or…?"

A family brushed past us on the boardwalk, an inflatable penguin almost smacking Will in the head. But he didn't crack a smile like he usually would. "Did something happen this afternoon? I thought we were…" He motioned between us. "Are you cross with me?"

I laughed genuinely, affection warming my chest. "No, I'm not 'cross.' Or any other cute words." I held out my hand. "Come on, let's go back."

But Will didn't take my hand. "Are you going to ghost me again?"

Dropping my arm, I struggled to inhale. I had to swallow hard. "Of course not!" As soon as I said it, guilt slammed me. I had no right to act like it was something I'd never done.

We stood on the boardwalk staring at each other as sunburned beachgoers shuffled by, the crowd starting to thin. The hurt shining in Will's eyes might as well have been a flashing neon billboard.

I'd owed him an explanation that first weekend at the glamping retreat—not to mention that I should never have ghosted him.

Because that's what I did even if I hadn't wanted to admit it. "I'm sorry," I said hoarsely. "I did ghost you. I didn't mean to, but—" Raising my hands, I shook my head. "No. It doesn't matter what I meant to do. The bottom line is that I stopped talking to you. I tried to pretend you didn't exist most of the time. Then I'd break down and look at your Facebook or Insta." I shook my head again, trying to find the right words.

"You didn't want me to exist?" Will asked. I could barely hear him, the words sounded like they were being dragged across a desert.

"No!" I reached for him, but he stepped back. I dropped my hands. "I'm doing this all wrong. What else is new?" Closing my eyes, I took a deep breath—maybe the deepest breath ever. Down to my soul. I opened my eyes and finally said it out loud.

"I loved you." *Loved, loves, will love.*

Will stared at me for the longest few seconds of my life. Then his brows met. "I loved you too. You're my best friend."

Oh, wow. He didn't get what I was saying. Okay. Another deep, soul-fortifying breath. In and out. My voice sounded far away. "I was *in* love with you. I still am. I love you. Like, right now. I'm in love with you."

Was it making sense? Will was still staring at me, his lips parted and his body completely frozen. So I kept talking.

"I've been in love with you for years. Since I was still with Zoe, honestly. But I knew it was never going to happen. At least, that's what I thought. And I just—I had to get over you. I was...wallowing. I think that's the right word?"

Will still stared like a statue, his eyes wide. I added, "You'd started seeing Kara, and I couldn't just keep wanting you uselessly."

"*Kara*? We barely dated a month. It was great to start, but it went downhill after a week. I would have ended it then, but I felt guilty and limped along for a while more. But even if I'd been mad about her, you got together with Jared and I was, what? Out of sight, out of mind?"

"*Never*. Jesus, I thought about you all the time. I ordered myself to face reality. It was like a mantra: I had to grow the fuck up and move on. I met Jared, and I thought if I kept my distance from you, I could get over you, and then we could go back to being best friends."

"Get over me," Will whispered.

God, was I making this all worse? I had no fucking clue. "Yeah, but I couldn't. I really tried, and then weeks went by, and then months, and I kept telling myself I just needed a little more time. Another week, and then we could hang out and watch a game or binge the latest murder show, and I'd be fine. I was going to make it work with Jared, and I'd stop loving you."

"You never said a word." He looked dazed. An ice cream vendor rode by with a freezer on the front of her bike, dinging her bell. Will didn't even blink.

"I couldn't." I shook my head, tears burning behind my eyes. "I was afraid you wouldn't want to be friends anymore."

He jolted like I'd slapped him. His voice rose. "Instead, you stopped being friends with me? How was that better?"

"It wasn't." I grabbed my Mets cap off my head and squeezed the brim down, needing something to break even if it would only bend. "I was a coward. And it got harder and harder to face that as time passed. To face you."

I raised my head to meet his eyes. "I missed you so fucking much. I told myself you were better off without me. I never thought in a million, billion years that you could ever want me the same way. You never said…"

"Because I didn't know!" Will practically shouted. His chest rose and fell, his breath shallow. He was definitely unfrozen now. "I didn't know that I'm…" His voice broke, and I reached for him again, but he raised his hands. I fell back.

After clearing his throat, Will asked, "Do you remember how my mum has a philosophy about taking leaps in life? Taking chances." At my nod, he added, "I think I've wanted to take this leap for ages, but I didn't know how." He squared his shoulders. "I'm bisexual. It's not just pretend, or for the weekend, or only the holidays. It's not a lark. It's who I am."

Not able to stop a smile, I wanted to twirl again—full *Sound of Music* vibes. "Thank you for telling me." I wanted to throw my arms around him, but I managed to stay put. I nodded encouragingly.

"I'd never fancied a bloke before. And when I started to, it wasn't anyone in particular. It was…just for me. Getting off alone. Fantasizing. But when you rang that night, and I picked you up on the road…"

I could barely breathe. My heart was going to actually explode this time. Or my head. Maybe both.

"Hey!" Olivia approached with a wave as she glanced up from her phone, and yep—my head exploded.

Chapter Nineteen
Will

OLIVIA ASKED, "ARE you guys going swimming? I want to get in quickly before the lifeguards go home. My hair's shit today anyway. Can you watch my stuff? Makayla's too sunburned from yesterday. I *told* her to put on more sunscreen after she got out of the water. She never listens to me."

Michael and I only stared at her, both of us apparently at a loss for words. My mind was a complete tangle.

She blinked, straightening her tote bag on her shoulder. "Shit, sorry. I'm interrupting."

"It's fine," I lied, managing to access my reserves of politeness.

Olivia lifted her hands. "You're obviously fighting."

Was that what we were doing? I honestly didn't know at this point.

With every ounce of strength, I tapped into that politeness. Mum and Dad would have been proud. "Don't be silly. We're happy to watch your things while you have a swim." I glanced at Michael, and he nodded. It wasn't Olivia's fault we were...

Confessing love to each other? Well, Michael had confessed. He'd said he was in love with me.

Michael was *in love with me.*

As we made our way through the thinning crowd, my loafers filled with sand until I had to stop and carry them. I fought to comprehend exactly what was happening.

My heart skipped erratically. A seismic shift was occurring, yet I felt as though I was hovering over the ground, watching cracks and fissures fan out from the epicenter.

Michael was in love with me.

Michael had been in love with me for years? *Years?* Was I completely daft? Mum had even said she'd suspected it! I'd laughed it off. I'd only thought about my own burgeoning curiosity about men and my secret wanking material. Michael had ghosted me, and I'd only considered my own pain, not his.

We had to sort this out, but for the moment, Olivia was there. Perhaps it was fortuitous timing, and Michael and I both needed to gather our thoughts.

Michael, who was in love with me.

Olivia was saying something I'd missed. Michael laughed weakly, not looking at me. She said, "Just don't break up— Mom'll be heartbroken. She totally ships you guys."

I tried to smile. I had to say something, and I couldn't talk about Michael and breaking up—those two words made me feel nauseous. So I said, "Angela does seem to get quite invested in queer relationships."

Olivia smiled ruefully and tucked her long hair—which looked smooth and lovely and not shit at all to my eyes—behind her ears. "She can be so cringe, I know. But she means well. My uncle was gay, and it was a massive family drama back in the day. He died before I was born."

"Oh. I'm sorry to hear that," I said. In all the office chatter about Angela, I'd never heard this mentioned.

"It's okay." Olivia pulled a face. "Not that it wasn't sad, obviously. He had AIDS. It was horrible. It was way different in the nineties, you know? Tons of people died."

Michael and I nodded.

"My grandpa sucked. He kicked out Uncle Andrew when Mom was just a kid. She always felt bad that she'd never said anything to defend him, but she was, like, eight. Years later, Uncle Andrew was sick, and he asked for help. Grandpa actually said no. Can you imagine?" She stopped on an empty area of sand near one of the red and yellow flags and unfurled her towel. "Here's good. You want to sit on my towel?"

We sat, and I asked, "What about your grandmother?"

Olivia took off her sunglasses and rolled her eyes. "One of those stereotypical white Southern ladies who never said shit to her husband. That house was a patriarchy, that's for sure. But Mom was like, fuck this. She moved out and worked two jobs while she looked after Uncle Andrew. Dad moved in to help as well. They were still teenagers and not married yet, which was a huge scandal. So ridiculous."

"Wow," Michael said. "She inherited the company, though?"

Olivia tugged her striped sundress over her head and rolled it neatly before straightening the straps on her bikini. "Yeah. Grandpa disowned her when she left, but he eventually put her back in the will. I think it was after Mom and Dad adopted me from Korea. I guess Grandma and Grandpa couldn't resist the lure of a baby."

She shrugged. "They sucked in a lot of ways, but they had good sides too. Aside from being insanely rich, I mean. I dunno. I couldn't totally write them off. Mom couldn't either."

"I get it," Michael said quietly. "It's hard not to love your family."

"They did eventually say they were wrong about Uncle Andrew. I mean, he was dead, so it didn't do him a lot of good. At least Grandpa gave a shit-ton of money to LGBTQ-plus charities and stuff. Mom does too. It wasn't her fault that they turned their backs on him, but she really tries to make up for it now."

"She's very generous," I agreed.

"Anyway, I'm going in. You guys are cool here?"

We nodded, barely looking at each other. I watched Olivia

navigate the shore break. There were still a fair number of people in the water, but her bright orange and red bikini made her easy to spot.

Michael and I sat watching, our shoulders only inches apart. I hugged my knees to my chest. I hadn't expected any of what Olivia had divulged about Angela and her brother. For long minutes, we were silent.

"Imagine your parents throwing you out like that," Michael finally said quietly. "Not even helping when you were dying. My folks can be really frustrating and distant, but I'm lucky to have them. I'm so glad Andrew had Angela."

"Me too."

We fell silent again. There was so much to say, but it seemed we both needed to catch our breath. Perhaps it should have been awkward, but... It wasn't. We'd known each other too many years.

The sun was lower in the sky, feeling close overhead as it began its slow descent to the horizon. There were still distant sounds of laughter and the steady heartbeat of the tide. A lifeguard slowly patrolled the shore, announcing on a megaphone that the tower would be closing soon.

"I'm sorry I left you alone," Michael whispered. The sun's caramel light reflected in his glistening eyes.

The air punched out of my lungs as I took his face in my hands. "I forgive you." I swiped his tears with my thumbs.

A sob escaped him, and he threw his arms around me, almost vaulting into my lap. I held him close, my throat too thick to speak.

Michael was in love with me—and I was in love with him.

"How was I so blind?" I eventually murmured, stroking a hand over Michael's hair. His breath was warm on my tear-damp neck.

He raised his head, sniffing loudly. "I guess I hid it well."

"My mum figured it out, so not that well. How did I not see it? How did I not realize I felt the same? What a bloody numpty I am."

Adam's apple bobbing, Michael sat back a few inches. Our knees bumped on the towel where we faced each other with legs bent to the side, and I ran my palm over his calf, needing to touch him.

Michael said solemnly, "You don't have to say that. Not that I don't—obviously I want you to love me. To be in love with me." He sniffed again and cleared his throat. "But we only kissed and stuff for the first time yesterday. Which is unreal. It's like Christmas had more than twenty-four hours. It seems like we've been hooking up for way longer."

"It does. Maybe it's the time change. We had Christmas Day here in the sun, and then had it all over again back in Eastern Time. In our hearts. That makes absolutely no sense whatsoever."

I loved to see the dimple in Michael's flushed cheek. His eyes were red-rimmed from crying, and he sniffed noisily, swiping his hand across his nose, and I'd never been so in love before. Not ever.

"I love you," I said with complete confidence. "It's not too soon. I'm not experimenting. I want you, and I'm in love with you. All those years, I was a fool."

"You weren't." Michael leaned in and caught my mouth in a sweet kiss. "You just didn't have all the information yet."

I chuckled. "I suppose not. I was rather slow on the uptake." I ran my thumb back and forth over the swell of his warm calf. "I always hated how people perceived me as such a player. It had been wonderful with Amelia, and I kept trying to recapture that. But none of the women I dated compared to her—or you. You were with Zoe, and maybe that's why I never thought of you that way? I'm not sure. All I knew was that you were my favorite person. Then you disappeared with no warning, no explanation—

nothing. You were my best friend, and we spoke almost every day, at least in texts, and then there was *nothing*. Which is what I felt like."

Michael made a plaintive sound of distress, his eyes shining with emotion. "I'm so sorry. It was all about me. I was selfish. I told myself you were happy with Kara. I couldn't tell my straight best friend I was in love with him. I imagined how horribly nice you'd have been about it. No, not nice—*kind*. You'd have been so understanding and felt sorry for me. It was torture. It hurt too much to be near you. Then it killed me to be away from you. But I convinced myself we were both better off."

"Meanwhile, I discovered gay porn and was desperately wanking to men and pretending it wasn't about you."

He exhaled sharply, his gaze flicking between my eyes and my mouth. He licked his lips. "I guess we make a good pair, huh?" He cupped my cheek, his fingers gentle against my rough stubble.

"We do. And we are, yes? A couple? Officially?"

Michael grinned before kissing me soundly. "We are," he mumbled against my lips before kissing me again and pulling back. I followed, nuzzling his jaw, leaning against him, trying to ease him back onto the towel.

Laughing softly, he stopped me with a firm palm on my chest. "This is a family show, remember?"

Blinking, I gazed around at the groups of people on the beach of all ages, some strolling the shore as the sun sank, others watching the sky blaze orange from their picnic blankets, still others splashing and playing as the lifeguards pulled up the flags, gathering their equipment and packing it away.

We disentangled ourselves, laughing as we straightened any clothing that had become askew. I lifted my hand over my eyes, searching for Olivia and finding her chatting with a young man in waist-deep water just beyond the shore break. The surf was calmer than it had been the day before.

With our arms around each other's backs, Michael and I watched the sunset. Michael played idly with the ends of my hair, rubbing the fuzzy, shorn area on the back of my neck and sending flickers down my spine.

"Why did you ring me that night?" I asked. "I suppose it was breaking up with Jared. Otherwise, you'd have called him."

Michael shuddered. "God, I'm so glad he dumped me. I was in so much denial." He rubbed my neck slowly. "I knew I could rely on you even though you couldn't rely on me. I honestly didn't expect you to pick me up, but I knew you'd understand why I was freaking out on the side of the road replaying every true crime story that took place in the woods. Even though I ghosted you, I knew when I needed help, you'd answer. At least, I'd prayed you would. I didn't deserve it, but you answered."

"I thought it had to be a pocket dial." I squeezed his shoulders. "It was so bloody good to hear your voice again." He opened his mouth, and I lifted my other hand to his lips. "I know you're sorry, and I forgive you. I've buggered up plenty of times in my life. Let's leave it all in the past."

He blew out a shaky breath. "Deal."

After kissing him softly, I nodded to the golden-orange sky, the sun reflecting on the water as it sank. "Time to leap into the future. Mum will be proud."

His hand was a comforting warm weight on my neck. "You're going to tell your parents? About being bi? About us?"

"Of course. Mum will be chuffed to bits that she was right."

"Glad to hear it." A fly buzzed around us, and he swatted it.

I swatted at it as well. "That's one thing about an Aussie Christmas I could do without—all the wee beasties."

Michael laughed. "The what?"

"Beasties. Insects. Not to mention the sharks, snakes, and crocodiles. And spiders! Kangaroos can be quite dangerous too, I understand. Everything's out to get you in Australia."

"Mmm." Michael's gaze dropped slowly over my body and back up. I could almost feel his gaze like a caress. "I can't blame them for being out to get you."

He ran his hand slowly down my back. I gasped softly as he slipped his fingers under the hem of my shirt, teasing the sensitive skin below my waistband.

Michael circled the dimple at the top of my arse and nuzzled under my ear, whispering, "We beasties can't resist you."

"Naw. You're too bonnie to be a beastie, lad," I said, thickening my accent.

He laughed, shaking lightly against me. "God, you're sexy when you go ultra Scottish. Not that you're not sexy all the time." He inched back, biting his lip. "'Bonnie' means pretty, right?"

"Aye." I traced his mouth with my finger. "You're beautiful."

He scoffed. "I mean, I wouldn't go that far. I'm no supermodel, but thank you."

"I mean it. It's not about being a supermodel—though you sell yourself short. There are a million attractive people in the world. Millions. But I don't want to actually be with them. I need to really care about the person."

Michael nodded. "I get it. I think there's a term for that on the asexual spectrum."

I frowned. "I like sex, though. I mean, Christ, if wanking was an Olympic sport…"

He laughed. "That's why it's a whole spectrum. I think it's demisexual when you really only want sex with other people if you're in love with them. Like with Amelia. Although I'm sure there's not just one way people experience being demi or anything else. There are a bunch of labels on the ace spectrum."

"Do I have to choose one?" My mind already felt as though it had run a marathon.

Michael smiled. "Nope. You don't have to do anything. There's no right or wrong way."

I exhaled in relief. "Okay. I'm bisexual. That's all I need for now." Saying it aloud gave me a thrill. "I'm bisexual," I repeated.

"You are." He grinned. "So am I. Just a couple of bi guys watching the sunset."

The horizon was now painted a deep orange-tinged pink as the sun disappeared. "You know, it really was different with Amelia than any other woman I dated. I wanted her all the time."

Michael licked his lips. "And with me?"

"Yes." The word rasped from my throat without hesitation. "All the bloody time. From the moment I saw you again on the side of that road. It was the same on one hand—familiar and easy the way it always had been. But something had changed. I wanted you. I think it was you I'd been wanting all along. It was you I'd been missing like a limb, so I watched men fucking, and I touched myself, wishing I was with you."

Michael gulped as he swept his fingertips back and forth across my lower back under my shorts. "If I'd known, I would have begged you to fuck me over the hood of my crappy car."

I laughed as my face blushed hot. "Naughty!"

With a sly smile, he dipped his fingers lower, barely touching me and still north of my arse crack but lighting my nerves on fire, my cock swelling. I glanced about guiltily, but there was no one nearby, and the sunset seemed to have everyone else's attention.

"Do you want me to fuck you like that?" I whispered. "Not over the hood of your car, but…"

He sucked in a shallow breath. "Yes."

"Have you thought about it?" My throat was dry. We were in public, but I couldn't stop myself from asking.

"Your cock in my ass? Oh, yeah." His hand was pressed flat on my lower back now, our skin damp. "I've thought about it a million times. Jerked off imagining you holding me down."

Lust flared red hot. "Christ," I muttered, the thought of Michael taking me, begging me for more was almost too much.

"I know you'll take care of me. I won't have to worry."

"You won't," I agreed, stroking his hair.

"I want you on top of me, inside me, giving it to me hard—"

We kissed, moaning into each other's mouths, our tongues meeting and—

"*Ahem.*" Olivia said, "Glad to see you guys made up, but can I have my towel?"

Chapter Twenty
Michael

I T WAS ONLY ten minutes back to the hotel, but it was an *eternity*. Olivia told us about the cute guy she'd met and given her number to while we smiled and nodded and tried not to say "fuck it!" and get arrested for public indecency.

Because we were going to get extremely indecent.

Will was bi, and most importantly, he *loved me back*. It was twilight, but it felt like the sun was lighting me up from the inside. Full-on twirling in my heart. These hills were *alive*.

We passed the huge Christmas tree in the lobby, where a jazzy version of "Joy to the World" played. I was about to start dancing to instrumental jazz if we didn't get back to our room.

Olivia was still talking as we rode the elevator. I watched the numbers tick up. It was only a small boutique hotel, and the doors slid open mercifully soon.

"So what do you guys think?" Olivia asked.

We'd already rushed out into the hallway, and I had nothing. Will looked at me with a hint of panic before saying, "Uh…"

She smirked. "Bless your hearts. I'll tell Mom and Dad you're doing your own thing for dinner. Bye!"

Safely behind our locked door with the privacy tag hanging on the knob, I laughed as Will flipped on the lamp beside the bed. Night had settled in beyond the windows. We stared at each other. Now that we could tear each other's clothes off, we weirdly hesitated.

Will said, "I found an open chemist after my meeting."

Was my brain fried? "Huh?"

"A drugstore."

"Oh! Oh. That's good."

He took off his loafers and tucked them under a chair where a paper bag sat. He dumped the contents onto the smooth bedspread: a bottle of lube, box of condoms, and a pack of mint gum.

Will picked up the gum. "That's for the plane ride home. I hate it when my ears pop."

"Me too."

Fiddling with the gum, he asked, "Do we need condoms? I haven't been with anyone in quite a while. I've been tested since at my physical."

"I've been tested too, and I never actually had sex with Jared without a condom. He doesn't like jizz."

"Oh. Right." Will nodded.

"Which is fine! To each their own, blah, blah, blah. I mean, we've been swallowing each other's cum, but the risk profile for oral is different. I'm good either way with condoms."

Will seemed to contemplate it, turning the thin gum package over and over. "So, you'd be open to having sex without them?"

"Wide open." I raised an eyebrow, and Will laughed, ducking his head. Was he blushing? I loved everything about this. "Seriously, though—I know you're new to this. We can totally use condoms, or we can keep doing other things. Don't need to rush."

He nodded. "But if I wanted to?"

"Um, hell yeah." I hesitated. "It can get messy. Just to make sure we're on the same page, do you want to fuck me without a condom?"

"Yes," he said in that low burr that made me hot all over.

Every available drop of blood flooded south to my dick. "You want to come inside me?"

"Oh, good Christ," he muttered as we lunged at each other.

Through laughter and kisses, it took longer than I wanted to get naked, but finally we made it. I shoved the covers down to the foot of the bed and stretched out on my back. With Will's dark eyes locked on me, I spread my legs and jerked my erection. He knelt between my knees with his knuckles white on the bottle of lube.

"You still down with this?" I asked, stroking myself slowly. "I want it to be good for you."

He smiled tenderly and pressed a kiss to my raised knee, his stubble scratchy. "Anything with you is good."

"Anything, huh?" I rubbed his hard dick with my foot. "What if I had a foot fetish?"

He laughed. "You can suck my toes to your heart's content, darling."

My chest swelled. "Or you could just call me sweet names. Maybe *that's* my kink."

"As opposed to?" Will lifted his brows. "Is there something you're not telling me, sweetheart?"

"Oh god, that sounds good."

He grinned. "You like it, my precious? Wait, that sounds like Gollum."

I sputtered, "Gollum is definitely not my kink!"

"So, is there something else that is?"

Despite myself, I could feel heat creeping up my face. "Just this." Why was I hesitating? Liking a rough pounding wasn't exactly an extreme kink, and Will definitely seemed into it.

"I'm going to have to start guessing outside the box." He frowned. "Do you want me to piss on you or something?"

Laughing, I shook my head. "No golden showers. Not my thing."

"All right. Do I need to google? Because I admit, I don't have much out-of-the-box experience."

"So to speak."

We burst out laughing, and I sat up, the need to touch my dick satisfied for the moment. We had all night, and I loved being like this with him. Naked and smiling and easy.

"No, not much experience outside the—what was that stupid name for it? *Vajayjay.*"

"My mom still says 'hoo-haw,' I think."

"I'm sure my mum still says 'fanny,' but it hasn't come up in conversation for some time. When I was a kid, my mates would say 'snatch' and 'muff.' 'Penis flytrap' was a personal favorite."

"Oh my god! That's amazing."

Somehow, we spent the next who-knew-how-long sitting together on the bed and listing off the most ridiculous names for genitalia. My sides hurt from laughing as Will rhymed off UK slang for a cock, beginning with "knob" and finishing with "tadger."

As we caught our breath, I ran my fingers through his chest hair. "Honestly, American imagination pales in comparison to the UK."

"Oh, I don't know." He ran his fingertip down my shaft from the head and back up again. "You said you imagined me while you got off."

I shivered. "Uh-huh."

"And you imagined me fucking you? Hard?" He watched me intensely, still lightly tracing the length of my dick.

"Yeah, I guess my biggest fantasy has always been bottoming. It's been a few years. Jared didn't like topping, and I do, so it was fine that way."

"'Fine' isn't exactly a ringing endorsement, honeybun."

I smiled. "I know. Honestly, though—I'm good with whatever. We can experiment."

"But what you'd like right now is to be fucked hard?"

I couldn't hold in a little moan. "I love hearing you say that.

And yeah. Like, rough and overpowered, but not anything extreme. Vanilla dom/sub stuff if that makes sense?"

"Mmm." Will dragged his finger up my belly, making it quiver. "It makes perfect sense."

Without warning, he shoved me flat on my back and pressed me into the mattress, heavy and muscled and *god*. He watched me carefully. "Do you like this, sugarplum?"

My throat was way too dry to talk or laugh at the silly name. I nodded.

He ran his hands down my arms and took my wrists, holding them over my head. "Maybe something like this?"

Another nod. My dick throbbed against Will's stomach.

Still holding down my wrists, he pushed his knee between my legs, and I eagerly spread them wide. He was hard too, and I was in danger of coming before he got anywhere near my ass.

Will asked, "Is it roughness or being held down?"

"Yes!" I gasped hoarsely.

A light brightened his beautiful face. "Both, then? All right. Like this? Or on your hands and knees? Or bent over something like the desk?"

All I could moan was, "*Yes*," and we laughed.

"Keep your hands there," he ordered before sliding back to kneel between my legs again. He picked up the lube and squeezed a glob onto his palm before looking at me. "Haven't moved. Good boy."

I moaned, keeping my hands high over my head. "Use your middle finger first." I rounded my back, giving him better access to my ass. "Just stick it in."

Will laughed. "Such sweet talk from my lover. Patience, pumpkin." He circled my hole with his slick fingertip, using his long middle finger as I suggested. "If it's been a few years, you'll be tight, won't you?"

My breath caught. "Yes. But I can take it. Please."

He pushed past my rim, the lube doing its job as his finger stretched me. I bore down eagerly, squeezing as his whole finger filled me. Will watched where it disappeared inside me, his chest rising and falling faster as he explored.

"Crook your finger. No, the other way, like—" Gasping, I arched my back and clutched at the sheets, keeping my hands in place. "Right there. You got it."

I wasn't sure if I'd ever talked so much during sex aside from the standard encouragement. I'd always enjoyed all kinds of sex with all kinds of people, but I couldn't remember ever feeling this free.

As Will rubbed my gland, I took my cock in hand and stroked, my other fingers circling my nipple. I didn't even think about the fact that I'd lowered my hands before Will pulled out his finger and jerked my wrists over my head again.

"Oh, god, *yes*." I bucked my hips up as we kissed desperately. "Fuck me, Will," I groaned into his mouth.

He pulled back, spit wet on his lips. "Pardon?"

"I said, *fuck me, Will*. Get your cock in me." We were closer to the end of the bed, and I grasped for one of the pillows above me with my outstretched hands. I squeezed the feathers tightly, my arms locked over my head. "I'll be good. I promise."

"I know, baby." Will kissed me, our tongues pushing and sliding. He held himself over me, one hand pushing back my sweaty hair. "We should have done this years ago. Why did I ever think I was straight?"

"I wish I knew."

We laughed and kissed until we could hardly breathe, and as Will finally slicked his cock and pushed into me, moments of joy and laughter switched back and forth with grunts and demands.

My legs were as wide as they could go, but I wanted more. Gripping the pillow above me, I hitched my knees higher, lifting my ass. Will groaned, buried all the way inside me, his pubes tickling me. Mouth open, he sucked on my neck.

He muttered, "You feel so good," against my skin. "*You're* so good, sweetheart."

Part of me could have stayed like that all day, or night or whatever time it was, with Will filling me, heavy and *real* on top of me. This wasn't a dream or my imagination. Will was inside, stretching me to the point that it was tough to take without wincing.

But it wasn't enough. I wanted everything. I wanted it to hurt. My muscles were already trembling, and I wanted more.

"Please fuck me," I moaned.

Will lifted his head and took my mouth in a rough kiss. "Tell me if it's too much, love."

The fact that he'd called me that so simply—"*love*"—had tears pricking my eyes. I blinked them back, groaning as he took both my wrists in one hand, squeezing them with his fingers.

He was really holding me down now as he pulled back and thrust deeply, his other hand powerful on my hip to keep me in place. All I could do was gasp and cry out, our skin slapping and the headboard thumping as he fucked me the way I needed.

"*Yes, god, yes,*" I chanted, fighting the urge to throw my head back and close my eyes, letting sensations carry me away. No, I had to watch him.

Sweat dampened his forehead, his face flushed and veins sticking out on his neck. His muscles bunched and strained, and he never tore his eyes from my face. I was spread open and stripped totally bare, the rough sensation of his raw cock pounding me hotter than I'd ever dreamed.

Since I didn't have to think about keeping my hands in place, his fingers like iron around my wrists, I could let go totally and wallow in being helpless.

I knew I wasn't—Will would stop in a heartbeat. But stopping was the last thing I wanted. Will would protect me.

I didn't have to think, or worry, or do anything but take him as he brought me to the edge. As much as I didn't want to stop, my balls were tight, and I needed to come. Pinned by Will, I couldn't touch my cock, and I could only whimper.

That and beg Will. "I need to come. Please." I squeezed my ass around his dick.

Panting, Will looked down at me in the golden light of the bedside lamp. "Are you sure I should let you?"

All I could do now was moan. He was amazing at this already. "Please."

He rocked into me, his movements smoother but still powerful. He dragged his hand from my hip up the side of my thigh. My legs were sweaty behind my bent knees. I squirmed, squeezing around his cock again.

Will sucked in a breath. "Naughty."

"God, please touch me."

He relented—of course he did—and it only took a few strokes of his hand for the pressure to blow, pleasure sweeping through me as I shot onto my stomach. Will was still in me, and I squeezed even harder, jerking with aftershocks.

Gasping my name, he thrust one last time and came deep inside me. Knowing there was nothing between us as he shuddered and emptied brought fresh tears to my eyes. I trusted him, and he trusted me, and I couldn't believe this was real.

Perfectly heavy on top of me, Will nuzzled my hair and eased my arms down. I closed my eyes as he pressed gentle kisses to the insides of my wrists. His cock was still partly inside my tender hole, and I had to clean up, but I couldn't move yet.

Will whispered something I couldn't make out across my cheek—before he inhaled sharply and went rigid. I opened my eyes.

His face pinched in concern as he wiped the tears that had leaked from my eyes. "Did I hurt you?"

"God, no. *No.*" I ran my hands over his shoulders to touch his face. "I promise. It was incredible, baby. It was exactly what I wanted. And more. Thank you." I paused. "Did you like it?"

He grinned. "Did I ever. I'll bugger you senseless morning, noon, and night as long as I'm not truly hurting you."

"You didn't. It was perfect."

"You're sure?" He kissed me softly.

"Positive. Ask Kevin. He'll tell you."

Will went still again. "Who?"

I nodded to the koala ornament hanging from the lamp beside us. "How could you forget our surfing Christmas koala already?"

Laughing, Will flopped onto me, his voice muffled in my neck. "Right, Kevin. Bloody hell. I thought I'd fucked you into insensibility."

"That does sound good though, doesn't it? Give me a few minutes and we can try it."

Will kissed me, a long, slow, deep sweep of his tongue. "Don't you think poor Kevin's seen enough tonight?"

"Good point. Also, I don't think you can get it up again after that."

"Oi!" Will seemed about to say something else but smiled ruefully. "Yeah, no chance in hell. But there's always tomorrow."

"Tomorrow and tomorrow and tomorrow." I punctuated each word with kisses.

"Are you quoting Shakespeare to me?"

"Huh. I don't know. Am I?"

"I think it's *MacBeth*."

"Shouldn't you know? I mean, you're Scottish, FYI."

"Ah dinnae ken."

I groaned. "If you start talking cute Scottish words, you'll definitely have to fuck me again."

"We can coorie doon in the meantime."

I had no clue what it meant, but we laughed and kissed, and I couldn't wait to find out.

Chapter Twenty-One
Will

"**A**CE! FOUR CARDS."

As I closed the door to our room behind me, I swallowed a flare of disappointment that we weren't alone. Through the screen door to the balcony, Michael, Makayla—who had apparently just laid down an ace—and Olivia sat around the small round table. I'd just have to wait a bit longer to be alone with Michael.

Granted, I'd buggered him over the end of the bed before I'd left in the morning, but I woke each day gagging for him. It hadn't even been a full week yet since we'd first touched, and this feverish, constant need for each other would surely wane.

Not today, though.

"Hiya," I called, tucking my work satchel away beside the desk. I hung my suit jacket in the closet and tugged on my tie as I joined them on the balcony. "What's the game?" I kissed Michael on the head before running my hands across his shoulders. This was innocent enough.

"Strip poker," Makayla said, straightening a stack of cards.

"Er, interesting choice?" I raised an eyebrow dramatically, but they were all still fully dressed, the girls in floral sundresses over their bikinis and Michael in his board shorts and a T-shirt. And obviously Michael wouldn't be playing that game with teenagers.

They'd clearly been swimming, their hair frizzy from having

dried in the sun. The table was littered with empty plates, crumpled napkins, and dark brown bottles of Bundaberg ginger beer, which was the best ginger ale I'd ever tasted.

Michael sputtered. "Strip Jack Naked!"

Makayla waved a dismissive hand, her nails glittering with new art that looked to be little lemons. "Same difference."

"Still sounds questionable," I said, giving Michael's shoulders a playful squeeze.

"It's what my grandfather called it! He was really old, okay?" Michael flipped over a card. "Ha! King."

Olivia muttered, "Son of a…" and laid down three cards on top of the king.

I watched them play, idly rubbing Michael's neck. Makayla had the biggest stack of cards, and sure enough, she soon had them all and declared victory.

I quickly said, "We should get ready for dinner!" before anyone could suggest another round.

Makayla picked up her phone. "Wait, I have to show you the pic I got with that lifeguard! You know, the Thor guy."

Olivia sighed. "You have zero chill."

"Great shot!" I said, looking at the picture of Makayla beaming beside Liam Fox, who towered over her and gave a thumbs-up to the camera with a handsome smile.

"Thanks! He was *so* nice. He's gay like you guys—remember that lady at the beach told us? Isn't that cool?"

"Zero. Chill," Olivia muttered as she tapped her phone.

I shared a glance with Michael, and he smiled encouragingly. It was nonsense that my pulse suddenly spiked, but it did as I said, "Actually, I'm bisexual. We're both bi." I nodded to Michael.

Makayla looked stricken and exclaimed, "Oh, sorry!"

"Nothing to be sorry for," I assured her.

I glanced at Olivia, and why was I nervous as to what she might say? I supposed because this was the first time I'd told anyone else. I'd been perceived by colleagues as bi at the retreat, but now it was real—well, it had always been real, but I'd been in deep denial.

Now I was announcing it officially. Which felt damn good.

Olivia thumbed off her phone, declared, "Hot," and added, "See you at dinner," before leading out Makayla.

Exhaling, I kissed Michael as he stood and asked, "Okay?"

"I'm grand."

"How'd the last meeting go?"

"Terrific. We're already discussing remote integration of BRK Sync systems so there'd be no need for a satellite office or anything. You should see Angela in action. She's a force of nature."

"I'm familiar. I'm here in Australia after all. With my best friend turned fake boyfriend but now real boyfriend. Also, I'm really glad she has a thing for mistletoe, or who knows if you would've had the guts to kiss me."

I chuckled, then gave Michael what I hoped was a seductive look. "I wouldn't have been able to wait much longer. Trust me."

"Mmm." He pulled me close, running his hands down over my arse. "Speaking of waiting, it's been a long day without you. I should get in the shower, though. Are you sure I don't need a tie for dinner?"

"Positive. It's 'smart casual.'" You'll be grand in your slacks and button-up shirt. And I'll join you in the shower. I need one."

Michael raised a dubious eyebrow. "You look exactly the same as you did when you left. All businessy and well-ironed." He nuzzled my neck, inhaling forcefully. "You smell good too."

"I'm filthy." I held his hips tightly against mine.

His warm breath tickled my ear. "Sure you don't want to shower with me so you can put your tongue in my ass?"

Lust gripped me. "Well, I did just say I'm filthy."

He bit my earlobe, scraping it with his teeth slowly. "Or maybe you want *my* tongue in your ass?"

"Do I have to choose?"

"Nope. Now let's get in there before we get carried away out here and there actually is stripping."

Under the rainfall shower in the blissfully huge shower stall, I braced a hand on the steamy tile as I stroked myself and pushed back against Michael's face.

I'd watched rimming in porn and had always gotten off on it, and I'd discovered the combination of wanking while Michael licked into me was a quick way to come.

He spread my arse cheeks wide with his hands, licking around my hole with rhythmic movements, pushing right into me every so often as I moaned.

"Christ, your mouth," I mumbled. I could feel him smile, and that was what tipped me over the edge.

Still on his knees, Michael suckled my twitching balls until I squirmed away from too much sensation. I eased him to his feet and pushed our tongues together in a lazy kiss before murmuring, "Your turn."

Michael spread his legs and braced with both hands as I knelt behind and licked and kissed his hole. It was shockingly intimate in a way that even cocksucking wasn't quite—at least to me.

"Wish I had time to fuck you," I muttered against his flesh.

He moaned. "We can just do New Year's Eve tomorrow, right? We'll stay in and fuck and then celebrate in twelve hours when it's midnight at home."

"Tempting, but Angela's surely paid for dinner and the concert already." I turned Michael, urging him to lean back against the tile.

He jolted. "Tiles are still cold." Smiling down at me, he ran his fingers over my wet hair. Water streamed down his body, which was marked with my love bites.

I slowly licked the length of his rigid cock, and he tightened his grip, tugging my hair just slightly.

"Get me off. Please," he full-on whined.

I chuckled. "Perhaps I should make you wait until next year."

Michael's eyes widened, his breath hitching and his hips jerking. Oh, he liked that idea. He liked that idea very much.

I stood and snapped off the water as I said, "We're out of time. I'm afraid you'll just have to wait all night to come, my darling."

A laugh punched out of him as he groaned. "This is cruel and unusual punishment!"

"And you fucking love it."

He grinned. "And I fucking love it."

I kissed him hard. "And I fucking love you." I slapped his bare, wet arse. "Now let's get moving."

DINNER IN THE hotel restaurant, which was still fully decked out in gold, red, and silver Christmas decorations, was fantastic. Between each of the seven courses on the tasting menu, I ran my palm across Michael's thigh beside me under the white tablecloth, inching toward his cock but then retreating while he bit his lip or sighed long-sufferingly.

As usual, Angela did most of the talking, Paul gazing at her affectionately and the girls chiming in from time to time.

As we ate a perfectly marshmallowy Pavlova for dessert, Angela exclaimed, "Don't you just love New Year's? A fresh start for all of us. Say, what does the song actually mean?" she asked me.

I knew she meant "Auld Lang Syne" and tried to think of the best way to summarize it. "It's about reconnecting with old friends. That the people who matter most should never be forgotten, and we should see them again if we can. That's my take at any rate."

Under the table, Michael took my hand and squeezed.

A concert started around ten in the park by Barking Beach, and we had VIP seats near the front in lawn chairs with drink holders. It was a perfect summer night, warm and close but with a cool sea breeze and a blanket of stars visible even with the fairy lights strung around the trees and lampposts. The couple next to us pointed out the stars of the Southern Cross and Seven Sisters.

I didn't recognize the Australian band, but their music was upbeat and fun, and they played plenty of covers of Elton John and the like. We all sang along to "Tiny Dancer," and even Olivia and Makayla somehow knew the words.

Beside me, Michael sipped his beer and idly ran his finger down my bare arm under the short sleeve of my linen shirt. As the band started a new song I didn't recognize, I took his hand and pressed a kiss to his palm.

"'Tis a perfect Hogmanay," I half shouted over the music. "I don't think my new beginnings have ever been quite this new before."

He smiled. "Me either. This is the fresh start to end all fresh starts." He checked his phone. "Only ten minutes to go."

I sat up straighter. "You know, I need to do something to make this a proper fresh start. I'll be back before midnight." I kissed him quickly.

"You'd better be. You're already making me wait—I expect a real kiss!"

I darted out, leaping over the Barkers' feet, glad we were near the end of the row. The boardwalk and beach were crowded with revelers, some people ignoring the extra signs warning that lifeguards weren't on duty at night.

Plugging one ear, I held my phone up to the other and paced a little section of the boardwalk as it rang.

Then Mum's voice echoed down the line. "Happy Hogmanay!" she exclaimed before calling, "It's Will!" to my dad.

"It's almost midnight, I said loudly. I can barely hear you, but

I have to tell you something before the new year begins."

"You've about six or seven hours left here, I think," Dad said, their phone now switched to the speaker.

"But I'm here, so I need to make it quick."

"All right, love." Mum chuckled. "What is it? Have the meetings gone well?"

"Aye, but it's no about work."

"Right. We're all ears," Dad said.

I was strangely calm. "I took a leap, Mum. The thing is, you were right—Michael does fancy me. He's in love with me, actually."

After a beat of silence, they exclaimed, "Oh!" in unison.

"And it turns out I'm in love with him. I'm bisexual."

The silence stretched out this time. I lifted the phone from my ear to check that we were still connected. My heart skipped. "Er, hello?"

"We're here, honey," Mum said. "Well, this is quite a leap indeed! You and Michael. How lovely!"

I hadn't expected any other reaction, but it was still a relief. "You think so?"

"Of course," Dad said. "As long as you're happy, we're happy."

"I should've known," Mum mused. "I was right, though, wasn't I? It was time for a leap."

I couldn't stop grinning. "Aye. It was."

With a minute to spare, I squeezed through the growing crowd on the boardwalk, showed my VIP badge to the security guards, and tripped into my chair. "Mum and Dad send their love," I told Michael.

"Yeah?" He raised his eyebrows in question. "Like..." He motioned between us.

"Aye."

He took my hand, threading our fingers together tightly.

On the screen behind the band, a countdown clock appeared, and as we all stood, Angela shouted to me, "Here's your song!"

Hundreds of people counted down with the clock: "Ten! Nine! Eight!"

When the clock struck midnight, Michael and I wrapped our arms around each other as our lips met in a long, sweet kiss. Then we sang my song—*our* song—at the top of our lungs, laughing and hugging the Barkers and wishing everyone nearby a happy new year.

Soon enough, we'd slip away to our bed, and I'd reward Michael's patience handsomely—a prize for us both, of course.

Until then, we sang and swayed in the warm night under bright constellations we'd never seen before, charting our future.

Epilogue
Michael

Two Years Later

WITH STRAY NEEDLES way too close to my face, I shifted my grip on the tree and kicked the heavy condo door open again with my right foot.

Because I was cursed, I kicked it too hard, and the door rebounded off the entry foyer wall and smacked back into me and the tree. I hit the hall closet on the left.

The hall closet with the mirrored, sliding door that I'd left open.

On my ass, fully in the closet, sitting on shoes and what had to be the handle of Will's tennis racket at an *interesting* angle, I was now in danger of being suffocated by the twine-bound tree on top of me.

"What on earth!"

I heard Will before I could see him thanks to the tree. His face appeared as he heaved the Douglas fir off me. He grunted, struggling to shift it enough to let the front door close as he asked, "Are you hurt, love?"

"Only my pride, I think?" I crawled out of the closet instead of trying to stand up under all our coats. I took the other side of the tree and kicked off my boots. "Mistakes were made."

Will laughed. "It's a little big, isn't it?"

"I might have gotten slightly carried away. Hey, we only have our first Christmas tree in our new home once."

He chuckled. "We did have a tree last year in the apartment, but fair enough."

We wrangled it into the corner of the living room and into the stand I'd set up earlier. The wall of glass to the right of the tree overlooked our balcony and the nature preserve beyond.

Up on the ninth floor, we weren't too low or too high. I couldn't wait to sit out on the balcony in the mornings to sip our coffee when it wasn't below freezing and snowing.

I'd assured Will the vertigo honestly didn't bother me here. It was only when I felt unstable, and with Will there, I'd almost be ready for rock climbing. Almost.

"It's gorgeous," Will said, drawing me in for a kiss. He caressed my face. "I love you with rosy cheeks."

I knew he meant from the cold, but of course my brain jumped farther south. "People will be here soon. Don't tease."

"Naughty!" He slapped my ass lightly and returned to the kitchen as a timer beeped. His dress shirt sleeves were rolled to his elbows and a red apron was knotted behind his waist.

The apron had been a gag gift from me last Christmas and said: *THIS GUY RUBS HIS OWN MEAT* with an arrow pointing up.

If we'd had more time, I would have dropped to my knees and sucked him under that apron.

Our condo was an open-plan living area, and we'd lucked out with an older building with character. We were still unpacking—the guest room was a maze of boxes—but we had the new couch, TV, side tables, and dining table and chairs ready. We'd gone with beachy neutrals. I couldn't wait to put up the gallery wall of photos in the dining area.

Will had blown up a few from Australia, including one of us and the Barkers smiling and sun-kissed on our last visit to Barking Beach, the beautiful turquoise blue of the Indian Ocean behind us. Our last visit for now. Will and I had already discussed Australia and New Zealand for our honeymoon.

Sure, we had to get married first, but we would.

"Rockin' Around the Christmas Tree" came on the holiday playlist we'd made, and I hummed as I quickly buttoned a nicer shirt over my jeans in the main bedroom.

We still had boxes to unpack, and most of our clothes were hanging in their garment bags in the closet, but we'd both taken time off over the holidays next week.

Still humming while Will put his cheese and crab dip in the oven, I carefully snipped the twine from the tree and fluffed the needles before winding the multicolored lights around the branches.

Snowflakes drifted down outside, but the roads had been okay. I checked the flight arrival info on my phone and smiled. On time.

"That all smells amazing," I said. "Can I help?"

"I think we're good. Cheese plate and first round of nibbles are ready to go. Are the decorations set?"

"Yep." I motioned to the boxes I'd laid out. "Actually, if you have a sec before everyone gets here…" I unwrapped the tissue paper from our most important ornament. The star went on last, and Kevin went on first.

Wiping his hands on a dishcloth before slinging it over his shoulder—how was that so damn sexy?—Will joined me in front of the tree.

He slipped his arm around my waist and said, "Cheers, Kevin. Where should we put you?"

"How about front and center." I waited for Will's nod, and because we were stupidly superstitious now apparently, we placed Kevin together, tugging his string over a branch by a pink light. He'd lost a bit of glitter, but still sparkled as he hung ten or whatever surfers did.

"Perfect," Will murmured just before our buzzer on the wall by the front door sounded. He quickly took off his apron while I tried unsuccessfully to bribe him into keeping it on.

Seth and Logan were first to arrive, with Matt and Becky right after. Matt insisted on referring to all of us as "Team Caper," and I supposed there were worse things to be called.

Seth raised his glass of Prosecco. "Congrats to you both on your promotions."

Will and I clinked our glasses with everyone. I said, "Thank you. Mine isn't such a big deal, but Angela's going to make Will vice-president of the whole company if she has her way."

"I'm goddamned shocked she hasn't convinced you to work for her too," Logan said.

I laughed. "Never say never." It had been extremely tempting given how generous the benefits were, but I didn't think it was a good idea at the moment. Maybe in a few years, but for now, I wanted my job to be independent from Will's even if we would have been in different departments.

While Will drifted to the kitchen with Becky and Matt, I asked Logan and Seth, "How's Connor doing in med school? Columbia, right? This is his first year?"

Seth answered, "It is. He's working very hard. It's a lot of stress."

"I bet. I can't even imagine."

"Had to practically beg him to come home for Christmas," Logan grumbled. "He stayed in New York for Thanksgiving and went to some fancy party with his buddy."

Seth absently rubbed Logan's back. "He *is* coming home for Christmas, though. We'll have to get used to him being too busy to visit as much as we'd like. Not to mention that we'll have to get used to him being a full-fledged adult. With a motorcycle."

Logan grudgingly agreed before ducking into the bathroom. Seth sighed heavily and polished his glasses on his buttoned shirt.

I said, "Sorry to bring up a sensitive subject."

Seth shook his head. "Not at all. We're just worried. It feels like there's something weighing on Connor, but he insists everything's well. Logan gets frustrated, and then they argue." He seemed to give himself a mental shake and forced a smile. "At least we don't have to worry about him being alone in New York—he's living with Angela's daughter Olivia."

"Oh! Are they a couple?"

Seth chuckled. "I don't think so, much to Angela's dismay. But she's paying for the apartment and charging Connor very reasonable rent for his room."

Sipping a festive cranberry and vodka cocktail, Becky joined us as Logan returned. She said, "But knowing Angela, I'm sure she'll be thrilled Connor's dating Reid Cabot."

I could have sworn an actual shockwave reverberated through the air. Logan and Seth stared at Becky for so long without saying anything that she laughed nervously.

"Um… At least, that's what I heard from my cousin in Manhattan? They were together at a party or something."

Logan demanded, "What the fuck are you talking about?"

That got Matt and Will's attention, and they approached warily. Matt slipped his arm around Becky's shoulders. "What's up?"

Seth raised one hand, his other on Logan's arm. "Everything's fine. It's a misunderstanding. Connor's best friend is Asher Cabot. Reid's his older brother." He frowned. "Connor isn't *dating* him. He isn't dating anyone. He's always been too busy with school."

Becky said, "I'm sure my cousin's wrong. She's an even bigger gossip than I am." She laughed weakly. "If you can believe it. I didn't mean to upset you."

Logan scrubbed a hand over his short hair. "Sorry I talked to you like that. I didn't expect to hear—" He turned to Seth. "That can't be true, right? Why the hell wouldn't he tell us? Asher's *brother?* Is this what he's been hiding?" He shook his head, muttering something I couldn't hear.

"I'm sure it's a misunderstanding," Seth soothed, taking Logan's hand. "Let's take a minute." He eased Logan away, and Will pointed them toward our bedroom.

When the door closed softly behind them, Will smiled awkwardly. "Brie bite, anyone?"

Keeping her voice low, Becky said, "I really am sorry! I didn't think it was a secret."

Matt hissed, "So, wait—Connor's really dating some older guy? His best friend's brother?"

Becky raised her eyebrows. "Well, you know Marcia *is* even more of a bigmouth than me, but… She's rarely wrong. That's all I'm saying."

"'Tis the season for drama-rama." Matt raised his glass, and we all ruefully cheered to that.

Jenna, Jun, and their boys arrived next, followed by Zoe and her husband Peter, and our other old friends from college who'd just had another baby.

Seth and Logan reappeared, and Seth was definitely better at pretending nothing was wrong, although Logan was clearly trying.

Soon, I could barely hear the music over the laughter and talking. It was perfect.

We ate and drank and slowly decorated the tree, everyone taking turns hanging ornaments while the youngest kids threw the shiny silver icicles everywhere but on the actual tree.

It was still perfect.

I gave Will a break in the kitchen, wincing at the waft of hot air as I pulled out a tray of cheese pastries. Zoe came around the island and opened the fridge, saying, "I'll just help myself."

"You always do."

We laughed as she topped her glass almost to the brim. "Whoops." She shrugged and took a gulp. "My mom says hi, by the way. She wants to see pics of the condo once you're finished decorating."

"She should just friend me on Insta."

Zoe groaned. "Don't encourage her, Mike." She took a sip and added, "Sorry. Michael. This place is great, by the way."

"Thanks. How's the bathroom reno going?'

"Well, my dad's not doing it, so better already. How are your folks?"

"The same. Maybe a little happier now I've co-purchased a condo and I'm an official grown-up by their standards."

She smiled. "Who would have thought back in the day that I'd still be living in that house and you'd be shacked up with Will?"

"Who even says 'shacked up' anymore?"

"Me, apparently. And hey, put a ring on it and I won't have to say it again. It's a win-win."

"Cute hair, by the way."

Zoe patted her sleek bob. "Thanks." She gazed around. "This place really is gorgeous. I really am so happy for you and Will. You know that, right?"

I grabbed the spatula from the pale quartz counter. "I know. You're not getting sentimental already, are you?"

"Oh god, I am." She held up her wine glass. "I'm such a lightweight these days."

My phone dinged, and I read the text with a grin and handed Zoe the spatula. "Can you put these on the platter for me? I've got to let someone else in." I hurried to the buzzer, opening the lobby door as quickly as I could.

Will somehow still heard the buzz and appeared in the short hallway. "I thought everyone was here?"

"Just about." I tried to hide my grin and failed miserably.

His brow furrowed. "Who's coming?"

I opened the door to Will's parents, and his jaw dropped. Judy yanked him into a fierce hug, Robert not far behind. Will stared at them, and then at me. He sputtered.

"You all planned this?"

"No, you numpty, it's a big coincidence," Judy said, giving Will another hug. "Merry Christmas, love. Now where's your guest room?" She nodded to the suitcases they'd squeezed into the hall behind them. "We need to unpack."

Will turned to me in horror. "But there's no bed yet!"

I said, "It's okay—they're cool with sleeping on the floor."

"Anything to be close to you, William," Robert said solemnly, his accent adorably thick.

As Will blinked and tried to smile, Judy and I couldn't stop from laughing. I assured him, "I booked the guest suite downstairs."

Shaking his head, Will laughed. "There's a guest suite downstairs?"

"Yep." I couldn't stop smiling. "You kept talking about wanting to see your parents, so I texted Judy."

"My partner in crime," Judy said, pulling me into a warm hug. "It's so good to see you again." She pulled away with a grimace, "But Christ, I must stink. We need to clean up before we join the party."

"You're not too tired from the flight?" I asked.

"Pour us a drink and we'll be up in no time," Robert said before hugging me too.

Will and I took his parents and their suitcases downstairs. I felt stupidly proud to lead the way to the guest suite we were able to rent from the building. In the elevator on the way back up, Will was quiet.

My happy, bubbly high burst as I looked at his serious expression. Shit. Had I totally screwed up? "It's a good surprise, right?"

His lips tugged up into a smile, and he hugged me close. "It's the best gift I could imagine, sweetheart. Thank you."

Our condo buzzed with laughter and music when we returned,

the old U2 version of "Christmas (Baby Please Come Home)" playing. Matt, Zoe, and Seth of all people were singing along loudly as they hung some of the final ornaments. Logan handed Seth a glittery candy cane, looking at him with such bare affection that my throat tightened.

I slipped my hand into Will's, and we paused on the threshold of our new home, watching our friends and their families talking and smiling and singing while snow floated down to blanket the world outside.

Lips brushing my ear, Will whispered, "There's only one thing you forgot."

I shivered. "What's that?"

"Mistletoe."

"It's in the bedroom. You'll have to wait to kiss me."

"Is that right?" Will took my face in his hands, and I melted into him as our lips met.

We'd waited long enough.

THE END

About the Author

Keira aims for the perfect mix of character, plot, and heat in her M/M romances. She writes everything from swashbuckling pirates to heartwarming holiday escapism. Her fave tropes are enemies to lovers, age gaps, forced proximity, and passionate virgins. Although she loves delicious angst along the way, Keira guarantees happy endings!

Find out more:
www.keiraandrews.com

Made in United States
North Haven, CT
03 February 2024

48246282R10146